D0472684

G F F s

GHOST FRIENDS FOREVER

charmz

MORE GRAPHIC NOVELS AVAILABLE FROM charmz

STITCHED
The First Day of the Rest of her Life
charmz

STITCHED #1
"THE FIRST DAY OF THE REST OF HER LIFE"

STITCHED
MARIAH McCOURT • AARON ALEXOVICH
Love in the Time of Assumption
charmz

STITCHED #2
"LOVE IN THE TIME OF ASSUMPTION"

GFFs
GHOST FRIENDS FOREVER
charmz

G.F.F.s #1
"MY HEART LIES IN THE 90s"

Ana
COSMIC RACE
THE RACE BEGINS
charmz

ANA AND THE COSMIC RACE #1
"THE RACE BEGINS"

Chloe
The New Girl
charmz

CHLOE #1
"THE NEW GIRL"

Chloe
The Queen of High School
charmz

CHLOE #2 "THE QUEEN OF HIGH SCHOOL"

Chloe
Frenemies
charmz

CHLOE #3
"FRENEMIES"

Chloe
Rainy Day
charmz

CHLOE #4
"RAINY DAY"

PATRICIA LYFOUNG
The Scarlet Rose
charmz

SCARLET ROSE #1
"I KNEW I'D MEET YOU"

PATRICIA LYFOUNG
The Scarlet Rose
I'll Go Where You Go
charmz

SCARLET ROSE #2
"I'LL GO WHERE YOU GO"

PATRICIA LYFOUNG
The Scarlet Rose
I Think I Love You
charmz

SCARLET ROSE #3
"I THINK I LOVE YOU"

PATRICIA LYFOUNG
The Scarlet Rose
charmz

SCARLET ROSE #4
"YOU WILL ALWAYS BE MINE"

Amy's Diary
Space Alien... Almost?
charmz

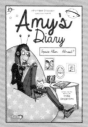

AMY'S DIARY #1
"SPACE ALIEN... ALMOST?"

Sweeties
CHERRY SKYE
charmz

SWEETIES #1
"CHERRY SKYE"

BEAUTY QUEEN
Jennifer De Guzman & Jamie Parreno

BEAUTY QUEEN

Charmz graphic novels are available for $9.99 in paperback, and $14.99 in hardcover. Available from booksellers everywhere. You can also order online from www.papercutz.com. Or call 1-800-886-1223, Monday through Friday, 9–5 EST. MC, Visa, and AmEx accepted. To order by mail, please add $5.00 for postage and handling for first book ordered, $1.00 for each additional book and make check payable to NBM Publishing.
Send to: Charmz, 160 Broadway, Suite 700, East Wing, New York, NY 10038.
Charmz graphic novels are also available wherever e-books are sold.

Gallagher, Monica, 1979–
GFFs: Ghost friends
forever. #2, Witches get
[2018]
33305244210016
gi   12/20/18

GFFs

GHOST FRIENDS FOREVER

#2 WITCHES GET THINGS DONE

STORY BY MONICA GALLAGHER

ART BY KATA KANE

NEW YORK

#2 "WITCHES GET THINGS DONE"

GFFs: GHOST FRIENDS FOREVER BY MONICA GALLAGHER & KATA KANE
©2018 MONICA GALLAGHER & KATA KANE
EDITORIAL ©2018 BY PAPERCUTZ
ALL RIGHTS RESERVED.

MONICA GALLAGHER — STORY
KATA KANE — ART & COVER
MATT HERMS — COLORS
WILSON RAMOS JR. — LETTERING

CHARMZ BOOKS MAY BE PURCHASED FOR BUSINESS OR PROMOTIONAL USE.
FOR INFORMATION ON BULK PURCHASES PLEASE CONTACT MACMILLAN
CORPORATE AND PREMIUM SALES DEPARTMENT AT (800) 221-7945 X5442

NO PART OF THIS BOOK MAY BE STORED, REPRODUCED OR TRANSMITTED IN ANY FORM OR BY
ANY MEANS, ELECTRONIC OR MECHANICAL, INCLUDING PHOTOCOPYING, RECORDING, OR BY ANY
INFORMATION STORAGE AND RETRIEVAL SYSTEM, WITHOUT WRITTEN PERMISSION FROM THE
COPYRIGHT HOLDER.

MARIAH McCOURT — ORIGINAL SERIES EDITOR
KATA KANE, JIM SALICRUP — EDITORS
JEFF WHITMAN — ASSISTANT MANAGING EDITOR
JIM SALICRUP
EDITOR-IN-CHIEF

PB ISBN: 978-1-5458-0151-2
HC ISBN: 978-1-5458-0150-5

PRINTED IN CHINA.
OCTOBER 2018

DISTRIBUTED BY MACMILLAN
FIRST PRINTING

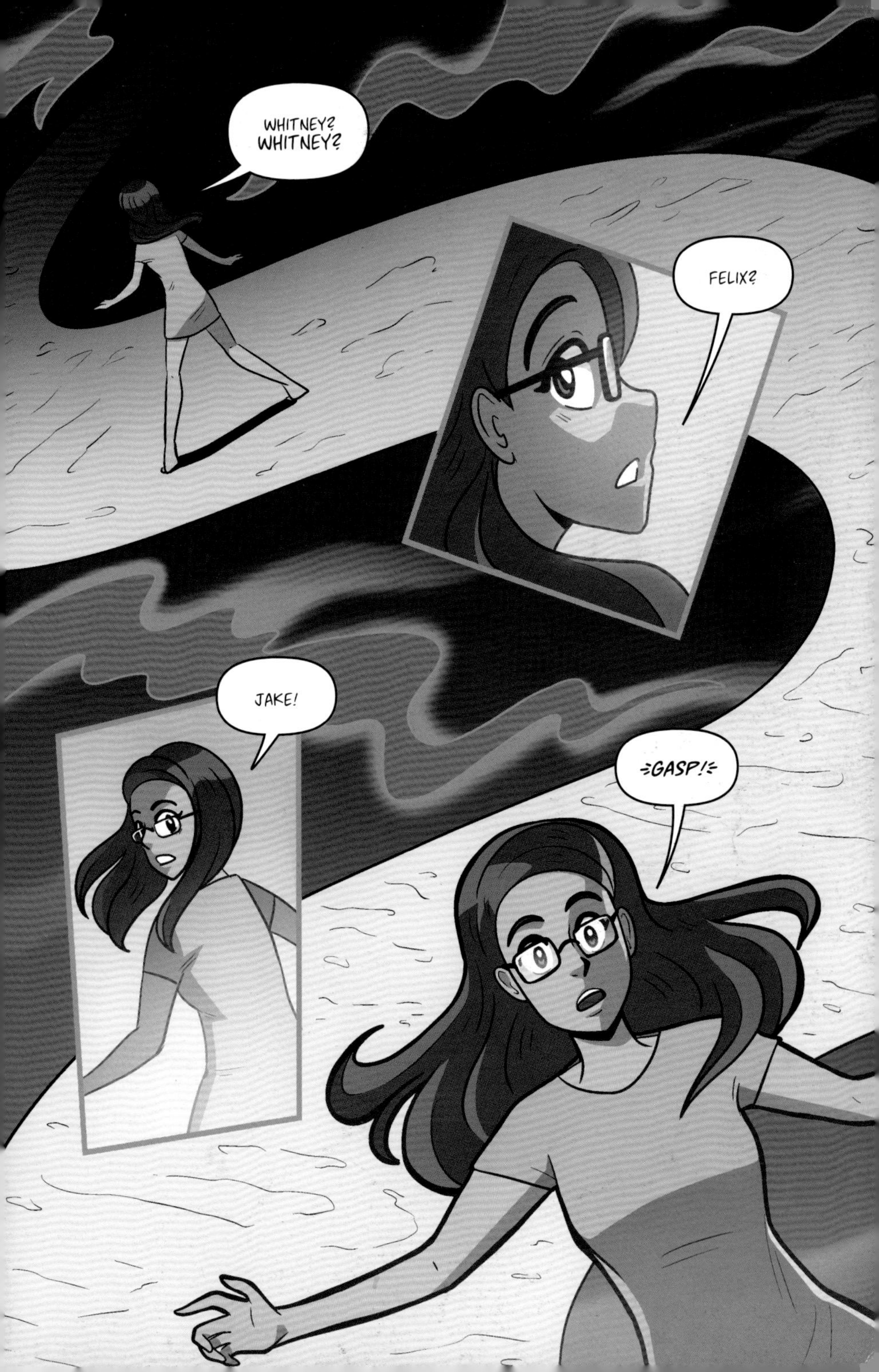
WHITNEY?
WHITNEY?
FELIX?
JAKE!
=GASP!=

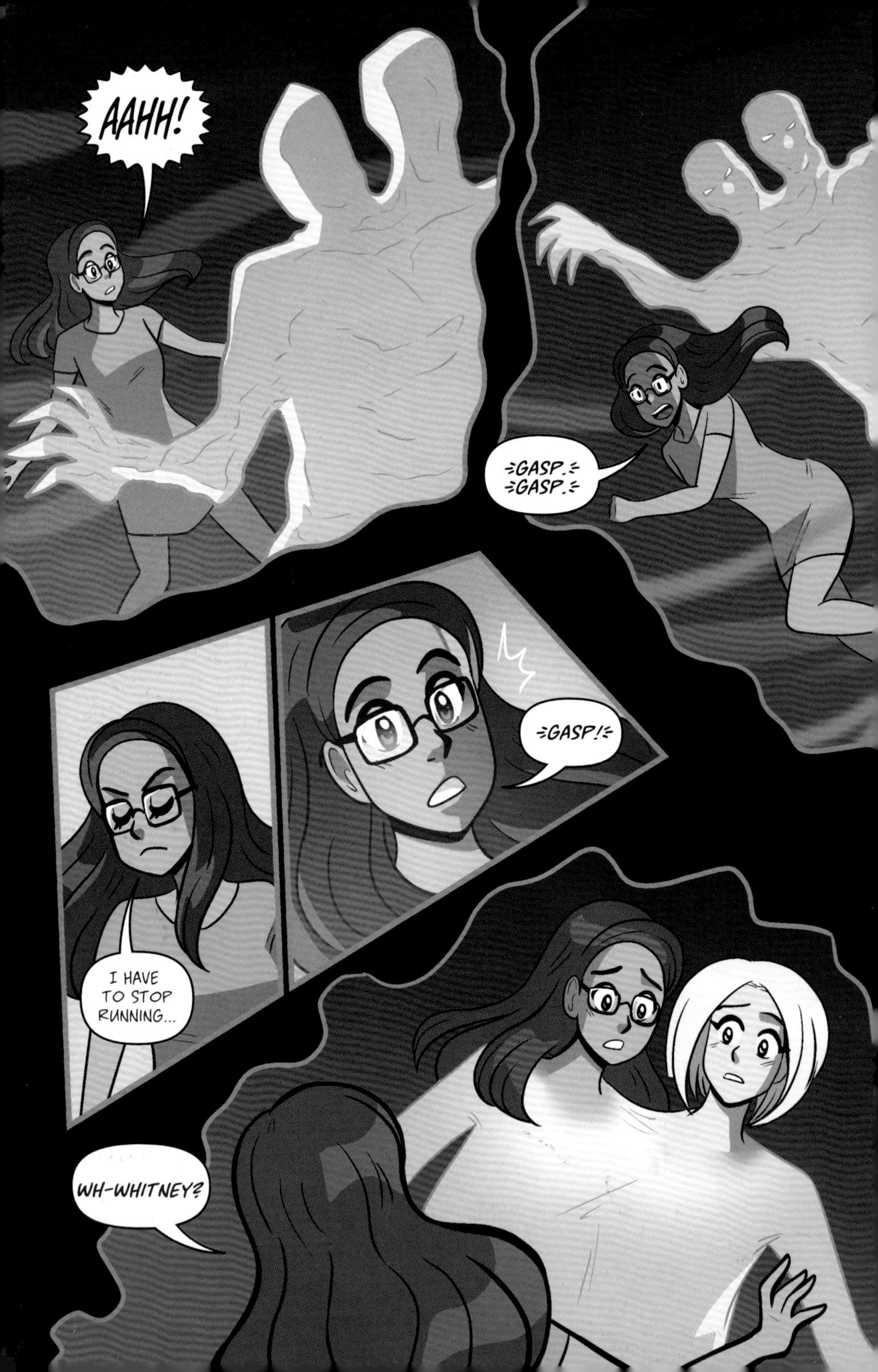
AAHH!
GASP. GASP.
GASP!
I HAVE TO STOP RUNNING...
WH-WHITNEY?

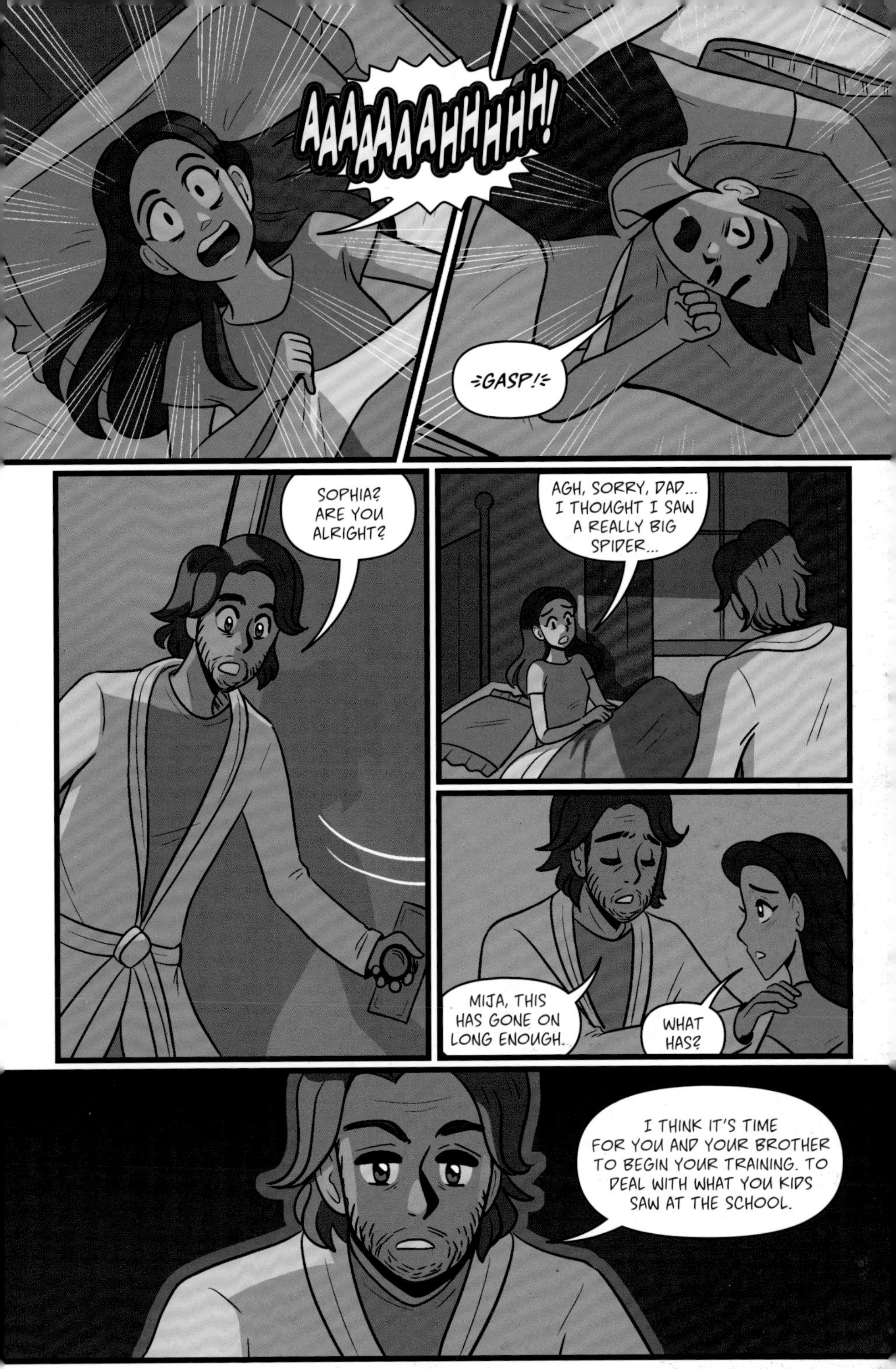
AAAAAAAHHHHH!
=GASP!=
SOPHIA? ARE YOU ALRIGHT?
AGH, SORRY, DAD... I THOUGHT I SAW A REALLY BIG SPIDER...
MIJA, THIS HAS GONE ON LONG ENOUGH.
WHAT HAS?
I THINK IT'S TIME FOR YOU AND YOUR BROTHER TO BEGIN YOUR TRAINING. TO DEAL WITH WHAT YOU KIDS SAW AT THE SCHOOL.

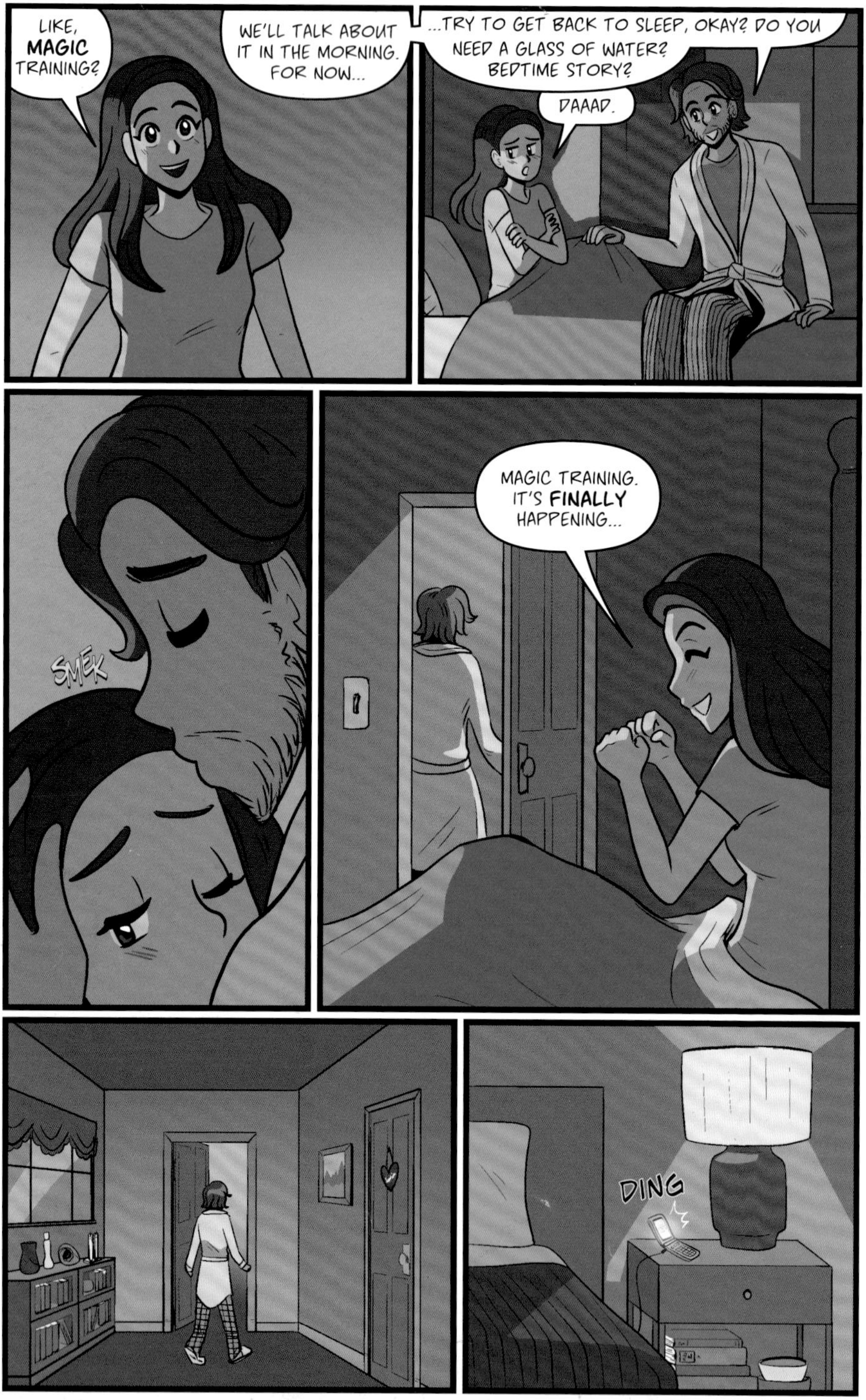
LIKE, **MAGIC** TRAINING?
WE'LL TALK ABOUT IT IN THE MORNING. FOR NOW...
...TRY TO GET BACK TO SLEEP, OKAY? DO YOU NEED A GLASS OF WATER? BEDTIME STORY?
DAAAD.
SMEK
MAGIC TRAINING. IT'S **FINALLY** HAPPENING...
DING

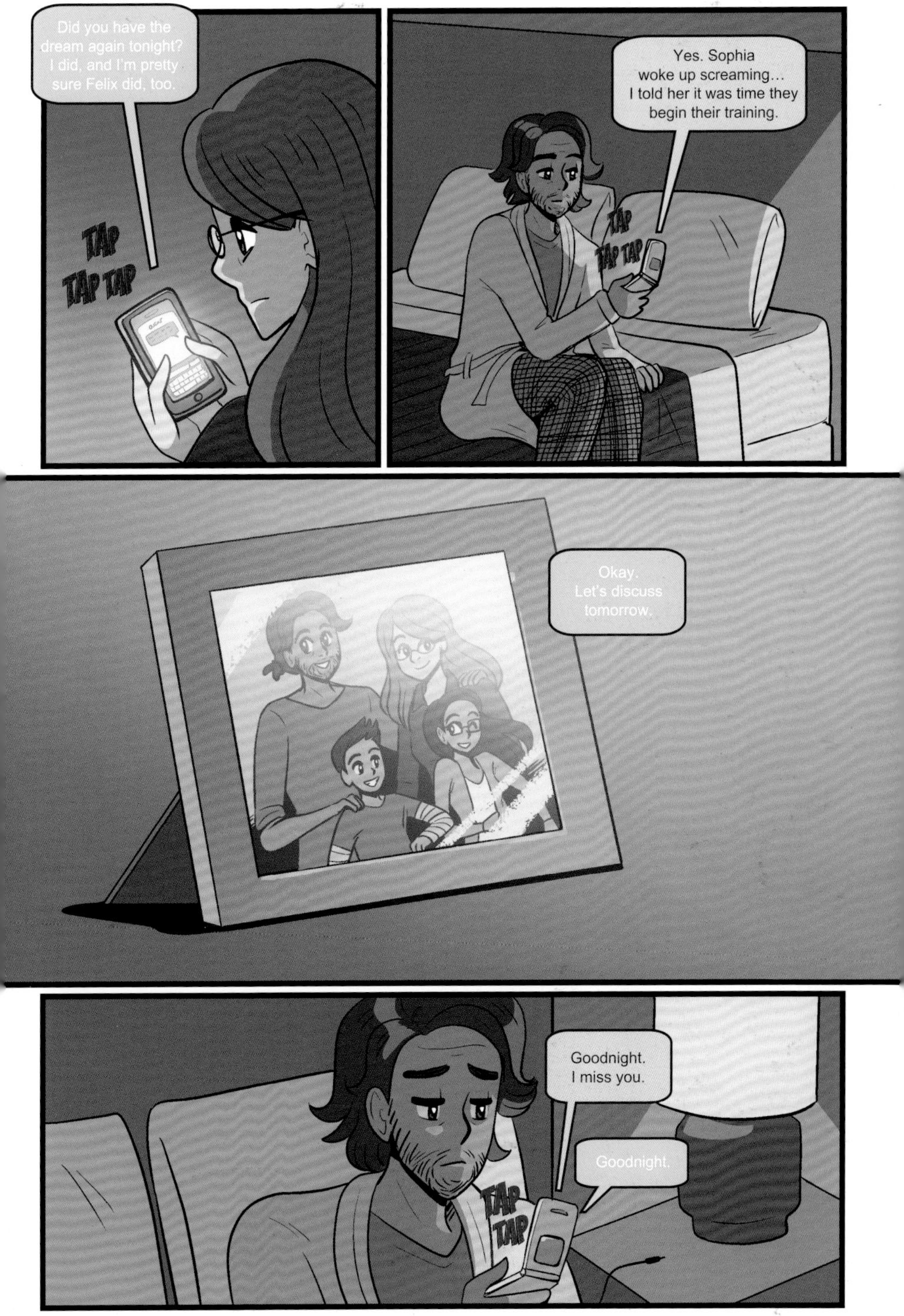

Did you have the dream again tonight? I did, and I'm pretty sure Felix did, too.
TAP TAP TAP
Yes. Sophia woke up screaming… I told her it was time they begin their training.
TAP TAP TAP
Okay. Let's discuss tomorrow.
Goodnight. I miss you.
Goodnight.
TAP TAP

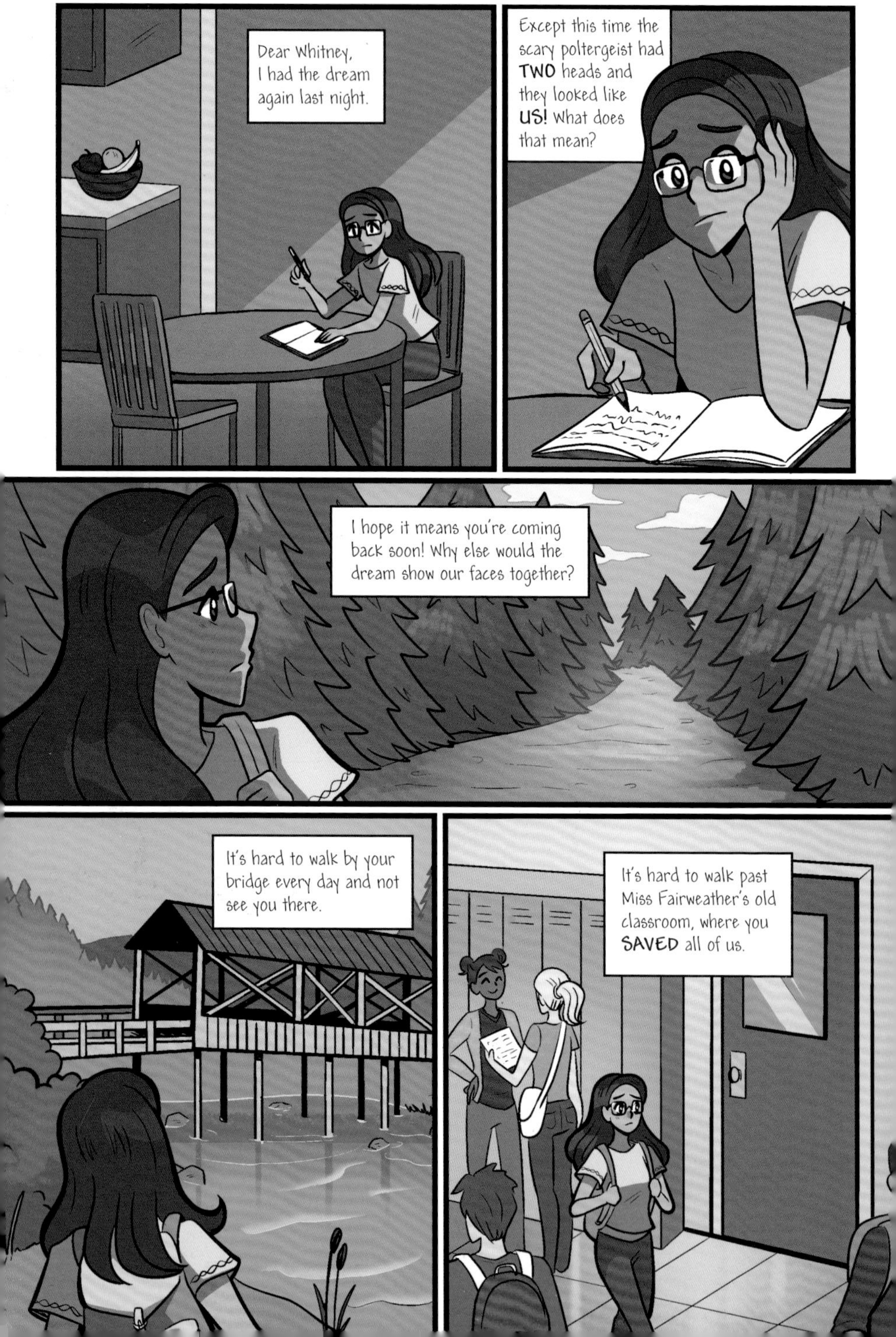
Dear Whitney,
I had the dream again last night.
Except this time the scary poltergeist had TWO heads and they looked like US! What does that mean?
I hope it means you're coming back soon! Why else would the dream show our faces together?
It's hard to walk by your bridge every day and not see you there.
It's hard to walk past Miss Fairweather's old classroom, where you SAVED all of us.

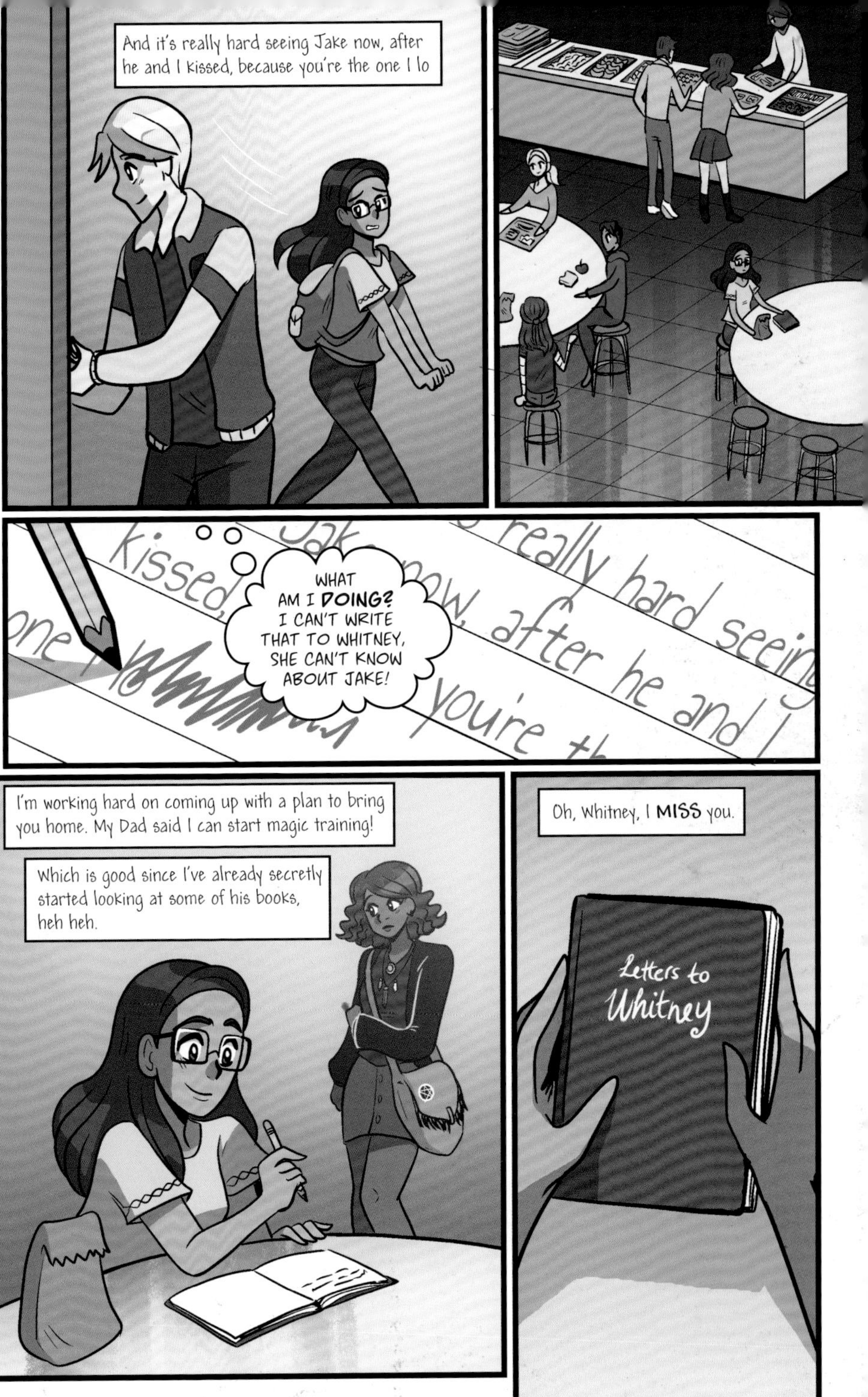

And it's really hard seeing Jake now, after he and I kissed, because you're the one I lo
WHAT AM I **DOING?** I CAN'T WRITE THAT TO WHITNEY, SHE CAN'T KNOW ABOUT JAKE!
I'm working hard on coming up with a plan to bring you home. My Dad said I can start magic training!
Which is good since I've already secretly started looking at some of his books, heh heh.
Oh, Whitney, I **MISS** you.
Letters to Whitney

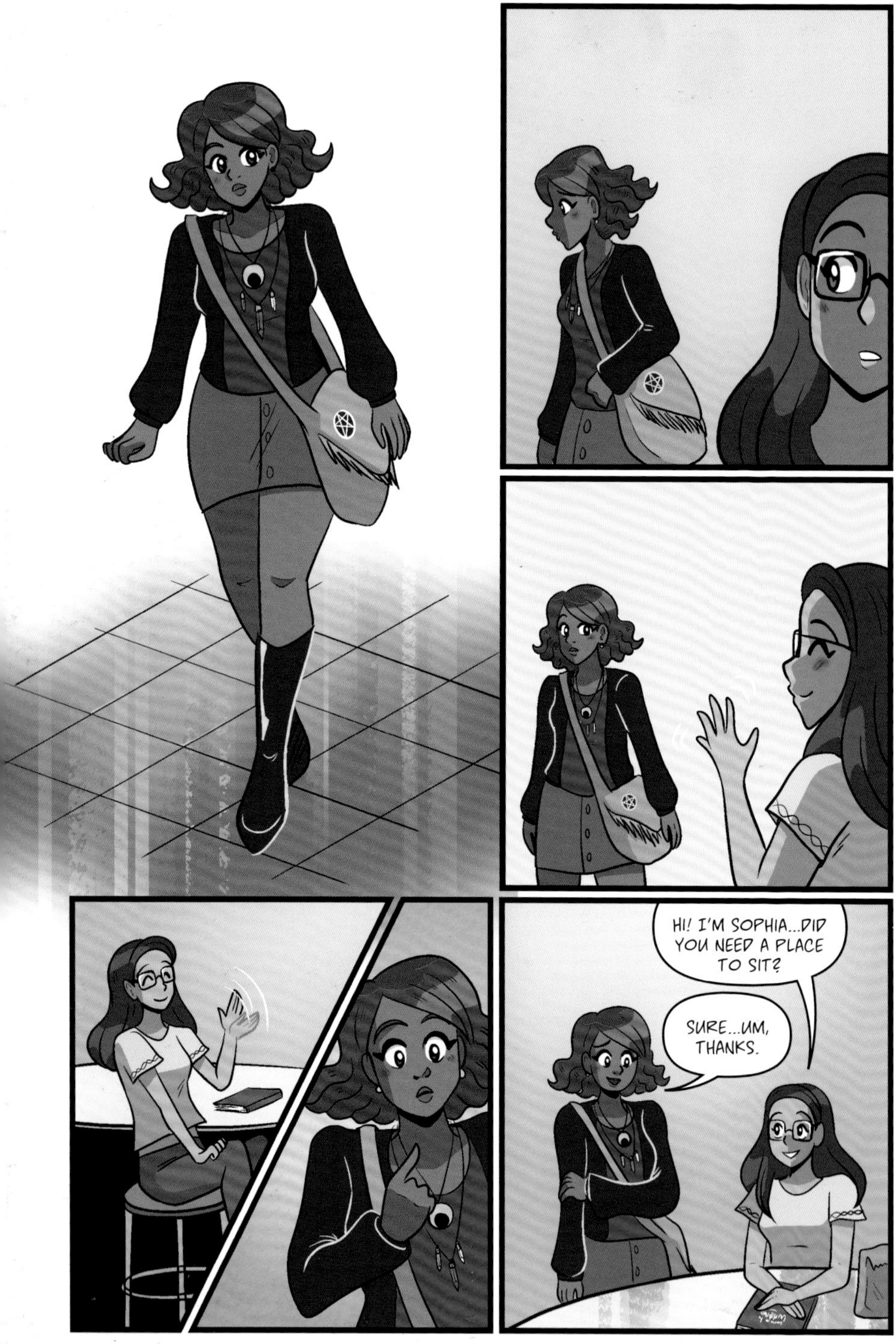
HI! I'M SOPHIA...DID YOU NEED A PLACE TO SIT?
SURE...UM, THANKS.

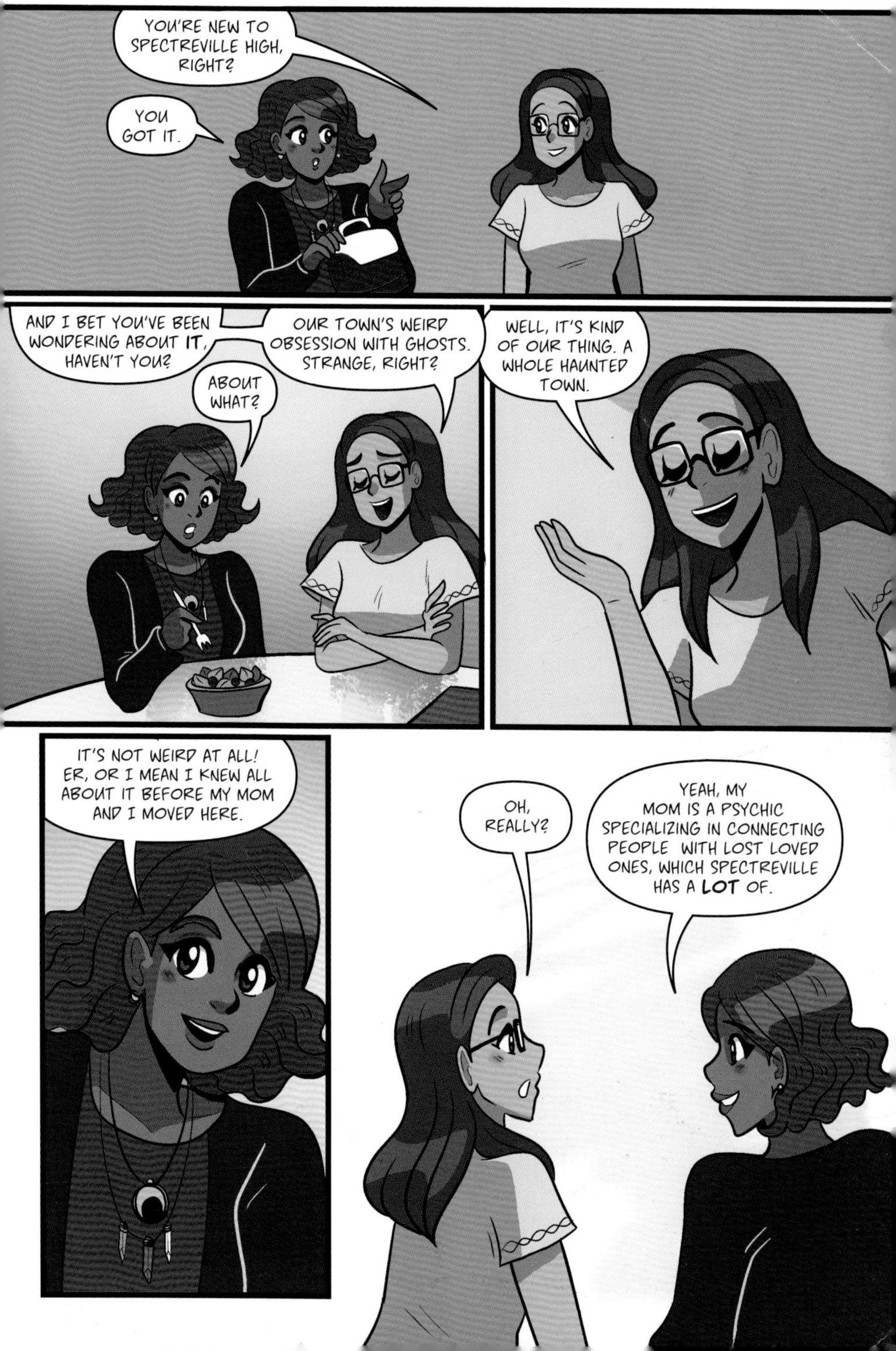
YOU'RE NEW TO SPECTREVILLE HIGH, RIGHT?
YOU GOT IT.
AND I BET YOU'VE BEEN WONDERING ABOUT IT, HAVEN'T YOU?
ABOUT WHAT?
OUR TOWN'S WEIRD OBSESSION WITH GHOSTS. STRANGE, RIGHT?
WELL, IT'S KIND OF OUR THING. A WHOLE HAUNTED TOWN.
IT'S NOT WEIRD AT ALL! ER, OR I MEAN I KNEW ALL ABOUT IT BEFORE MY MOM AND I MOVED HERE.
OH, REALLY?
YEAH, MY MOM IS A PSYCHIC SPECIALIZING IN CONNECTING PEOPLE WITH LOST LOVED ONES, WHICH SPECTREVILLE HAS A LOT OF.

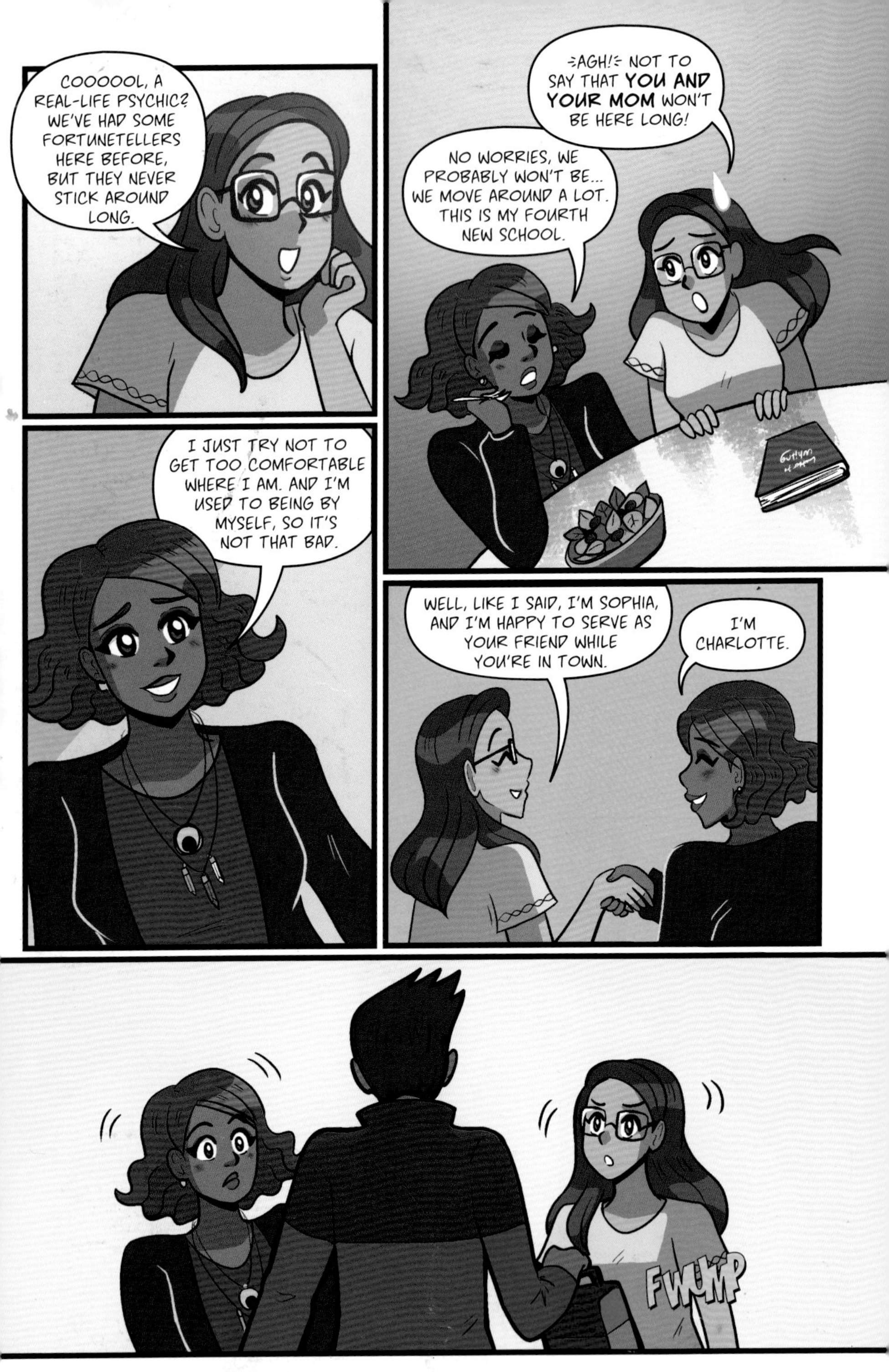
COOOOOL, A REAL-LIFE PSYCHIC? WE'VE HAD SOME FORTUNETELLERS HERE BEFORE, BUT THEY NEVER STICK AROUND LONG.
NO WORRIES, WE PROBABLY WON'T BE... WE MOVE AROUND A LOT. THIS IS MY FOURTH NEW SCHOOL.
AGH! NOT TO SAY THAT **YOU AND YOUR MOM** WON'T BE HERE LONG!
I JUST TRY NOT TO GET TOO COMFORTABLE WHERE I AM. AND I'M USED TO BEING BY MYSELF, SO IT'S NOT THAT BAD.
WELL, LIKE I SAID, I'M SOPHIA, AND I'M HAPPY TO SERVE AS YOUR FRIEND WHILE YOU'RE IN TOWN.
I'M CHARLOTTE.
FWUMP

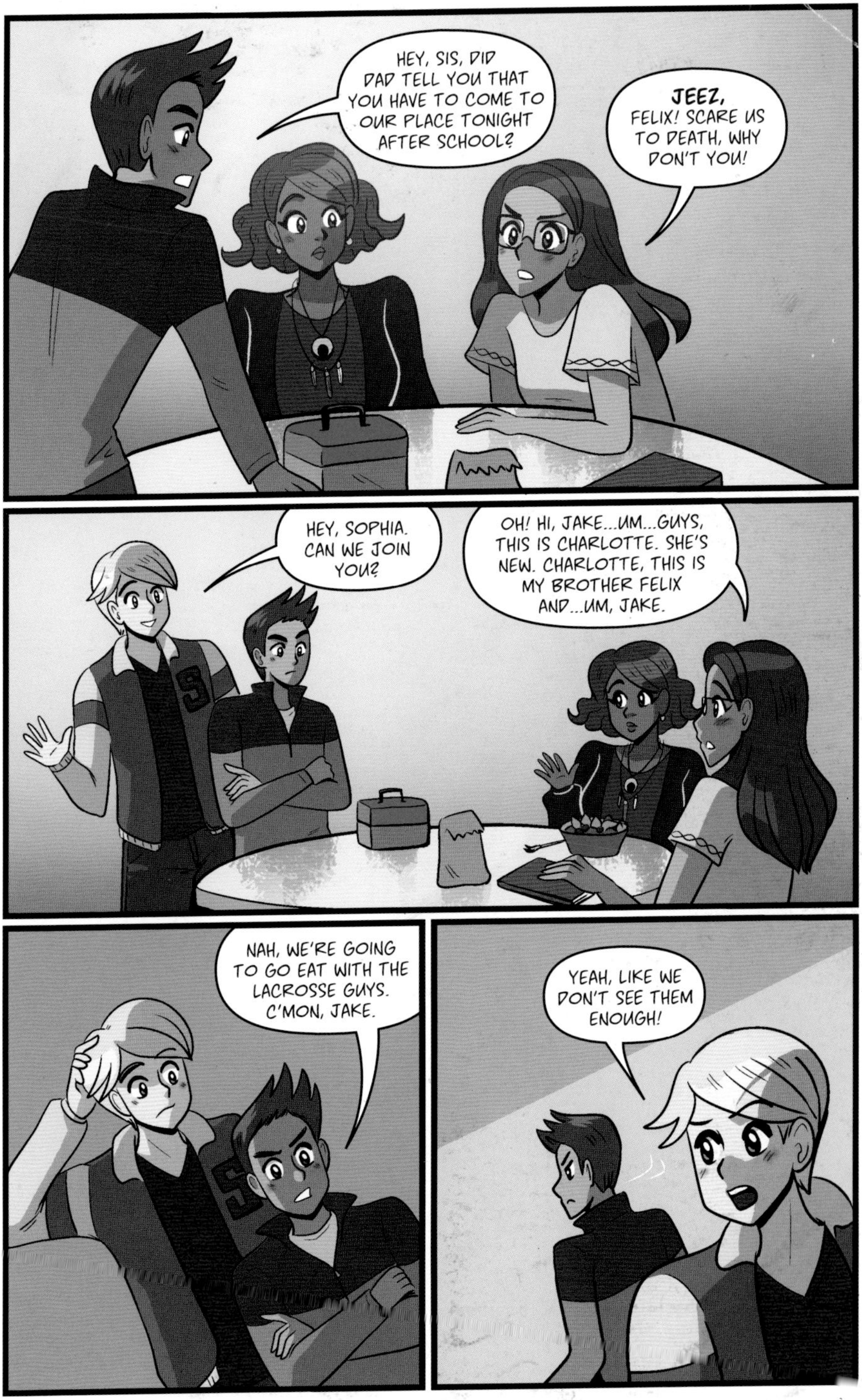
HEY, SIS, DID DAD TELL YOU THAT YOU HAVE TO COME TO OUR PLACE TONIGHT AFTER SCHOOL?
JEEZ, FELIX! SCARE US TO DEATH, WHY DON'T YOU!
HEY, SOPHIA. CAN WE JOIN YOU?
OH! HI, JAKE...UM...GUYS, THIS IS CHARLOTTE. SHE'S NEW. CHARLOTTE, THIS IS MY BROTHER FELIX AND...UM, JAKE.
NAH, WE'RE GOING TO GO EAT WITH THE LACROSSE GUYS. C'MON, JAKE.
YEAH, LIKE WE DON'T SEE THEM ENOUGH!

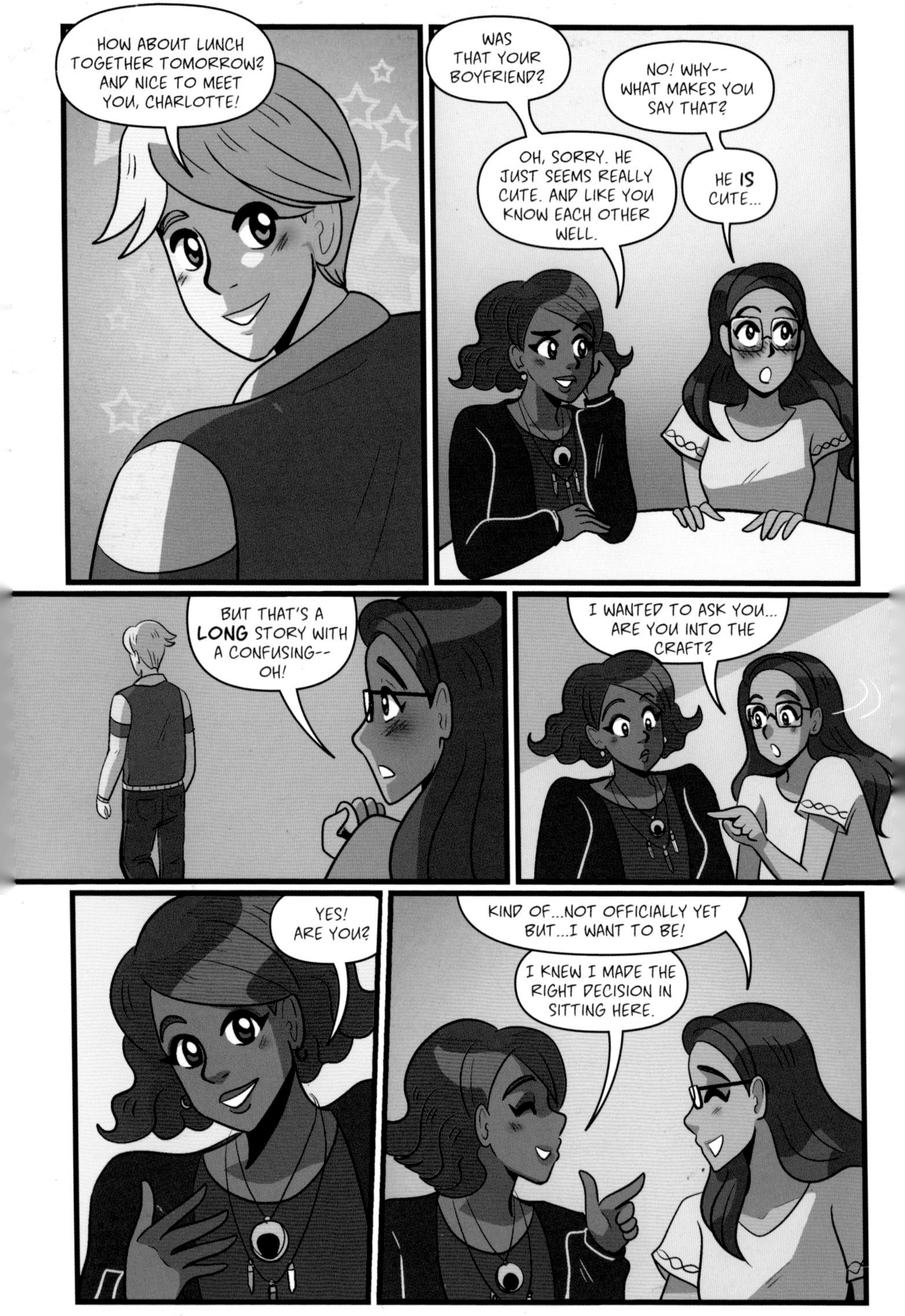
HOW ABOUT LUNCH TOGETHER TOMORROW? AND NICE TO MEET YOU, CHARLOTTE!
WAS THAT YOUR BOYFRIEND?
NO! WHY-- WHAT MAKES YOU SAY THAT?
OH, SORRY. HE JUST SEEMS REALLY CUTE. AND LIKE YOU KNOW EACH OTHER WELL.
HE **IS** CUTE...
BUT THAT'S A **LONG** STORY WITH A CONFUSING-- OH!
I WANTED TO ASK YOU... ARE YOU INTO THE CRAFT?
YES! ARE YOU?
KIND OF...NOT OFFICIALLY YET BUT...I WANT TO BE!
I KNEW I MADE THE RIGHT DECISION IN SITTING HERE.

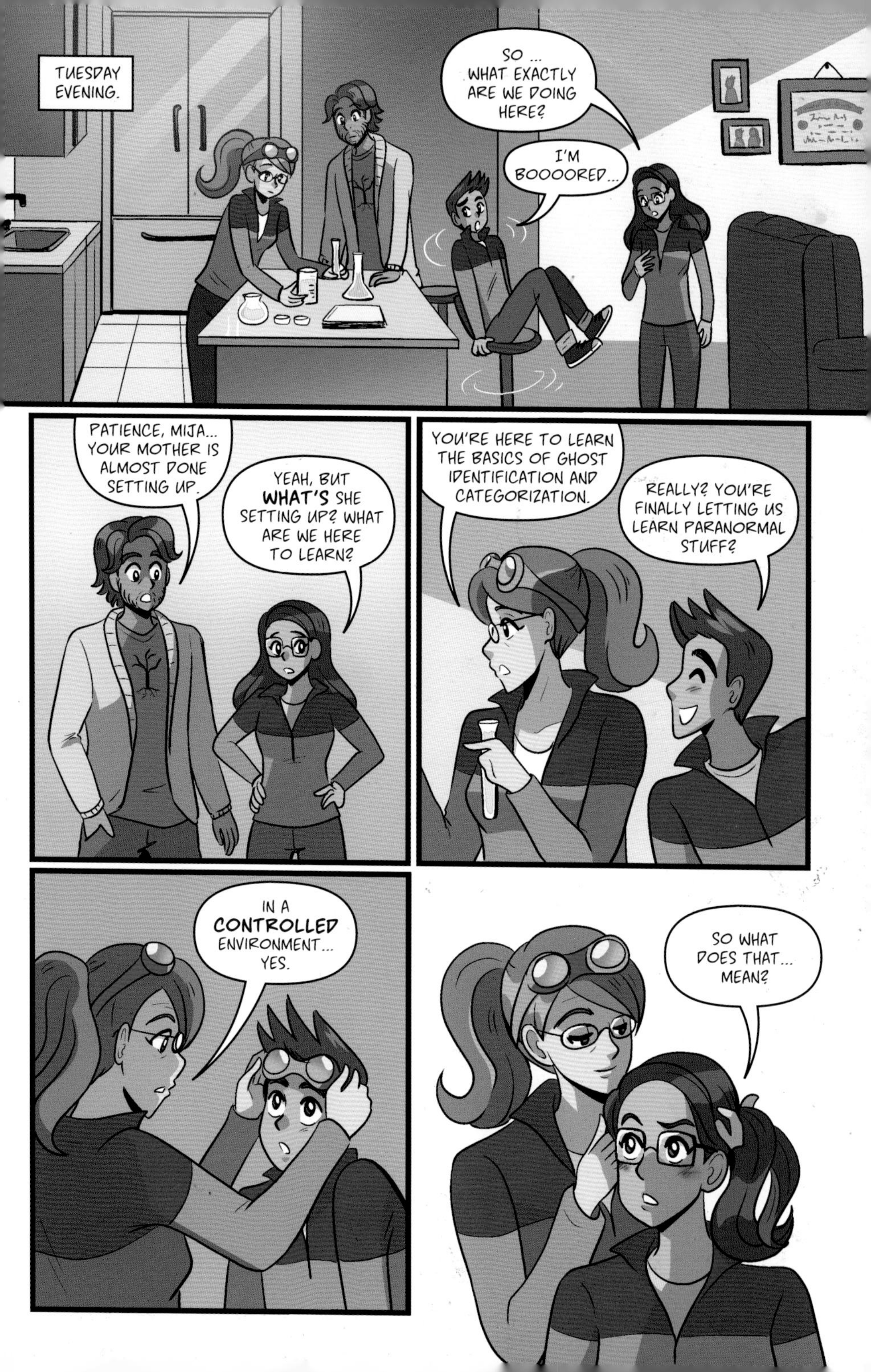
TUESDAY EVENING.
SO ... WHAT EXACTLY ARE WE DOING HERE?
I'M BOOOORED...
PATIENCE, MIJA... YOUR MOTHER IS ALMOST DONE SETTING UP.
YEAH, BUT WHAT'S SHE SETTING UP? WHAT ARE WE HERE TO LEARN?
YOU'RE HERE TO LEARN THE BASICS OF GHOST IDENTIFICATION AND CATEGORIZATION.
REALLY? YOU'RE FINALLY LETTING US LEARN PARANORMAL STUFF?
IN A CONTROLLED ENVIRONMENT... YES.
SO WHAT DOES THAT... MEAN?

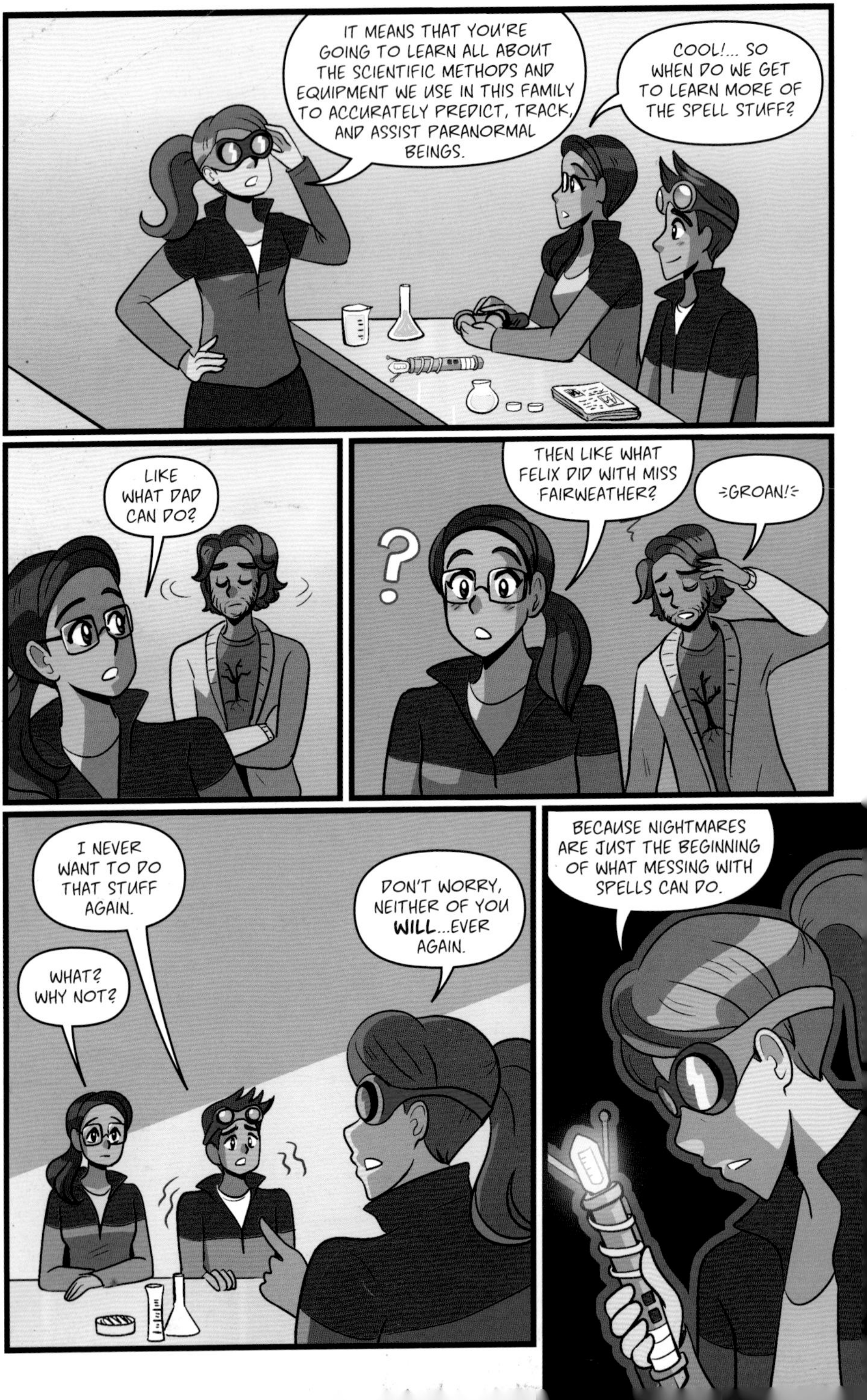
IT MEANS THAT YOU'RE GOING TO LEARN ALL ABOUT THE SCIENTIFIC METHODS AND EQUIPMENT WE USE IN THIS FAMILY TO ACCURATELY PREDICT, TRACK, AND ASSIST PARANORMAL BEINGS.
COOL!... SO WHEN DO WE GET TO LEARN MORE OF THE SPELL STUFF?
LIKE WHAT DAD CAN DO?
THEN LIKE WHAT FELIX DID WITH MISS FAIRWEATHER?
GROAN!
I NEVER WANT TO DO THAT STUFF AGAIN.
WHAT? WHY NOT?
DON'T WORRY, NEITHER OF YOU **WILL**...EVER AGAIN.
BECAUSE NIGHTMARES ARE JUST THE BEGINNING OF WHAT MESSING WITH SPELLS CAN DO.

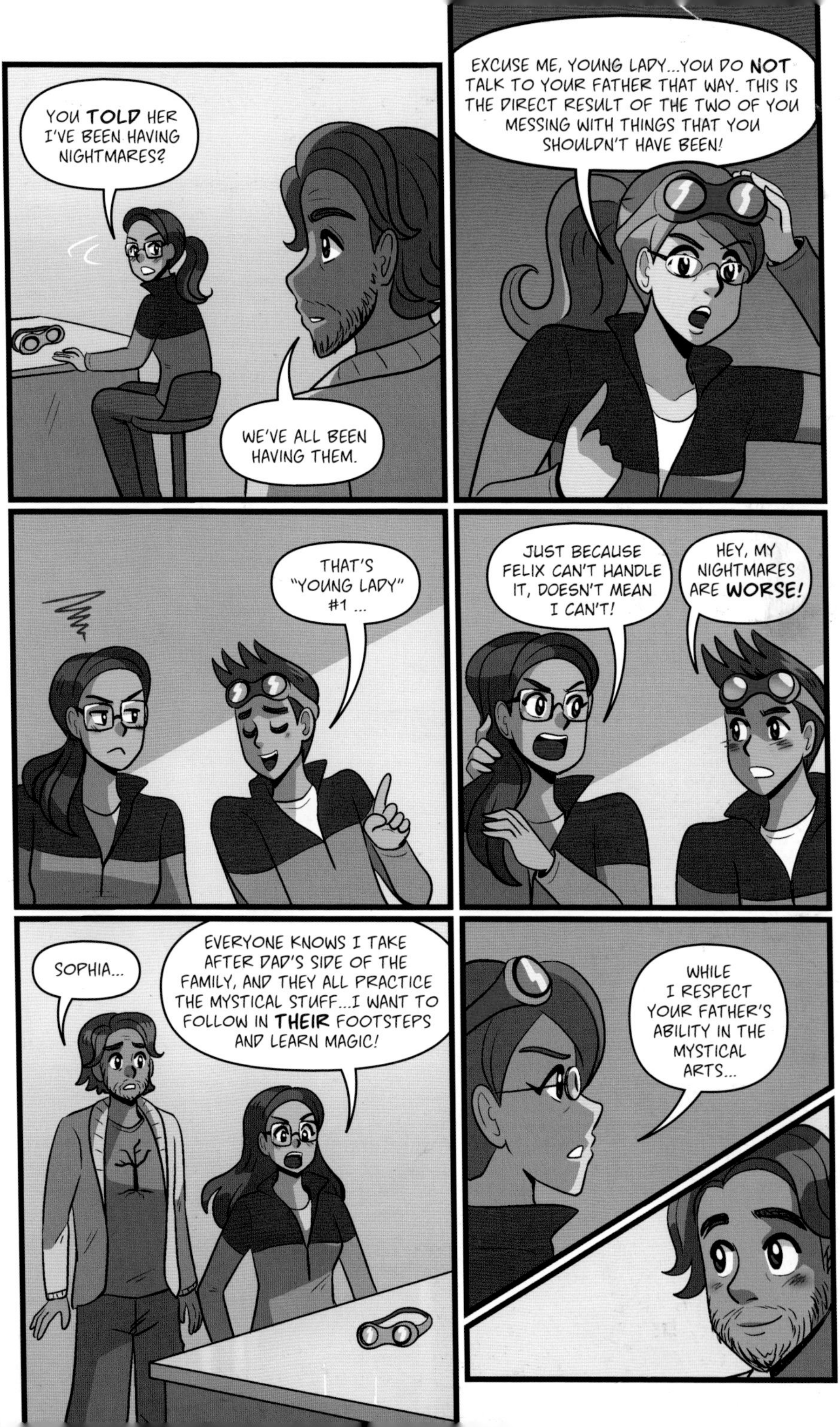

YOU TOLD HER I'VE BEEN HAVING NIGHTMARES?
WE'VE ALL BEEN HAVING THEM.
EXCUSE ME, YOUNG LADY...YOU DO NOT TALK TO YOUR FATHER THAT WAY. THIS IS THE DIRECT RESULT OF THE TWO OF YOU MESSING WITH THINGS THAT YOU SHOULDN'T HAVE BEEN!
THAT'S "YOUNG LADY" #1 ...
JUST BECAUSE FELIX CAN'T HANDLE IT, DOESN'T MEAN I CAN'T!
HEY, MY NIGHTMARES ARE WORSE!
SOPHIA...
EVERYONE KNOWS I TAKE AFTER DAD'S SIDE OF THE FAMILY, AND THEY ALL PRACTICE THE MYSTICAL STUFF...I WANT TO FOLLOW IN THEIR FOOTSTEPS AND LEARN MAGIC!
WHILE I RESPECT YOUR FATHER'S ABILITY IN THE MYSTICAL ARTS...

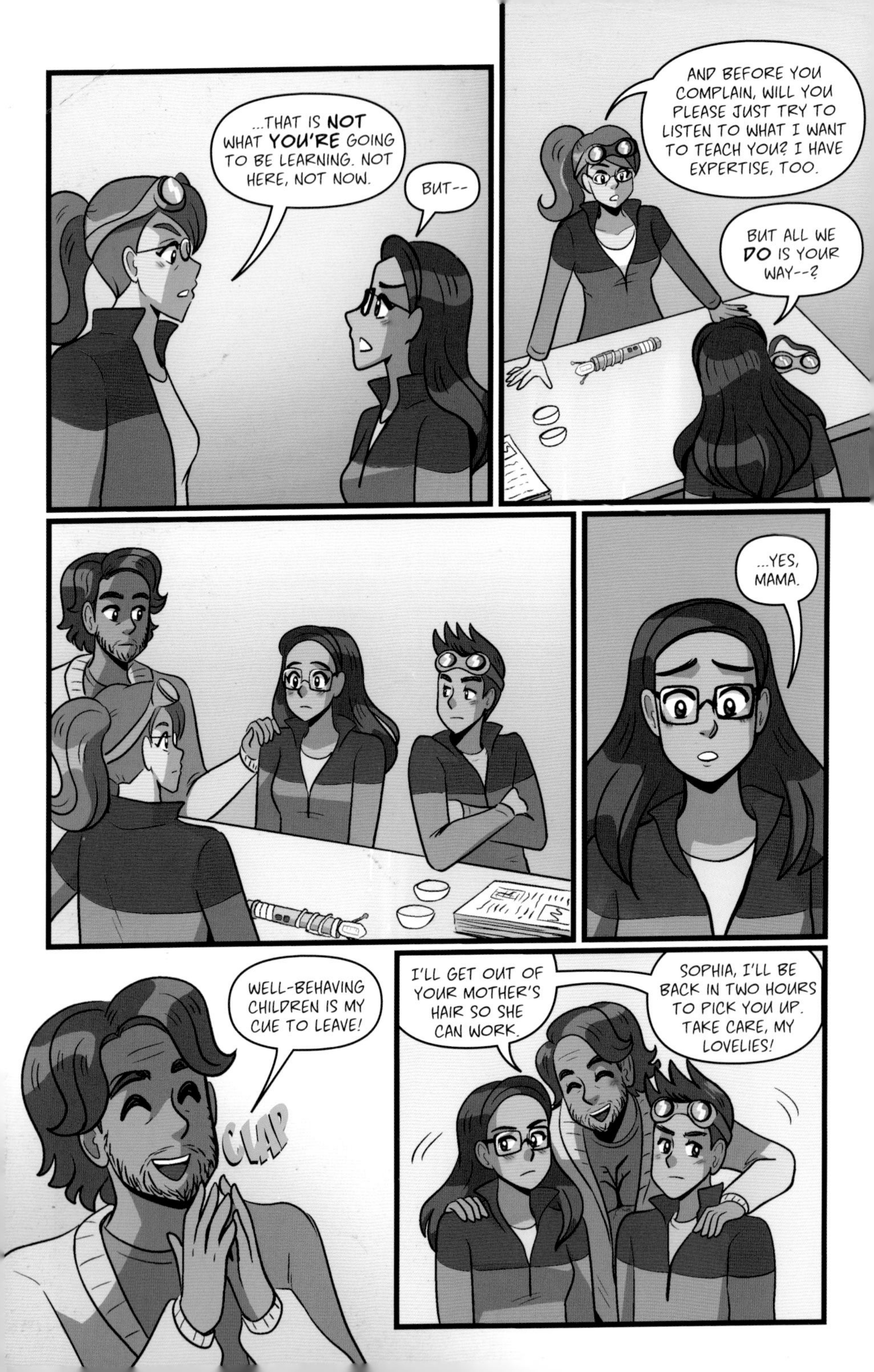
...THAT IS NOT WHAT YOU'RE GOING TO BE LEARNING. NOT HERE, NOT NOW.
BUT--
AND BEFORE YOU COMPLAIN, WILL YOU PLEASE JUST TRY TO LISTEN TO WHAT I WANT TO TEACH YOU? I HAVE EXPERTISE, TOO.
BUT ALL WE DO IS YOUR WAY--?
...YES, MAMA.
WELL-BEHAVING CHILDREN IS MY CUE TO LEAVE!
CLAP
I'LL GET OUT OF YOUR MOTHER'S HAIR SO SHE CAN WORK.
SOPHIA, I'LL BE BACK IN TWO HOURS TO PICK YOU UP. TAKE CARE, MY LOVELIES!

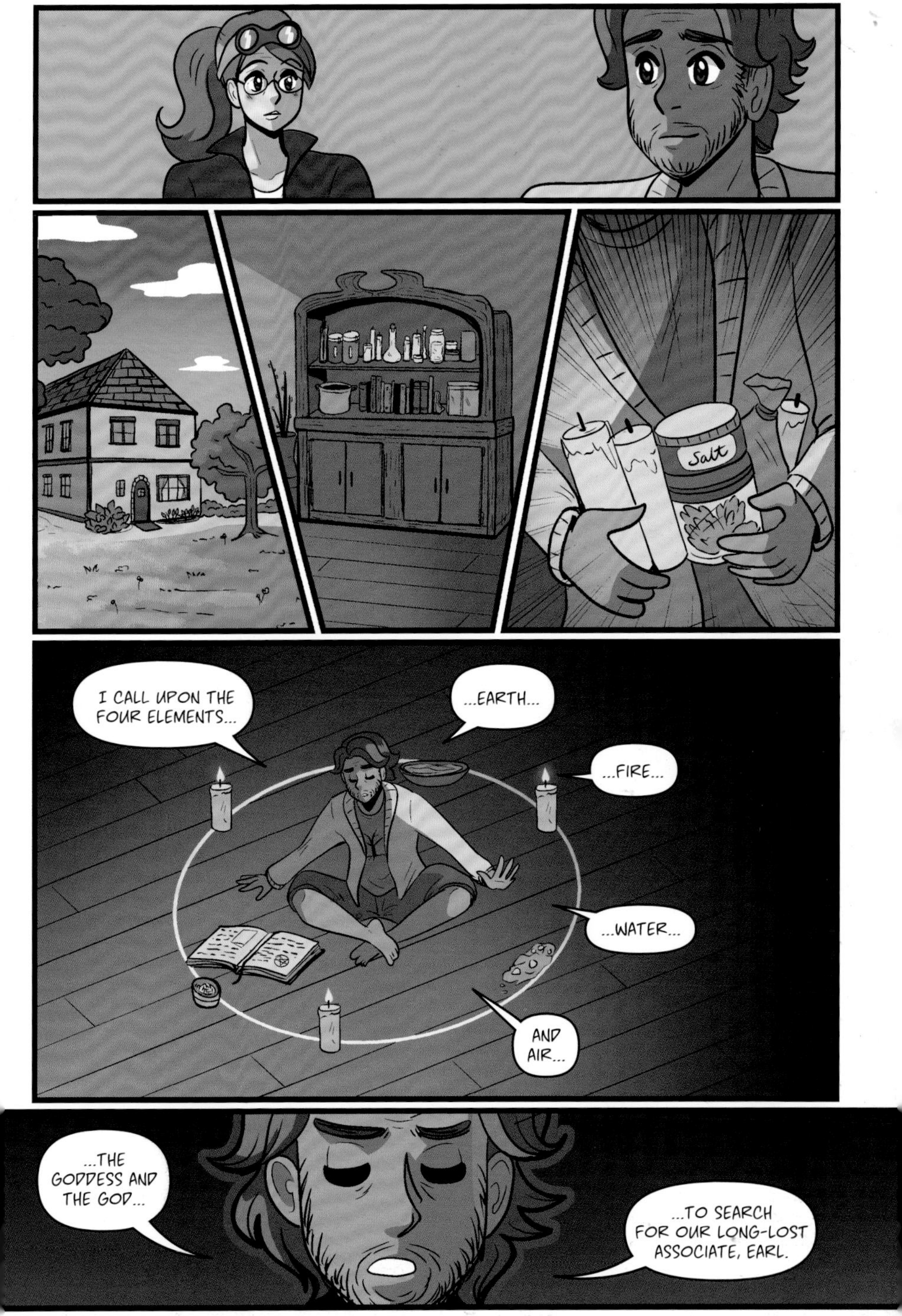
Salt
I CALL UPON THE FOUR ELEMENTS...
...EARTH...
...FIRE...
...WATER...
AND AIR...
...THE GODDESS AND THE GOD...
...TO SEARCH FOR OUR LONG-LOST ASSOCIATE, EARL.

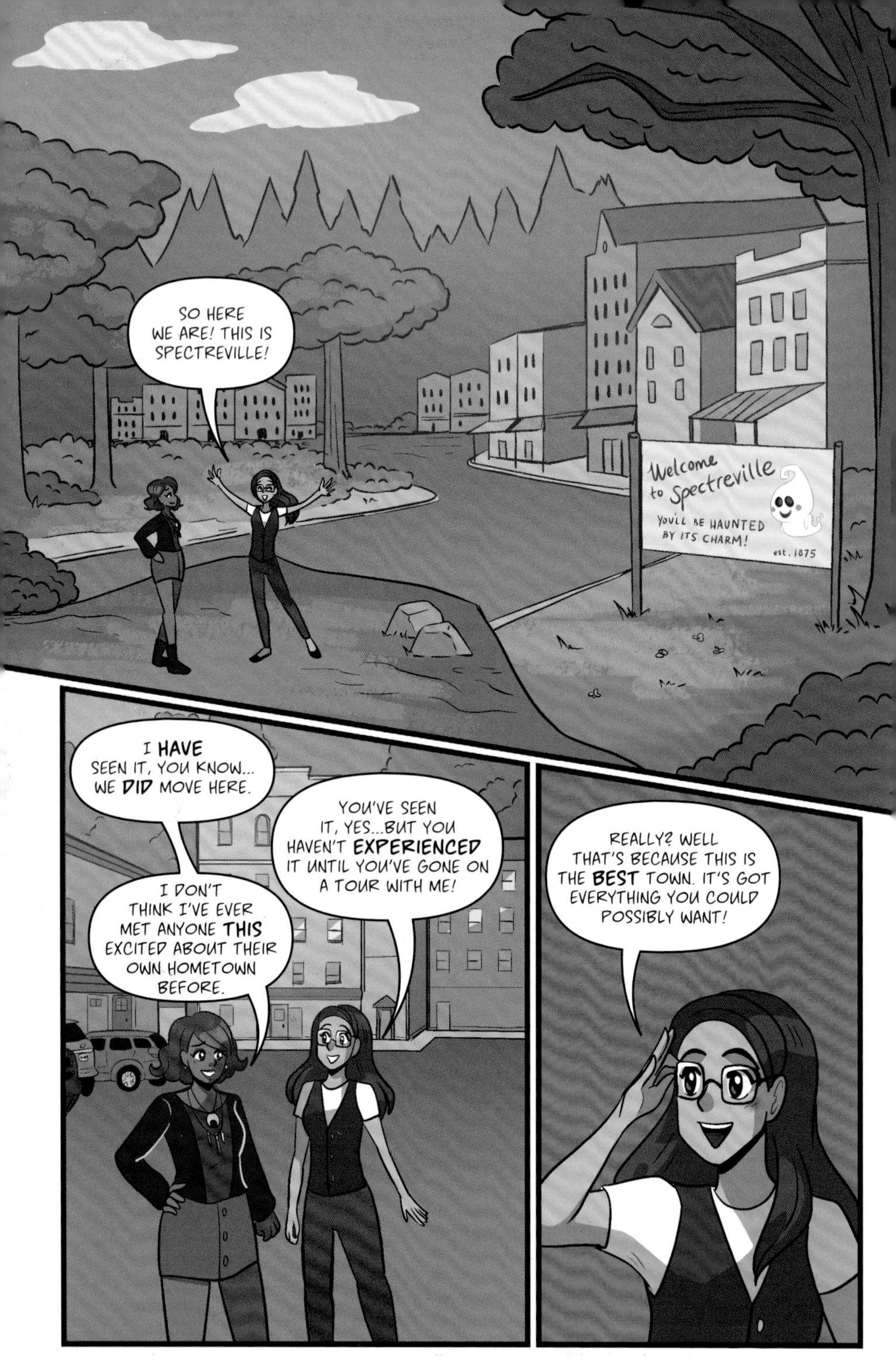

SO HERE WE ARE! THIS IS SPECTREVILLE!
Welcome to Spectreville
YOU'LL BE HAUNTED BY ITS CHARM!
est. 1875
I HAVE SEEN IT, YOU KNOW... WE DID MOVE HERE.
I DON'T THINK I'VE EVER MET ANYONE THIS EXCITED ABOUT THEIR OWN HOMETOWN BEFORE.
YOU'VE SEEN IT, YES...BUT YOU HAVEN'T EXPERIENCED IT UNTIL YOU'VE GONE ON A TOUR WITH ME!
REALLY? WELL THAT'S BECAUSE THIS IS THE BEST TOWN. IT'S GOT EVERYTHING YOU COULD POSSIBLY WANT!

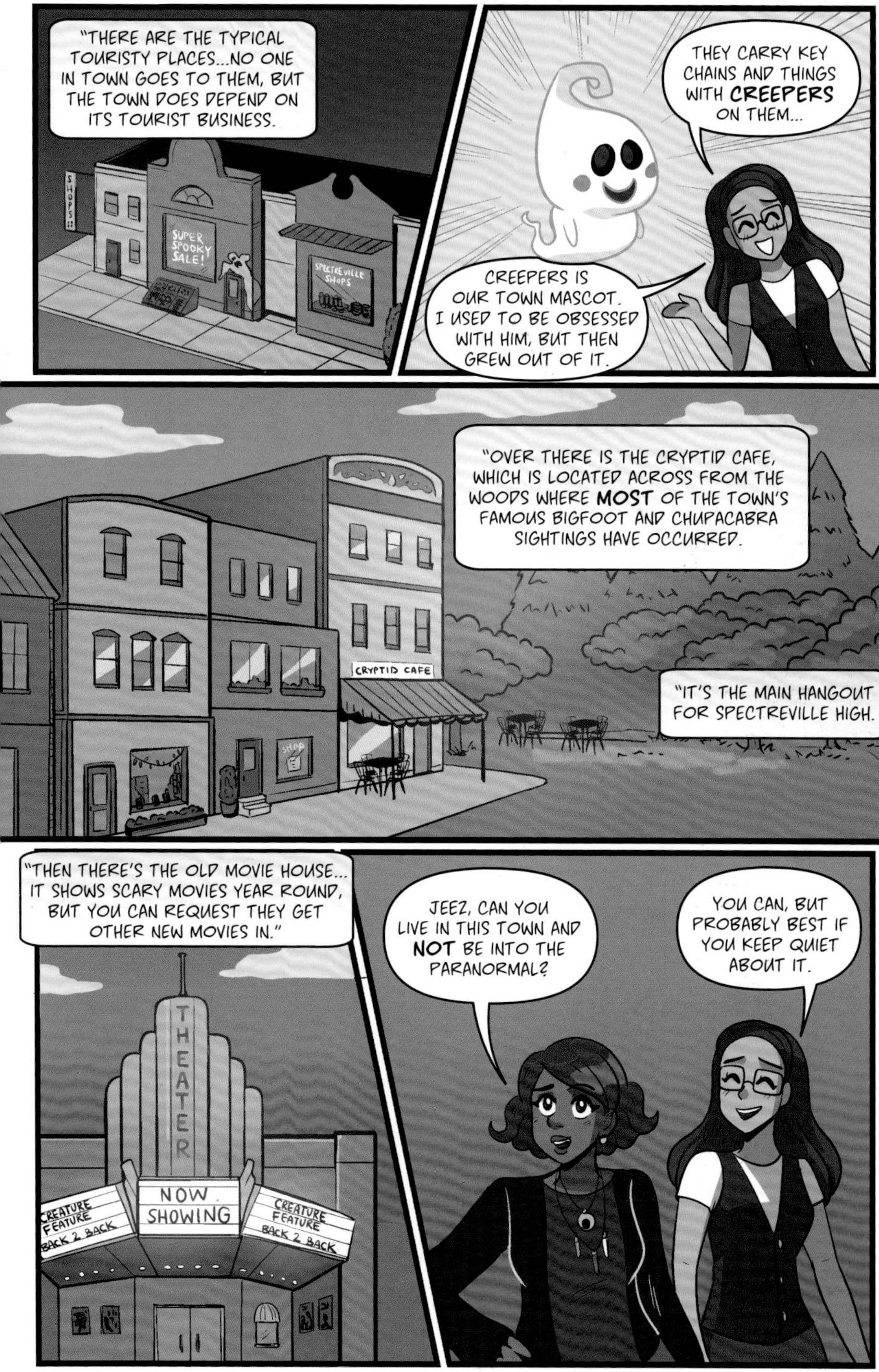
"THERE ARE THE TYPICAL TOURISTY PLACES...NO ONE IN TOWN GOES TO THEM, BUT THE TOWN DOES DEPEND ON ITS TOURIST BUSINESS.
SHOPS!!
SUPER SPOOKY SALE!
SPECTREVILLE SHOPS
THEY CARRY KEY CHAINS AND THINGS WITH **CREEPERS** ON THEM...
CREEPERS IS OUR TOWN MASCOT. I USED TO BE OBSESSED WITH HIM, BUT THEN GREW OUT OF IT.
"OVER THERE IS THE CRYPTID CAFE, WHICH IS LOCATED ACROSS FROM THE WOODS WHERE **MOST** OF THE TOWN'S FAMOUS BIGFOOT AND CHUPACABRA SIGHTINGS HAVE OCCURRED.
CRYPTID CAFE
SHOP
"IT'S THE MAIN HANGOUT FOR SPECTREVILLE HIGH.
"THEN THERE'S THE OLD MOVIE HOUSE... IT SHOWS SCARY MOVIES YEAR ROUND, BUT YOU CAN REQUEST THEY GET OTHER NEW MOVIES IN."
THEATER
CREATURE FEATURE BACK 2 BACK
NOW SHOWING
CREATURE FEATURE BACK 2 BACK
JEEZ, CAN YOU LIVE IN THIS TOWN AND **NOT** BE INTO THE PARANORMAL?
YOU CAN, BUT PROBABLY BEST IF YOU KEEP QUIET ABOUT IT.

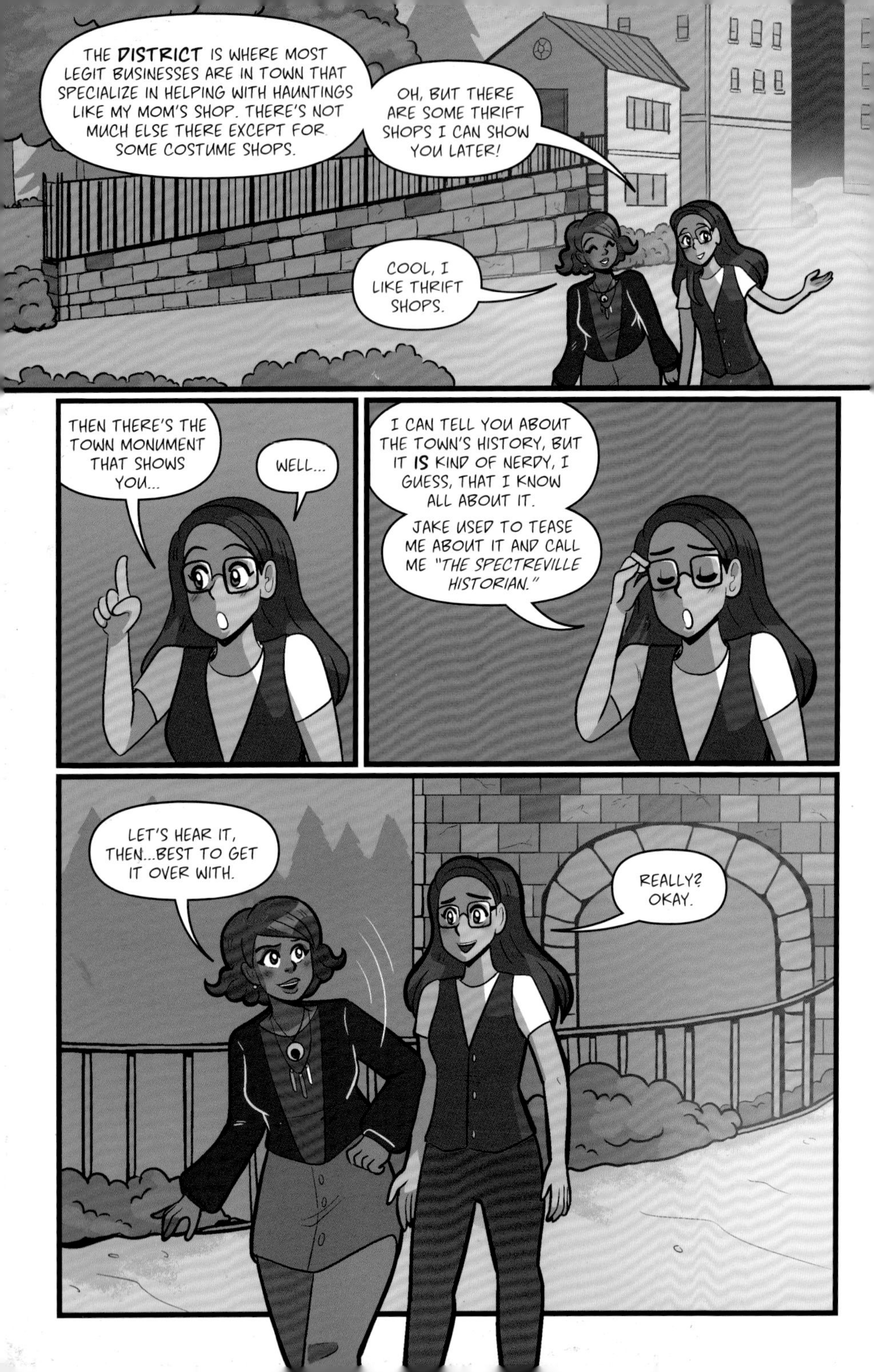
THE **DISTRICT** IS WHERE MOST LEGIT BUSINESSES ARE IN TOWN THAT SPECIALIZE IN HELPING WITH HAUNTINGS LIKE MY MOM'S SHOP. THERE'S NOT MUCH ELSE THERE EXCEPT FOR SOME COSTUME SHOPS.
OH, BUT THERE ARE SOME THRIFT SHOPS I CAN SHOW YOU LATER!
COOL, I LIKE THRIFT SHOPS.
THEN THERE'S THE TOWN MONUMENT THAT SHOWS YOU...
WELL...
I CAN TELL YOU ABOUT THE TOWN'S HISTORY, BUT IT **IS** KIND OF NERDY, I GUESS, THAT I KNOW ALL ABOUT IT.
JAKE USED TO TEASE ME ABOUT IT AND CALL ME *"THE SPECTREVILLE HISTORIAN."*
LET'S HEAR IT, THEN...BEST TO GET IT OVER WITH.
REALLY? OKAY.

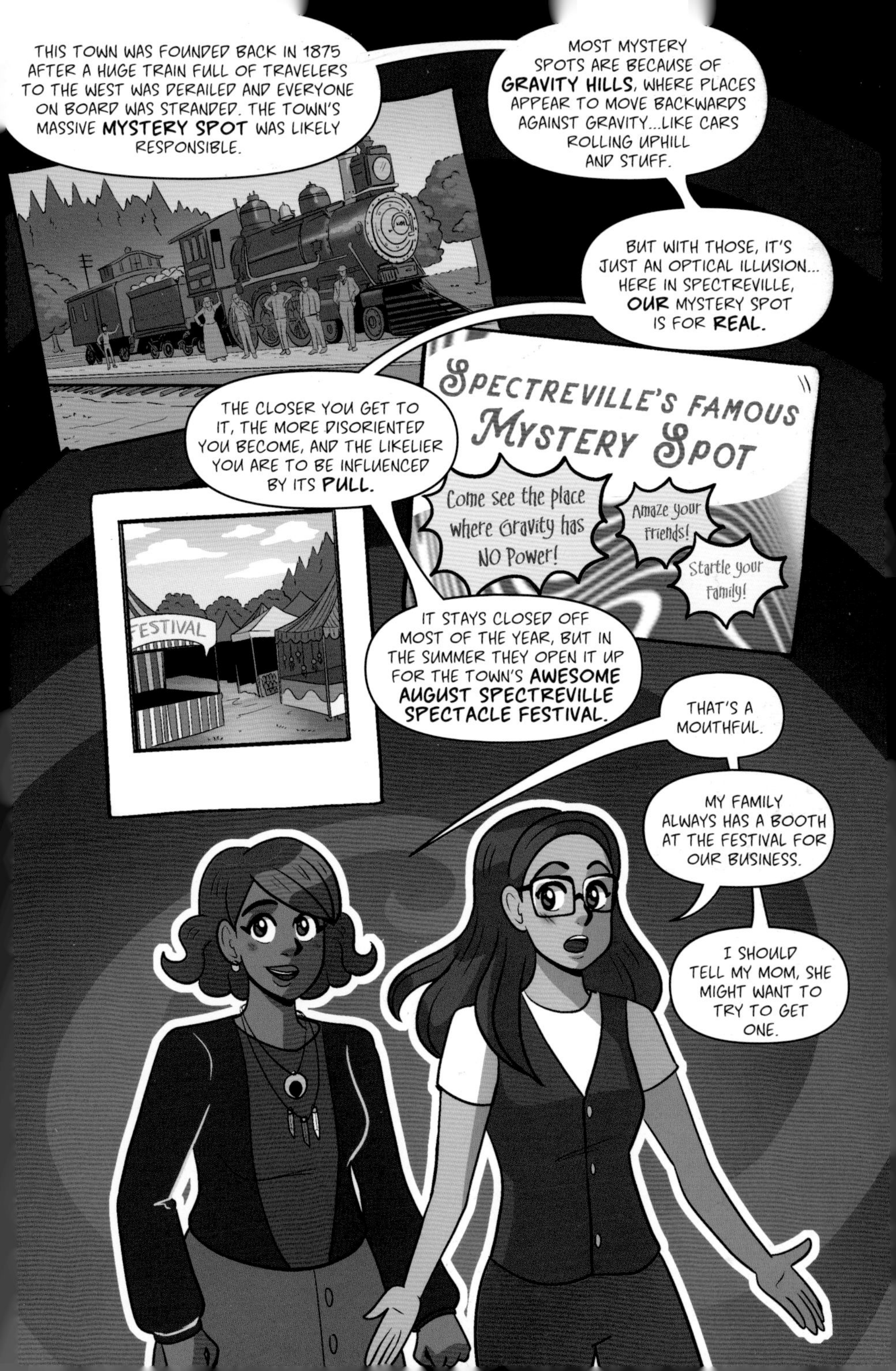
THIS TOWN WAS FOUNDED BACK IN 1875 AFTER A HUGE TRAIN FULL OF TRAVELERS TO THE WEST WAS DERAILED AND EVERYONE ON BOARD WAS STRANDED. THE TOWN'S MASSIVE **MYSTERY SPOT** WAS LIKELY RESPONSIBLE.
MOST MYSTERY SPOTS ARE BECAUSE OF **GRAVITY HILLS**, WHERE PLACES APPEAR TO MOVE BACKWARDS AGAINST GRAVITY...LIKE CARS ROLLING UPHILL AND STUFF.
BUT WITH THOSE, IT'S JUST AN OPTICAL ILLUSION... HERE IN SPECTREVILLE, **OUR** MYSTERY SPOT IS FOR **REAL**.
SPECTREVILLE'S FAMOUS MYSTERY SPOT
Come see the place where Gravity has NO Power!
Amaze your Friends!
Startle your Family!
THE CLOSER YOU GET TO IT, THE MORE DISORIENTED YOU BECOME, AND THE LIKELIER YOU ARE TO BE INFLUENCED BY ITS **PULL**.
FESTIVAL
IT STAYS CLOSED OFF MOST OF THE YEAR, BUT IN THE SUMMER THEY OPEN IT UP FOR THE TOWN'S **AWESOME AUGUST SPECTREVILLE SPECTACLE FESTIVAL**.
THAT'S A MOUTHFUL.
MY FAMILY ALWAYS HAS A BOOTH AT THE FESTIVAL FOR OUR BUSINESS.
I SHOULD TELL MY MOM, SHE MIGHT WANT TO TRY TO GET ONE.

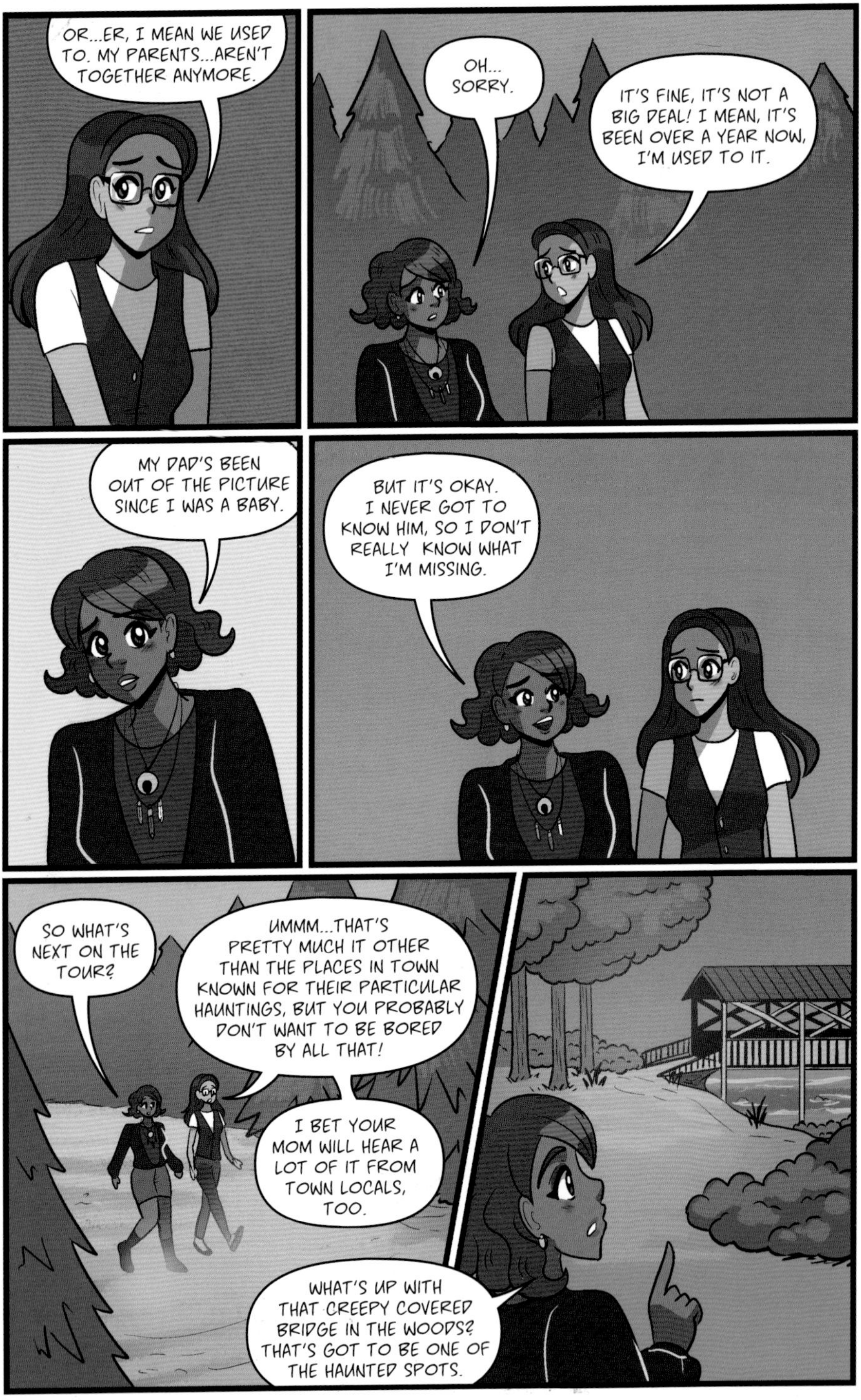
OR...ER, I MEAN WE USED TO. MY PARENTS...AREN'T TOGETHER ANYMORE.
OH... SORRY.
IT'S FINE, IT'S NOT A BIG DEAL! I MEAN, IT'S BEEN OVER A YEAR NOW, I'M USED TO IT.
MY DAD'S BEEN OUT OF THE PICTURE SINCE I WAS A BABY.
BUT IT'S OKAY. I NEVER GOT TO KNOW HIM, SO I DON'T REALLY KNOW WHAT I'M MISSING.
SO WHAT'S NEXT ON THE TOUR?
UMMM...THAT'S PRETTY MUCH IT OTHER THAN THE PLACES IN TOWN KNOWN FOR THEIR PARTICULAR HAUNTINGS, BUT YOU PROBABLY DON'T WANT TO BE BORED BY ALL THAT!
I BET YOUR MOM WILL HEAR A LOT OF IT FROM TOWN LOCALS, TOO.
WHAT'S UP WITH THAT CREEPY COVERED BRIDGE IN THE WOODS? THAT'S GOT TO BE ONE OF THE HAUNTED SPOTS.

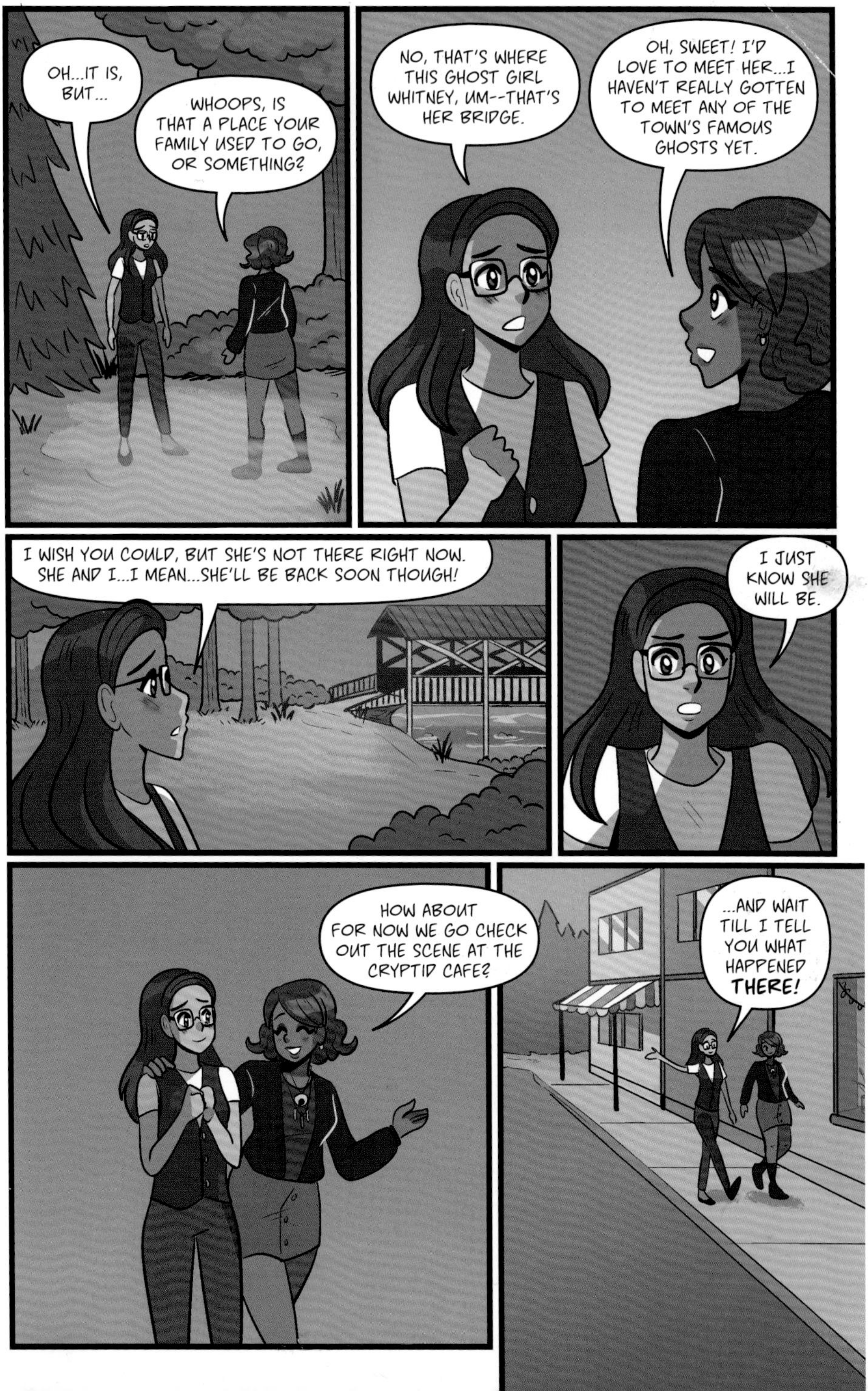

OH...IT IS, BUT...
WHOOPS, IS THAT A PLACE YOUR FAMILY USED TO GO, OR SOMETHING?
NO, THAT'S WHERE THIS GHOST GIRL WHITNEY, UM--THAT'S HER BRIDGE.
OH, SWEET! I'D LOVE TO MEET HER...I HAVEN'T REALLY GOTTEN TO MEET ANY OF THE TOWN'S FAMOUS GHOSTS YET.
I WISH YOU COULD, BUT SHE'S NOT THERE RIGHT NOW. SHE AND I...I MEAN...SHE'LL BE BACK SOON THOUGH!
I JUST KNOW SHE WILL BE.
HOW ABOUT FOR NOW WE GO CHECK OUT THE SCENE AT THE CRYPTID CAFE?
...AND WAIT TILL I TELL YOU WHAT HAPPENED **THERE!**

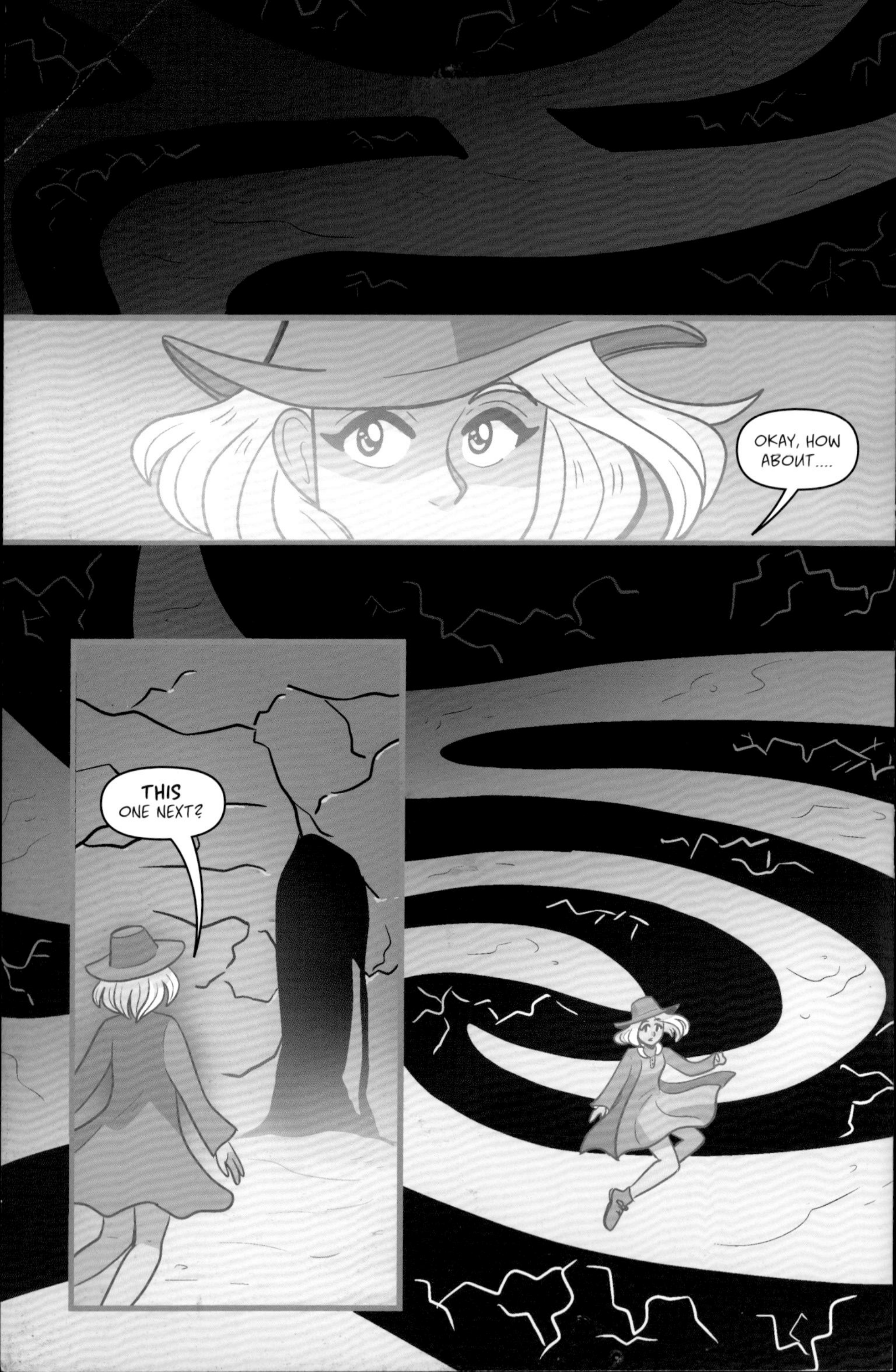
OKAY, HOW ABOUT....
THIS ONE NEXT?

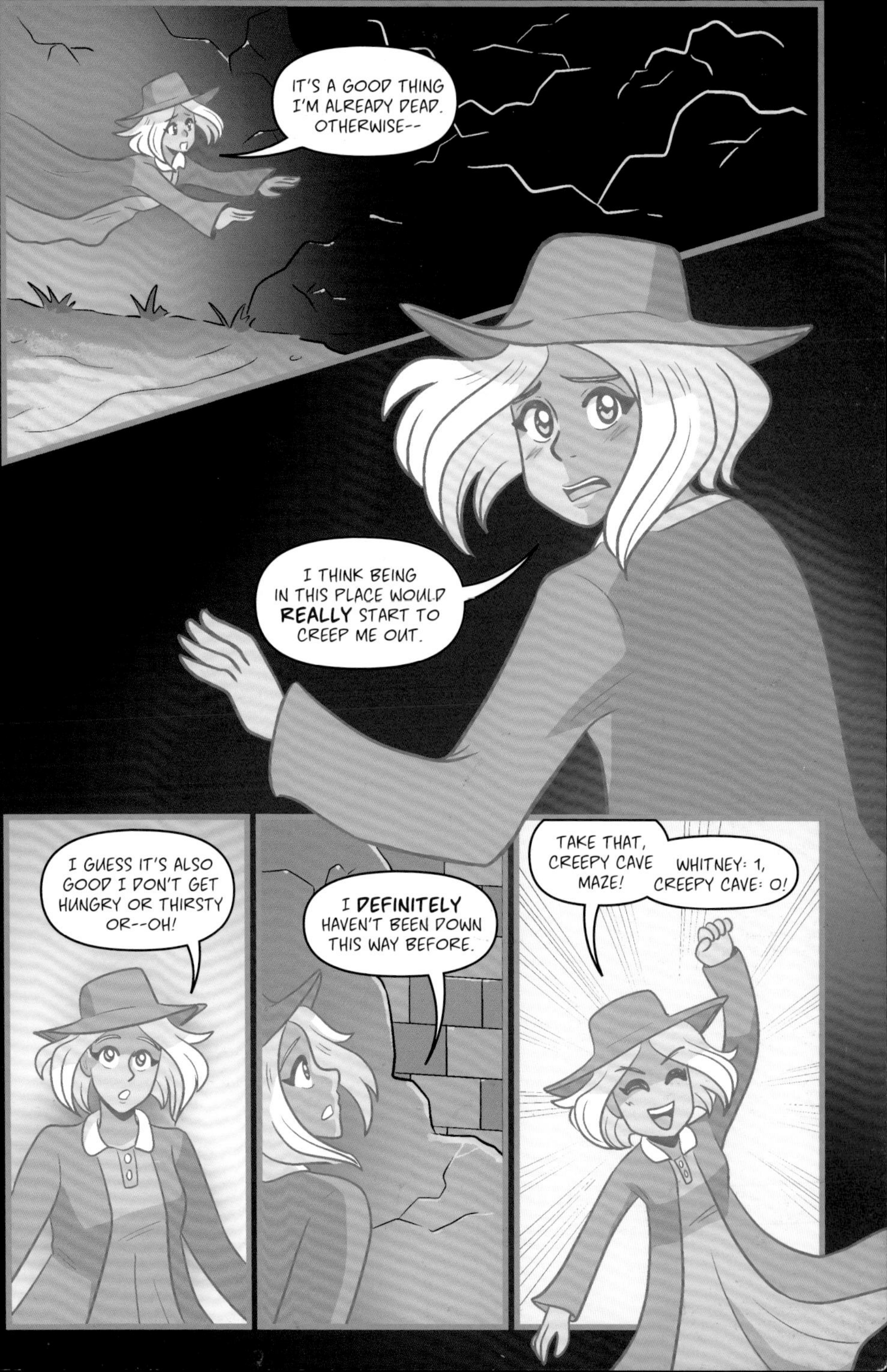
IT'S A GOOD THING I'M ALREADY DEAD. OTHERWISE--
I THINK BEING IN THIS PLACE WOULD **REALLY** START TO CREEP ME OUT.
I GUESS IT'S ALSO GOOD I DON'T GET HUNGRY OR THIRSTY OR--OH!
I **DEFINITELY** HAVEN'T BEEN DOWN THIS WAY BEFORE.
TAKE THAT, CREEPY CAVE MAZE!
WHITNEY: 1, CREEPY CAVE: 0!

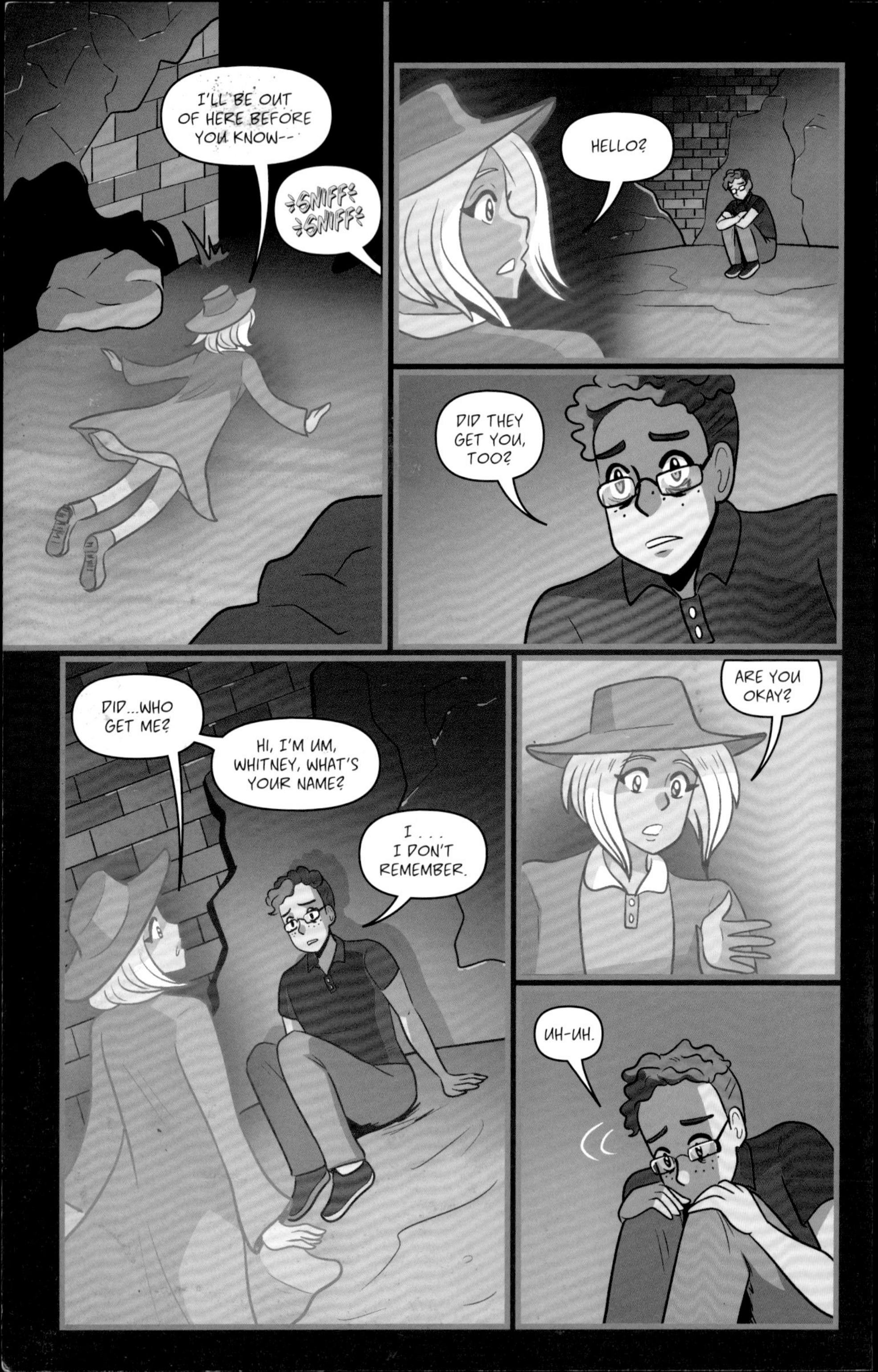
I'LL BE OUT OF HERE BEFORE YOU KNOW--
SNIFF SNIFF
HELLO?
DID THEY GET YOU, TOO?
DID...WHO GET ME?
HI, I'M UM, WHITNEY, WHAT'S YOUR NAME?
I . . . I DON'T REMEMBER.
ARE YOU OKAY?
UH-UH.

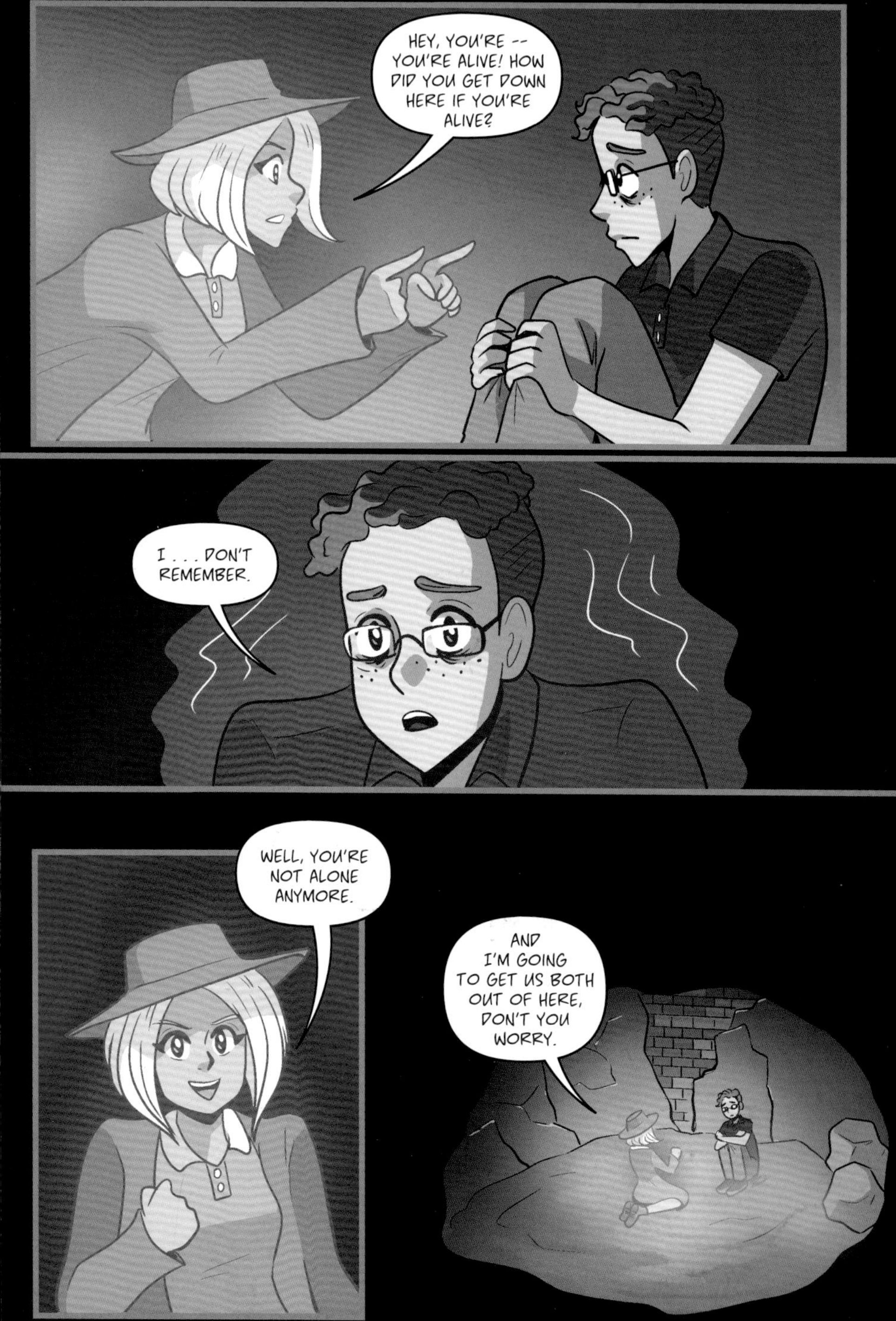
HEY, YOU'RE -- YOU'RE ALIVE! HOW DID YOU GET DOWN HERE IF YOU'RE ALIVE?
I . . . DON'T REMEMBER.
WELL, YOU'RE NOT ALONE ANYMORE.
AND I'M GOING TO GET US BOTH OUT OF HERE, DON'T YOU WORRY.

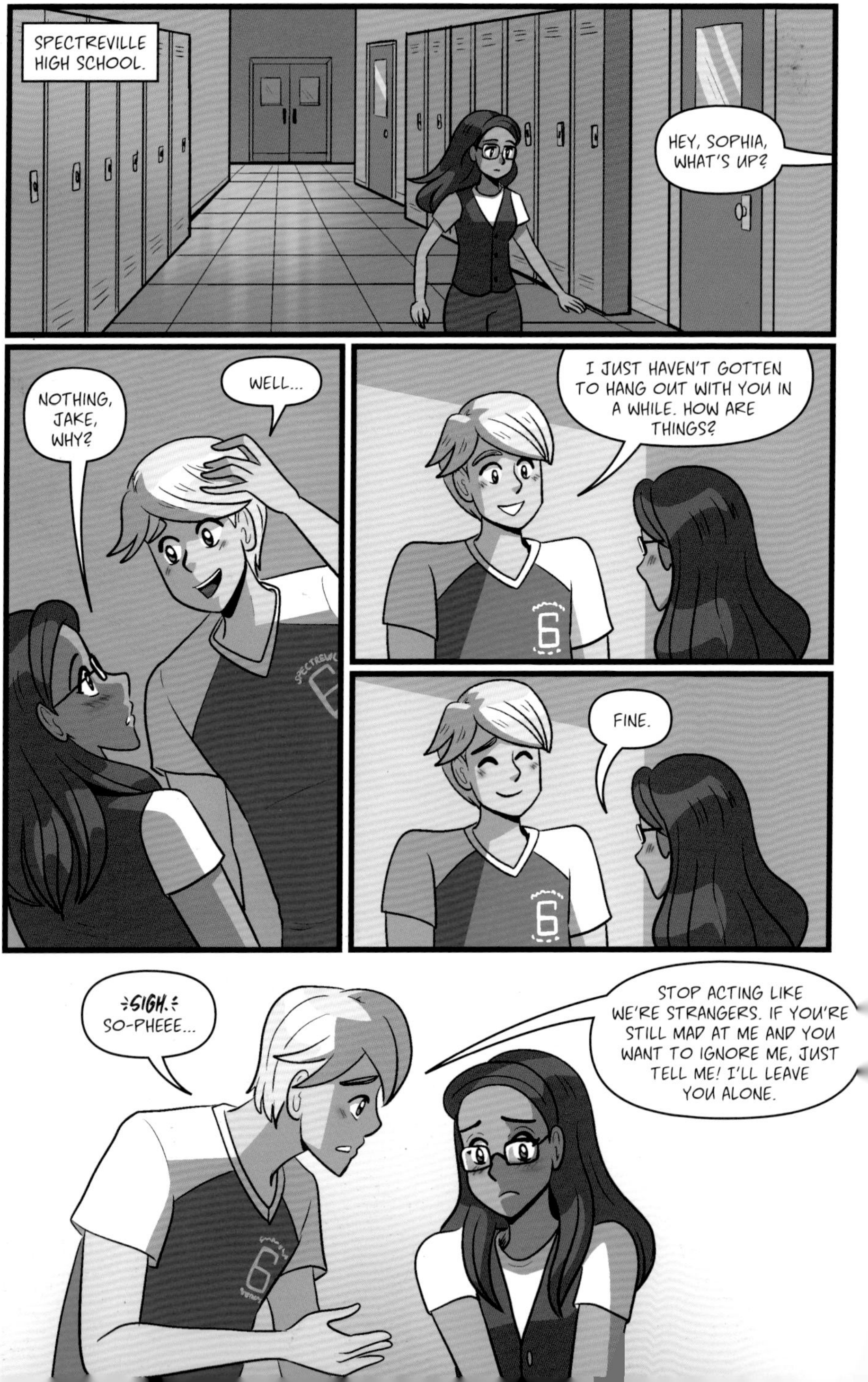
SPECTREVILLE HIGH SCHOOL.
HEY, SOPHIA, WHAT'S UP?
NOTHING, JAKE, WHY?
WELL...
I JUST HAVEN'T GOTTEN TO HANG OUT WITH YOU IN A WHILE. HOW ARE THINGS?
FINE.
SIGH. SO-PHEEE...
STOP ACTING LIKE WE'RE STRANGERS. IF YOU'RE STILL MAD AT ME AND YOU WANT TO IGNORE ME, JUST TELL ME! I'LL LEAVE YOU ALONE.

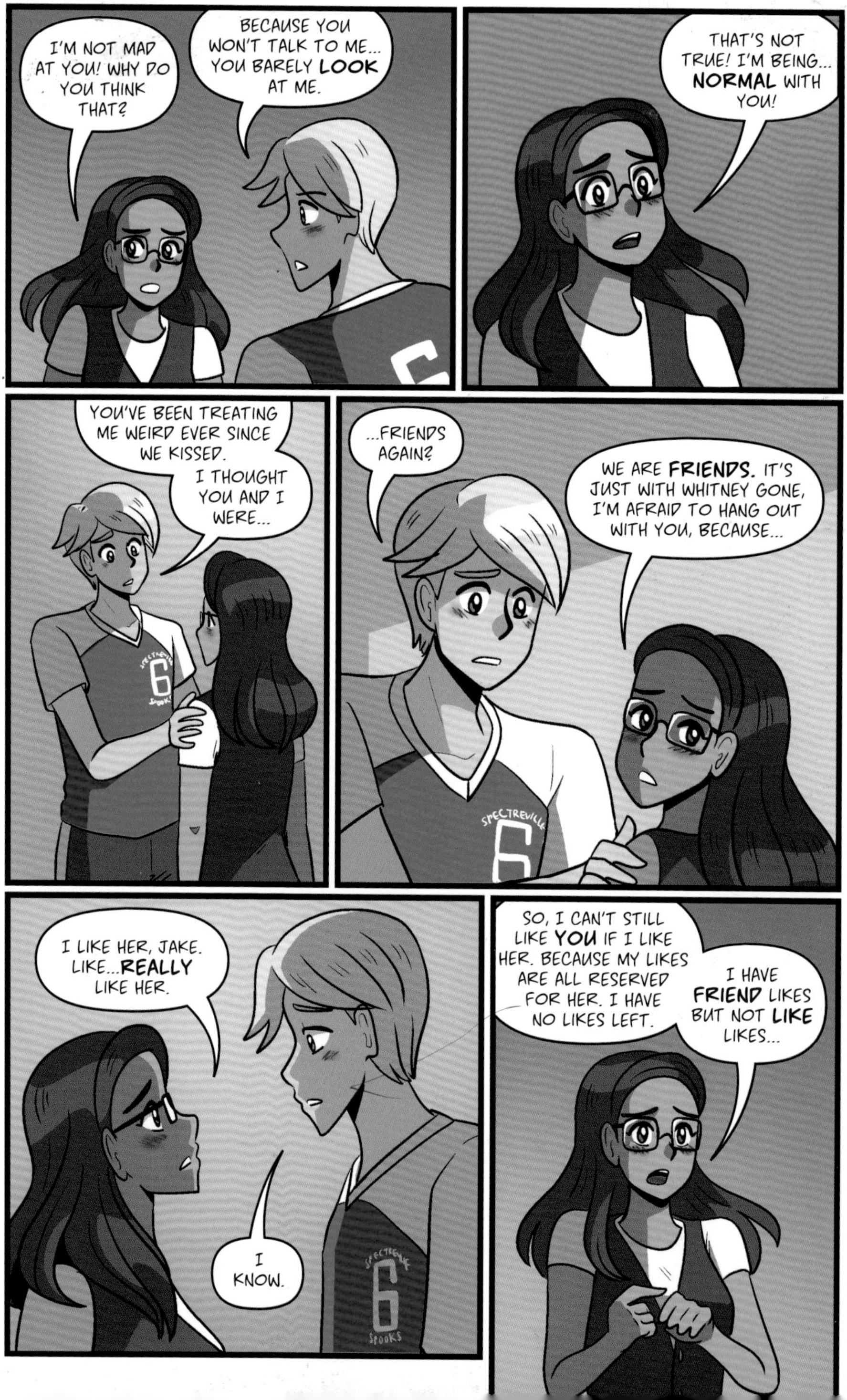
I'M NOT MAD AT YOU! WHY DO YOU THINK THAT?
BECAUSE YOU WON'T TALK TO ME... YOU BARELY LOOK AT ME.
THAT'S NOT TRUE! I'M BEING... NORMAL WITH YOU!
YOU'VE BEEN TREATING ME WEIRD EVER SINCE WE KISSED.
I THOUGHT YOU AND I WERE...
...FRIENDS AGAIN?
WE ARE FRIENDS. IT'S JUST WITH WHITNEY GONE, I'M AFRAID TO HANG OUT WITH YOU, BECAUSE...
SPECTREVILLE
6
I LIKE HER, JAKE. LIKE...REALLY LIKE HER.
I KNOW.
SO, I CAN'T STILL LIKE YOU IF I LIKE HER. BECAUSE MY LIKES ARE ALL RESERVED FOR HER. I HAVE NO LIKES LEFT.
I HAVE FRIEND LIKES BUT NOT LIKE LIKES...

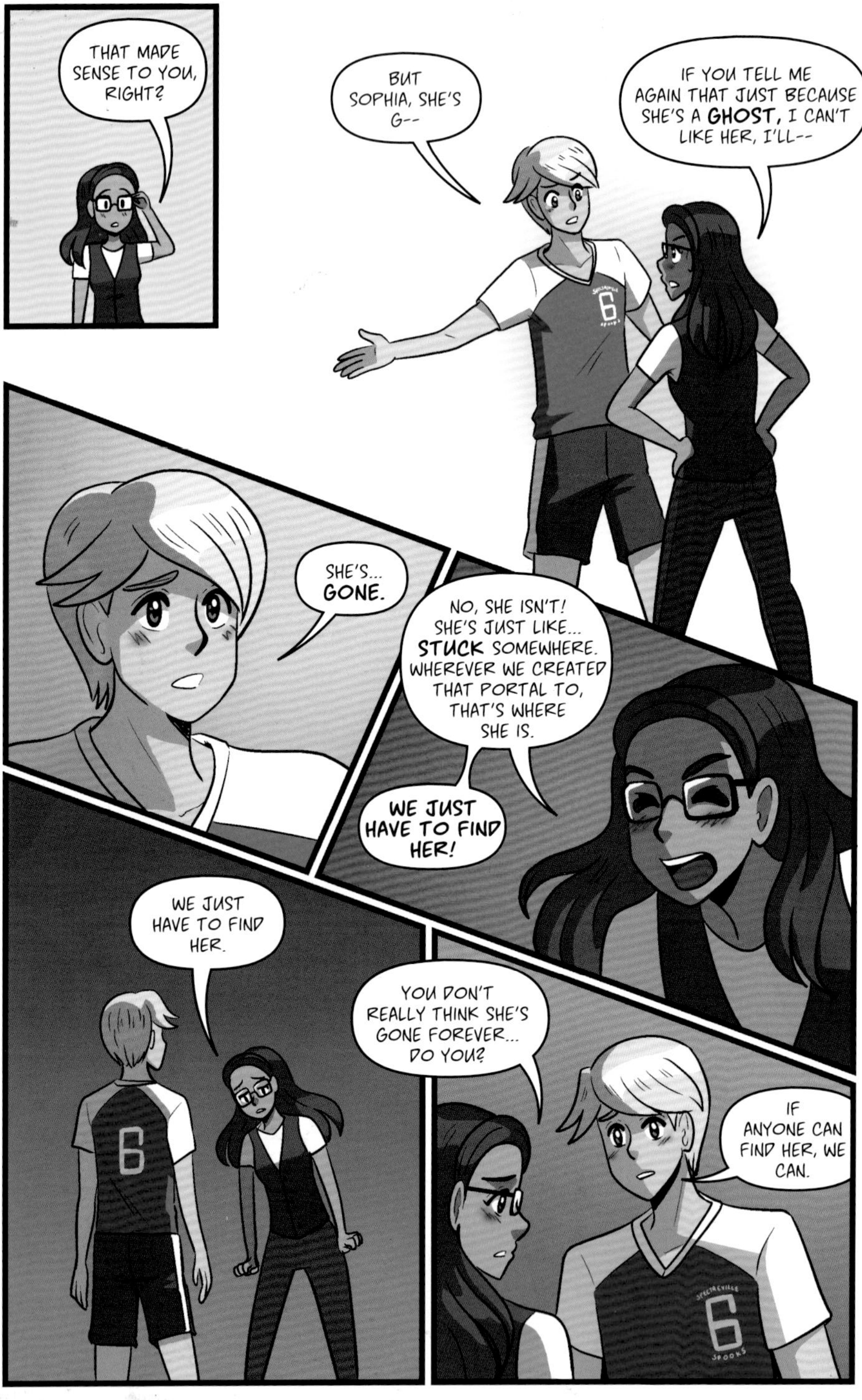
THAT MADE SENSE TO YOU, RIGHT?
BUT SOPHIA, SHE'S G--
IF YOU TELL ME AGAIN THAT JUST BECAUSE SHE'S A GHOST, I CAN'T LIKE HER, I'LL--
SHE'S... GONE.
NO, SHE ISN'T! SHE'S JUST LIKE... STUCK SOMEWHERE. WHEREVER WE CREATED THAT PORTAL TO, THAT'S WHERE SHE IS.
WE JUST HAVE TO FIND HER!
WE JUST HAVE TO FIND HER.
YOU DON'T REALLY THINK SHE'S GONE FOREVER... DO YOU?
IF ANYONE CAN FIND HER, WE CAN.

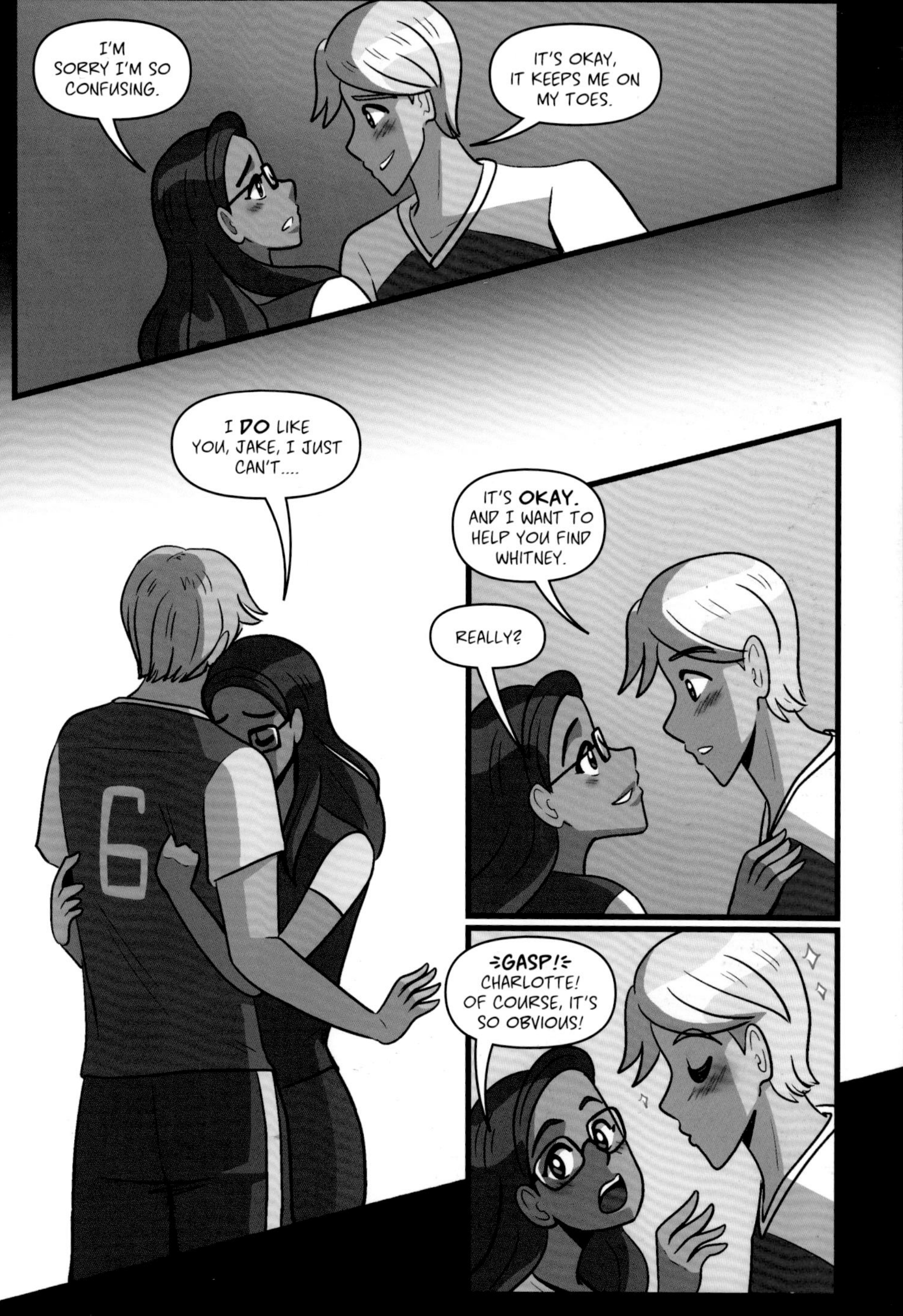
I'M SORRY I'M SO CONFUSING.
IT'S OKAY, IT KEEPS ME ON MY TOES.
I **DO** LIKE YOU, JAKE, I JUST CAN'T....
IT'S **OKAY.** AND I WANT TO HELP YOU FIND WHITNEY.
REALLY?
GASP! CHARLOTTE! OF COURSE, IT'S SO OBVIOUS!

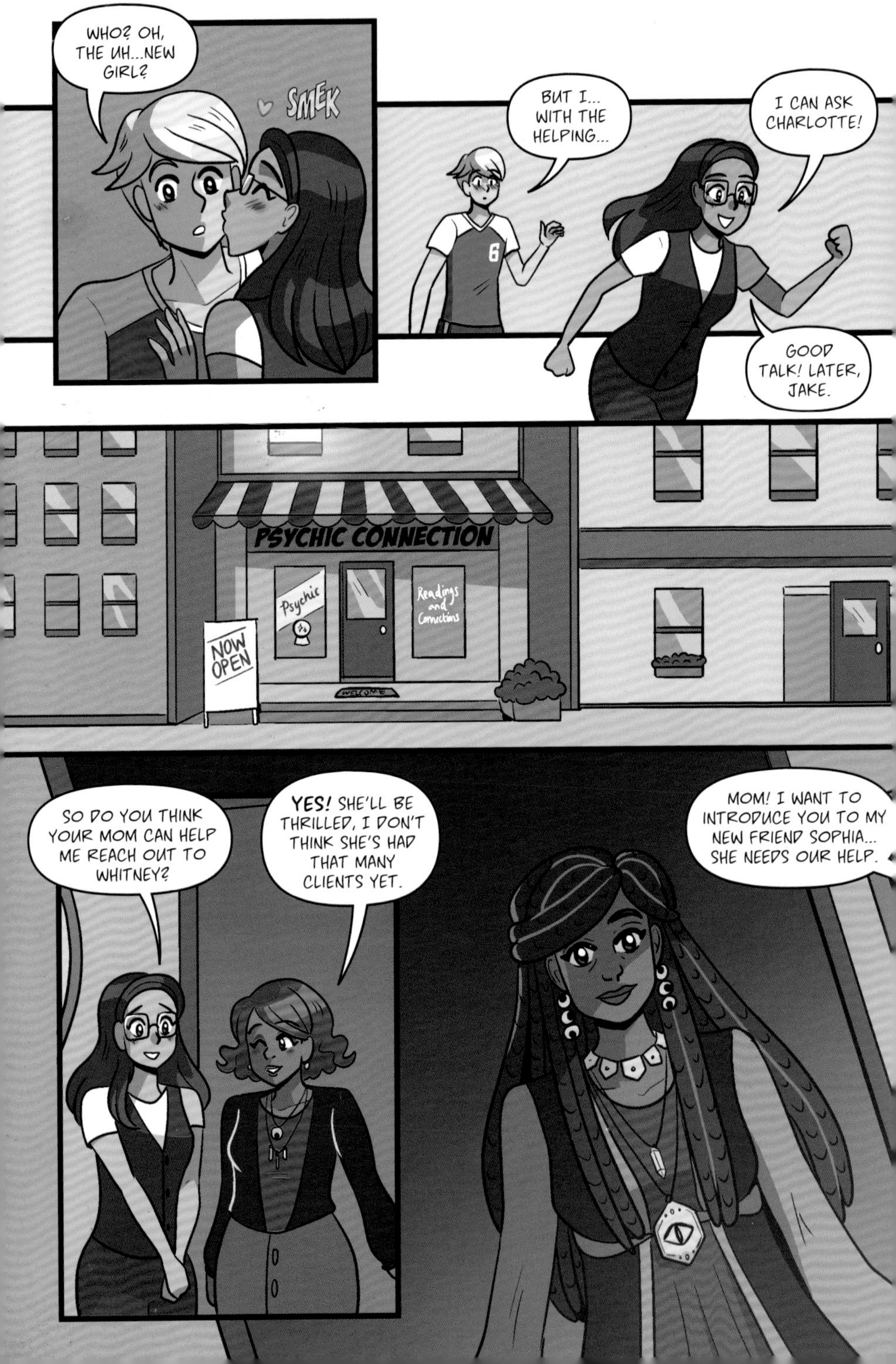
WHO? OH, THE UH...NEW GIRL?
SMEK
BUT I... WITH THE HELPING...
I CAN ASK CHARLOTTE!
GOOD TALK! LATER, JAKE.
PSYCHIC CONNECTION
Psychic
Readings and Connections
NOW OPEN
WELCOME
SO DO YOU THINK YOUR MOM CAN HELP ME REACH OUT TO WHITNEY?
YES! SHE'LL BE THRILLED, I DON'T THINK SHE'S HAD THAT MANY CLIENTS YET.
MOM! I WANT TO INTRODUCE YOU TO MY NEW FRIEND SOPHIA... SHE NEEDS OUR HELP.

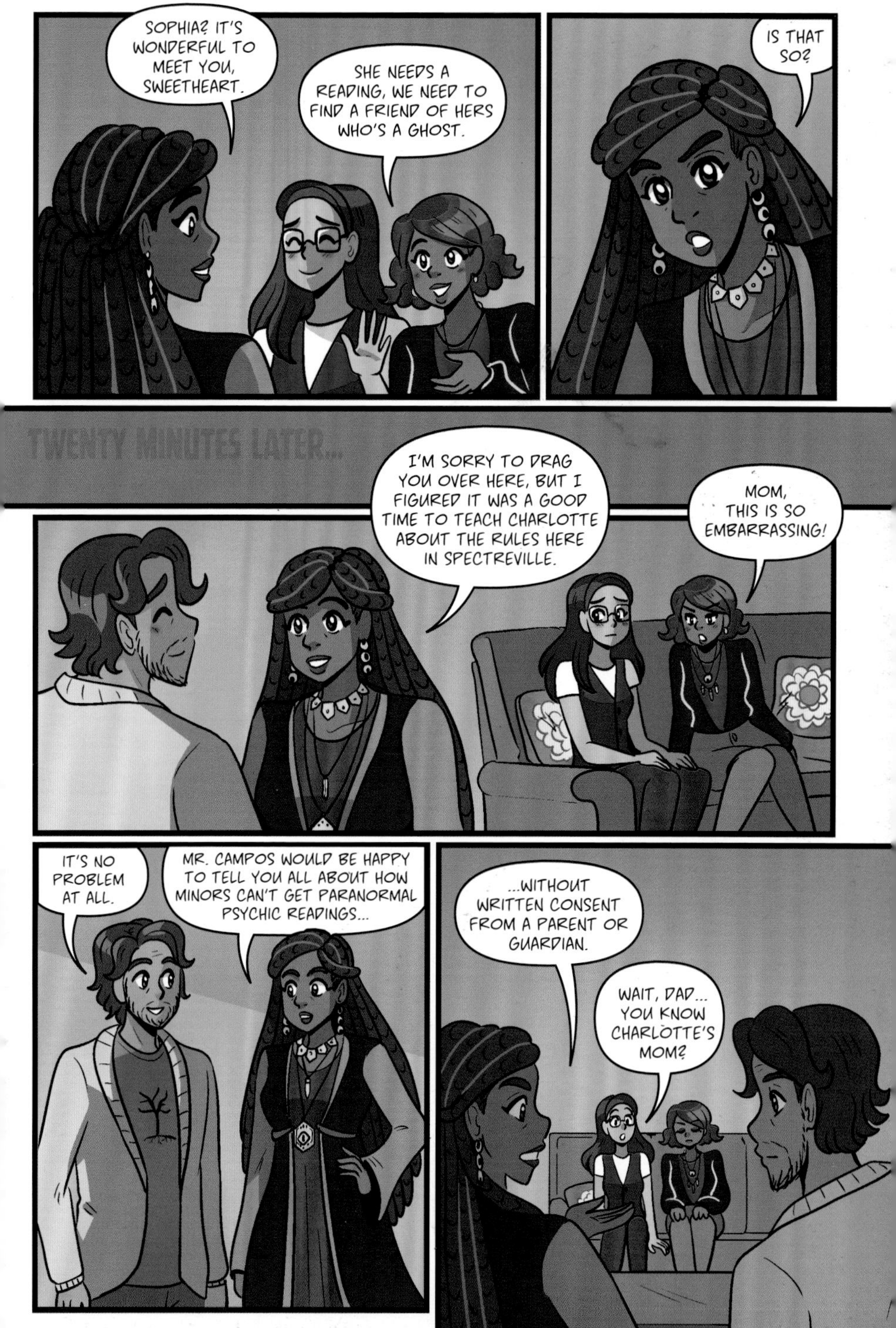
SOPHIA? IT'S WONDERFUL TO MEET YOU, SWEETHEART.
SHE NEEDS A READING, WE NEED TO FIND A FRIEND OF HERS WHO'S A GHOST.
IS THAT SO?
TWENTY MINUTES LATER...
I'M SORRY TO DRAG YOU OVER HERE, BUT I FIGURED IT WAS A GOOD TIME TO TEACH CHARLOTTE ABOUT THE RULES HERE IN SPECTREVILLE.
MOM, THIS IS SO EMBARRASSING!
IT'S NO PROBLEM AT ALL.
MR. CAMPOS WOULD BE HAPPY TO TELL YOU ALL ABOUT HOW MINORS CAN'T GET PARANORMAL PSYCHIC READINGS...
...WITHOUT WRITTEN CONSENT FROM A PARENT OR GUARDIAN.
WAIT, DAD... YOU KNOW CHARLOTTE'S MOM?

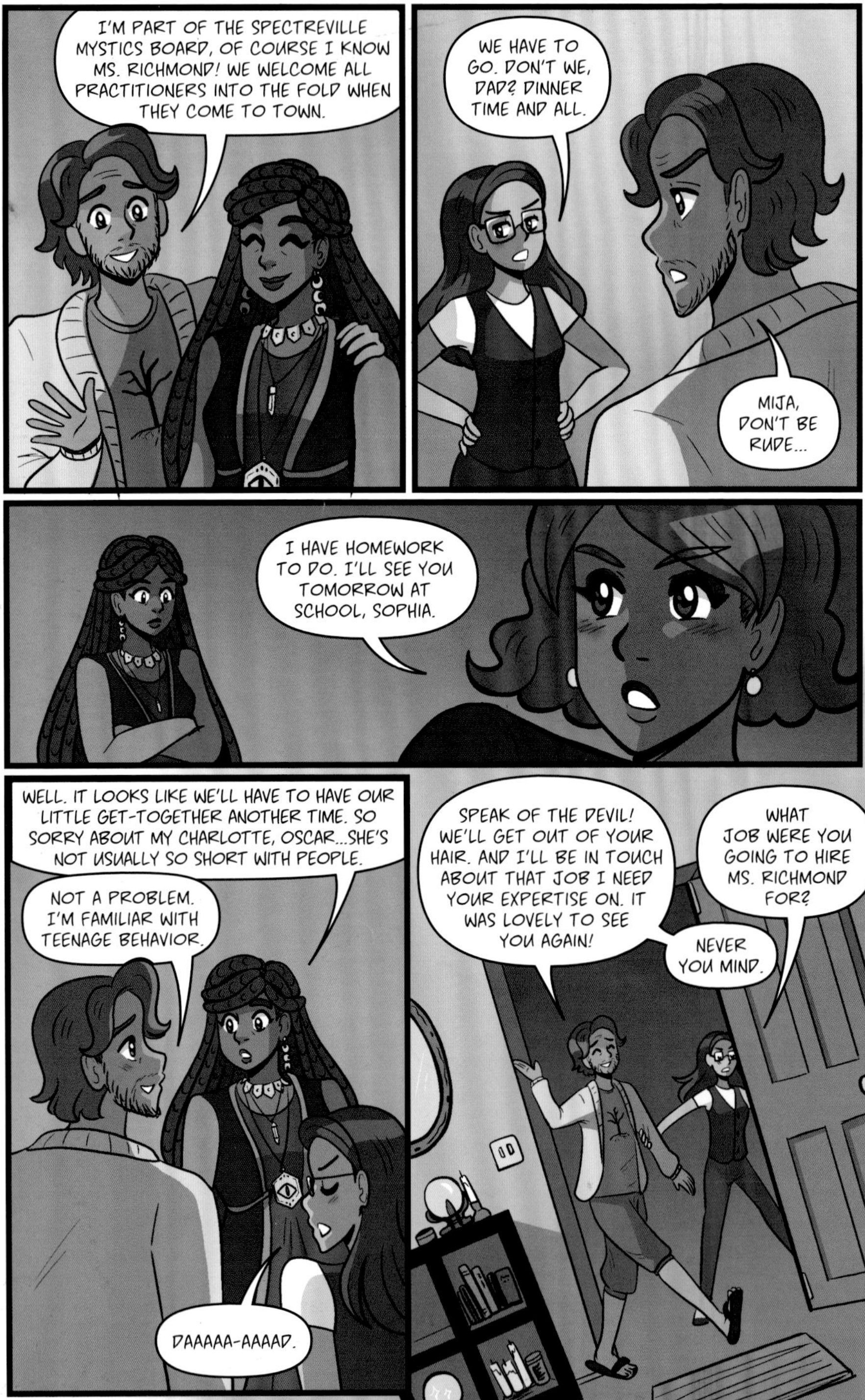
I'M PART OF THE SPECTREVILLE MYSTICS BOARD, OF COURSE I KNOW MS. RICHMOND! WE WELCOME ALL PRACTITIONERS INTO THE FOLD WHEN THEY COME TO TOWN.
WE HAVE TO GO. DON'T WE, DAD? DINNER TIME AND ALL.
MIJA, DON'T BE RUDE...
I HAVE HOMEWORK TO DO. I'LL SEE YOU TOMORROW AT SCHOOL, SOPHIA.
WELL. IT LOOKS LIKE WE'LL HAVE TO HAVE OUR LITTLE GET-TOGETHER ANOTHER TIME. SO SORRY ABOUT MY CHARLOTTE, OSCAR...SHE'S NOT USUALLY SO SHORT WITH PEOPLE.
NOT A PROBLEM. I'M FAMILIAR WITH TEENAGE BEHAVIOR.
DAAAAA-AAAAD.
SPEAK OF THE DEVIL! WE'LL GET OUT OF YOUR HAIR. AND I'LL BE IN TOUCH ABOUT THAT JOB I NEED YOUR EXPERTISE ON. IT WAS LOVELY TO SEE YOU AGAIN!
WHAT JOB WERE YOU GOING TO HIRE MS. RICHMOND FOR?
NEVER YOU MIND.

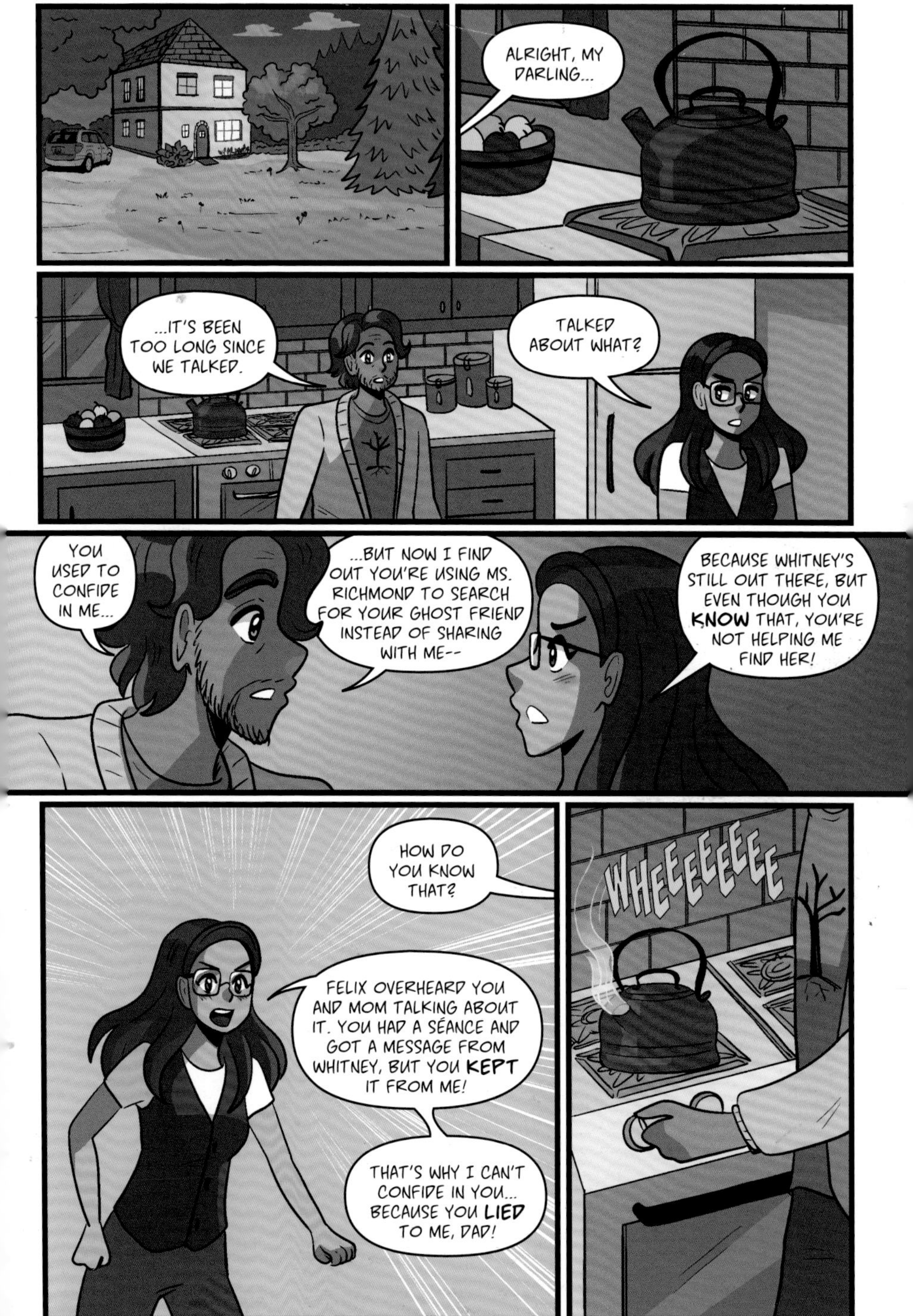
ALRIGHT, MY DARLING...
...IT'S BEEN TOO LONG SINCE WE TALKED.
TALKED ABOUT WHAT?
YOU USED TO CONFIDE IN ME...
...BUT NOW I FIND OUT YOU'RE USING MS. RICHMOND TO SEARCH FOR YOUR GHOST FRIEND INSTEAD OF SHARING WITH ME--
BECAUSE WHITNEY'S STILL OUT THERE, BUT EVEN THOUGH YOU KNOW THAT, YOU'RE NOT HELPING ME FIND HER!
HOW DO YOU KNOW THAT?
WHEEEEEEEE
FELIX OVERHEARD YOU AND MOM TALKING ABOUT IT. YOU HAD A SÉANCE AND GOT A MESSAGE FROM WHITNEY, BUT YOU KEPT IT FROM ME!
THAT'S WHY I CAN'T CONFIDE IN YOU... BECAUSE YOU LIED TO ME, DAD!

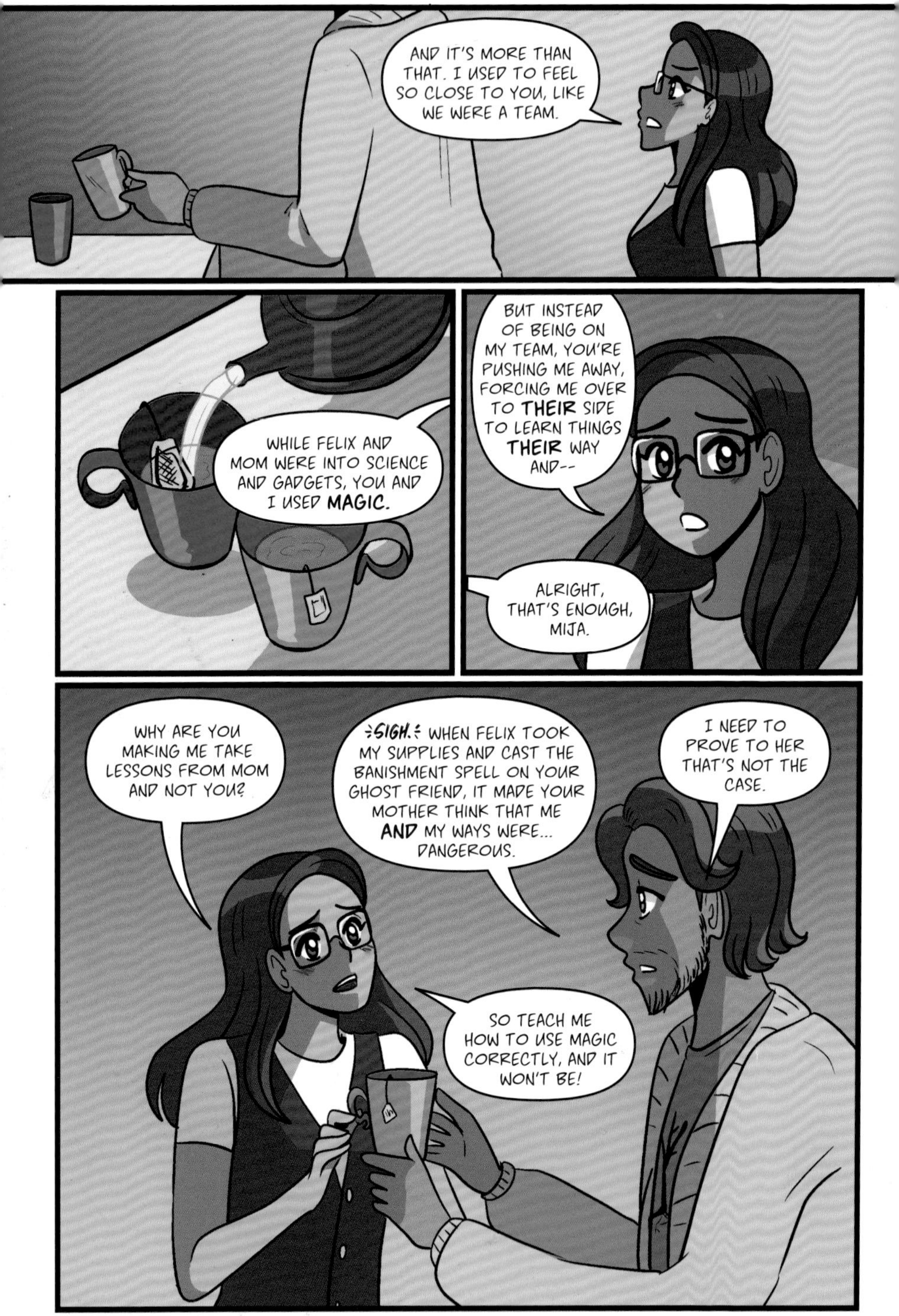
AND IT'S MORE THAN THAT. I USED TO FEEL SO CLOSE TO YOU, LIKE WE WERE A TEAM.
WHILE FELIX AND MOM WERE INTO SCIENCE AND GADGETS, YOU AND I USED **MAGIC.**
BUT INSTEAD OF BEING ON MY TEAM, YOU'RE PUSHING ME AWAY, FORCING ME OVER TO **THEIR** SIDE TO LEARN THINGS **THEIR** WAY AND--
ALRIGHT, THAT'S ENOUGH, MIJA.
WHY ARE YOU MAKING ME TAKE LESSONS FROM MOM AND NOT YOU?
SIGH. WHEN FELIX TOOK MY SUPPLIES AND CAST THE BANISHMENT SPELL ON YOUR GHOST FRIEND, IT MADE YOUR MOTHER THINK THAT ME **AND** MY WAYS WERE... DANGEROUS.
I NEED TO PROVE TO HER THAT'S NOT THE CASE.
SO TEACH ME HOW TO USE MAGIC CORRECTLY, AND IT WON'T BE!

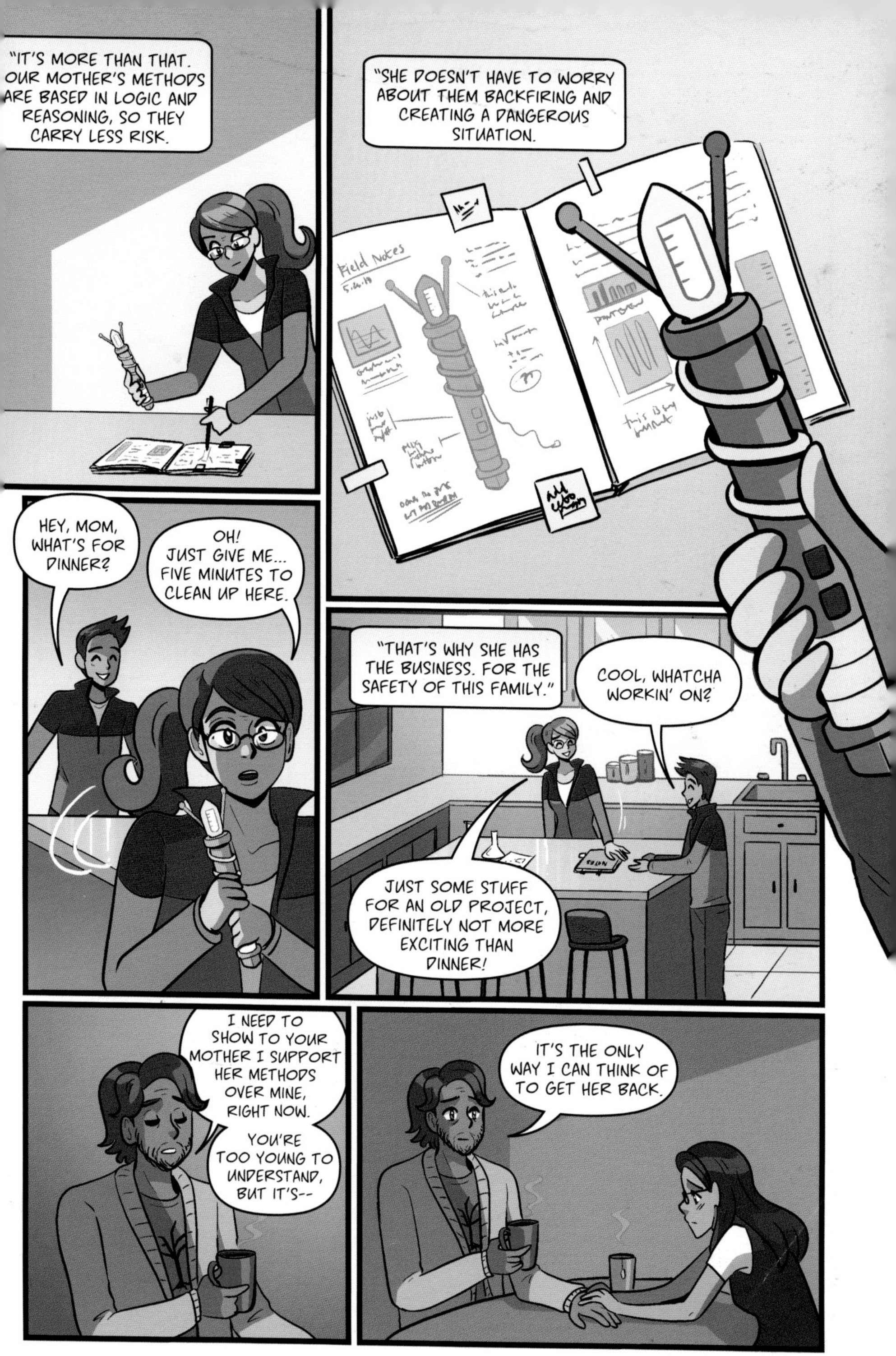
"IT'S MORE THAN THAT. OUR MOTHER'S METHODS ARE BASED IN LOGIC AND REASONING, SO THEY CARRY LESS RISK.
"SHE DOESN'T HAVE TO WORRY ABOUT THEM BACKFIRING AND CREATING A DANGEROUS SITUATION.
Field Notes
HEY, MOM, WHAT'S FOR DINNER?
OH! JUST GIVE ME... FIVE MINUTES TO CLEAN UP HERE.
"THAT'S WHY SHE HAS THE BUSINESS. FOR THE SAFETY OF THIS FAMILY."
COOL, WHATCHA WORKIN' ON?
JUST SOME STUFF FOR AN OLD PROJECT, DEFINITELY NOT MORE EXCITING THAN DINNER!
I NEED TO SHOW TO YOUR MOTHER I SUPPORT HER METHODS OVER MINE, RIGHT NOW.
YOU'RE TOO YOUNG TO UNDERSTAND, BUT IT'S--
IT'S THE ONLY WAY I CAN THINK OF TO GET HER BACK.

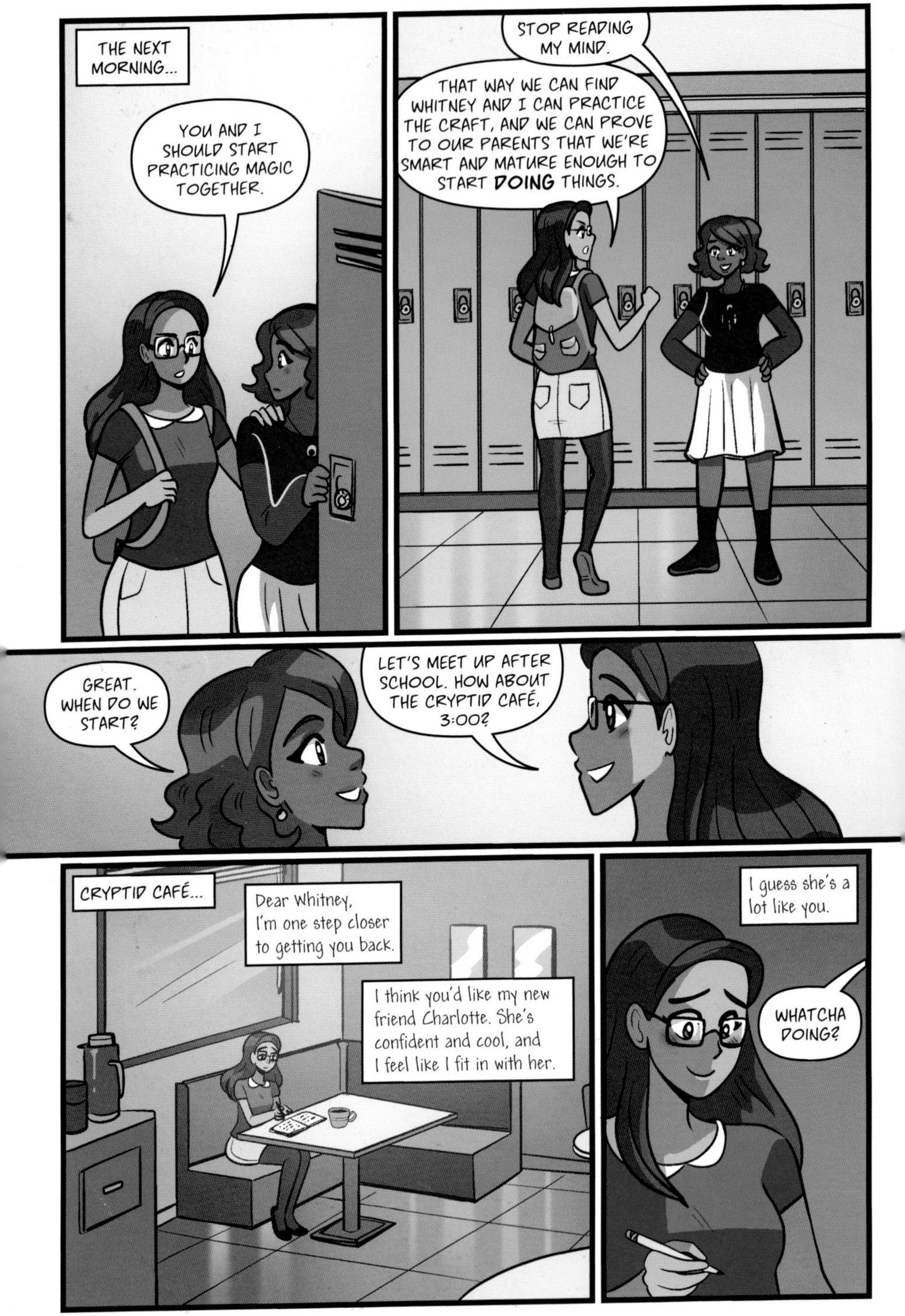
THE NEXT MORNING...
YOU AND I SHOULD START PRACTICING MAGIC TOGETHER.
THAT WAY WE CAN FIND WHITNEY AND I CAN PRACTICE THE CRAFT, AND WE CAN PROVE TO OUR PARENTS THAT WE'RE SMART AND MATURE ENOUGH TO START DOING THINGS.
STOP READING MY MIND.
GREAT. WHEN DO WE START?
LET'S MEET UP AFTER SCHOOL. HOW ABOUT THE CRYPTID CAFÉ, 3:00?
CRYPTID CAFÉ...
Dear Whitney, I'm one step closer to getting you back.
I think you'd like my new friend Charlotte. She's confident and cool, and I feel like I fit in with her.
I guess she's a lot like you.
WHATCHA DOING?

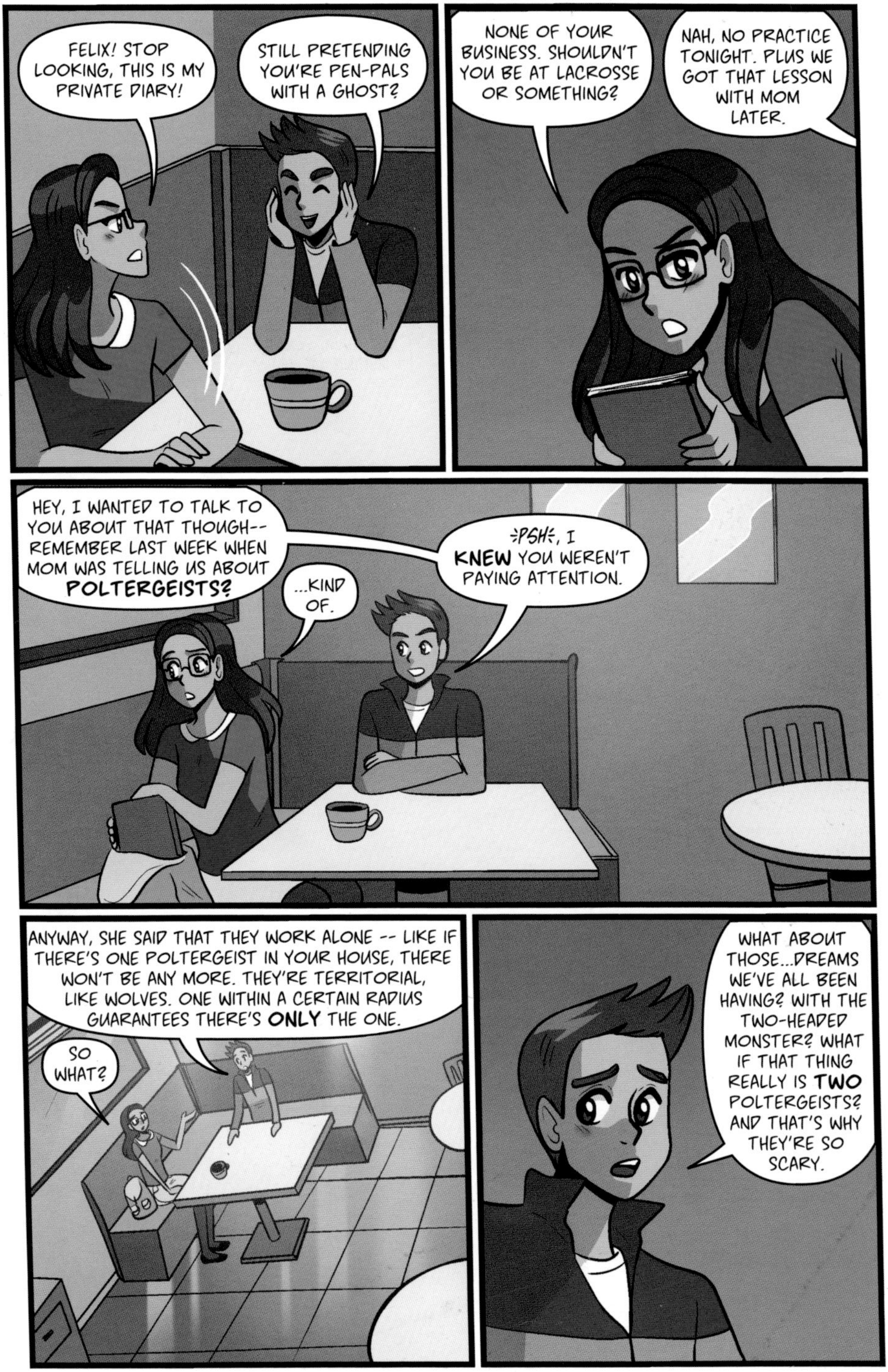
FELIX! STOP LOOKING, THIS IS MY PRIVATE DIARY!
STILL PRETENDING YOU'RE PEN-PALS WITH A GHOST?
NONE OF YOUR BUSINESS. SHOULDN'T YOU BE AT LACROSSE OR SOMETHING?
NAH, NO PRACTICE TONIGHT. PLUS WE GOT THAT LESSON WITH MOM LATER.
HEY, I WANTED TO TALK TO YOU ABOUT THAT THOUGH-- REMEMBER LAST WEEK WHEN MOM WAS TELLING US ABOUT POLTERGEISTS?
...KIND OF.
PSH, I KNEW YOU WEREN'T PAYING ATTENTION.
ANYWAY, SHE SAID THAT THEY WORK ALONE -- LIKE IF THERE'S ONE POLTERGEIST IN YOUR HOUSE, THERE WON'T BE ANY MORE. THEY'RE TERRITORIAL, LIKE WOLVES. ONE WITHIN A CERTAIN RADIUS GUARANTEES THERE'S ONLY THE ONE.
SO WHAT?
WHAT ABOUT THOSE...DREAMS WE'VE ALL BEEN HAVING? WITH THE TWO-HEADED MONSTER? WHAT IF THAT THING REALLY IS TWO POLTERGEISTS? AND THAT'S WHY THEY'RE SO SCARY.

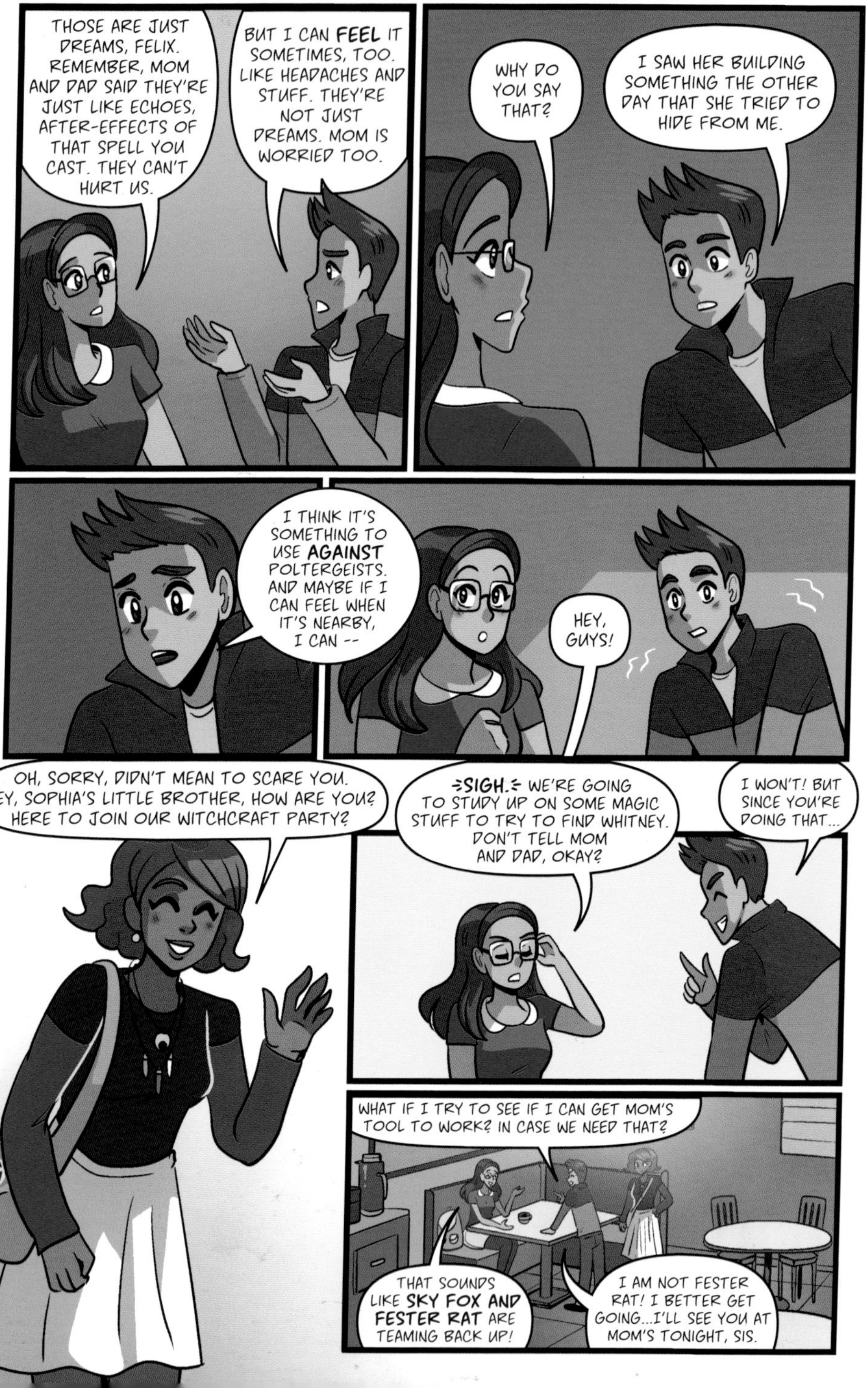
THOSE ARE JUST DREAMS, FELIX. REMEMBER, MOM AND DAD SAID THEY'RE JUST LIKE ECHOES, AFTER-EFFECTS OF THAT SPELL YOU CAST. THEY CAN'T HURT US.
BUT I CAN FEEL IT SOMETIMES, TOO. LIKE HEADACHES AND STUFF. THEY'RE NOT JUST DREAMS. MOM IS WORRIED TOO.
WHY DO YOU SAY THAT?
I SAW HER BUILDING SOMETHING THE OTHER DAY THAT SHE TRIED TO HIDE FROM ME.
I THINK IT'S SOMETHING TO USE AGAINST POLTERGEISTS. AND MAYBE IF I CAN FEEL WHEN IT'S NEARBY, I CAN --
HEY, GUYS!
OH, SORRY, DIDN'T MEAN TO SCARE YOU. HEY, SOPHIA'S LITTLE BROTHER, HOW ARE YOU? HERE TO JOIN OUR WITCHCRAFT PARTY?
SIGH. WE'RE GOING TO STUDY UP ON SOME MAGIC STUFF TO TRY TO FIND WHITNEY. DON'T TELL MOM AND DAD, OKAY?
I WON'T! BUT SINCE YOU'RE DOING THAT...
WHAT IF I TRY TO SEE IF I CAN GET MOM'S TOOL TO WORK? IN CASE WE NEED THAT?
THAT SOUNDS LIKE SKY FOX AND FESTER RAT ARE TEAMING BACK UP!
I AM NOT FESTER RAT! I BETTER GET GOING...I'LL SEE YOU AT MOM'S TONIGHT, SIS.

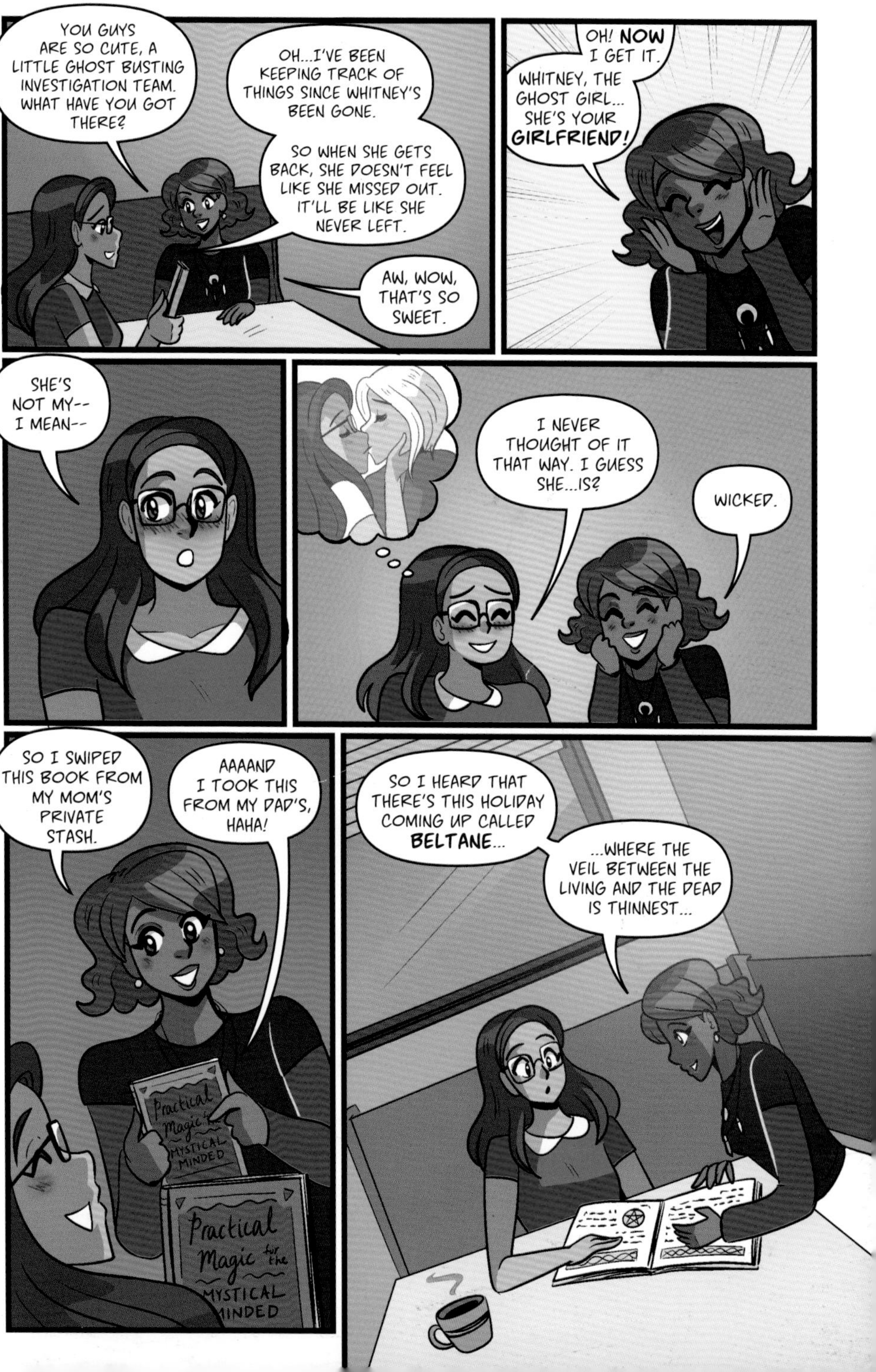
YOU GUYS ARE SO CUTE, A LITTLE GHOST BUSTING INVESTIGATION TEAM. WHAT HAVE YOU GOT THERE?
OH...I'VE BEEN KEEPING TRACK OF THINGS SINCE WHITNEY'S BEEN GONE.
SO WHEN SHE GETS BACK, SHE DOESN'T FEEL LIKE SHE MISSED OUT. IT'LL BE LIKE SHE NEVER LEFT.
AW, WOW, THAT'S SO SWEET.
OH! NOW I GET IT.
WHITNEY, THE GHOST GIRL... SHE'S YOUR GIRLFRIEND!
SHE'S NOT MY-- I MEAN--
I NEVER THOUGHT OF IT THAT WAY. I GUESS SHE...IS?
WICKED.
SO I SWIPED THIS BOOK FROM MY MOM'S PRIVATE STASH.
AAAAND I TOOK THIS FROM MY DAD'S, HAHA!
Practical Magic for the MYSTICAL MINDED
Practical Magic for the MYSTICAL MINDED
SO I HEARD THAT THERE'S THIS HOLIDAY COMING UP CALLED BELTANE...
...WHERE THE VEIL BETWEEN THE LIVING AND THE DEAD IS THINNEST...

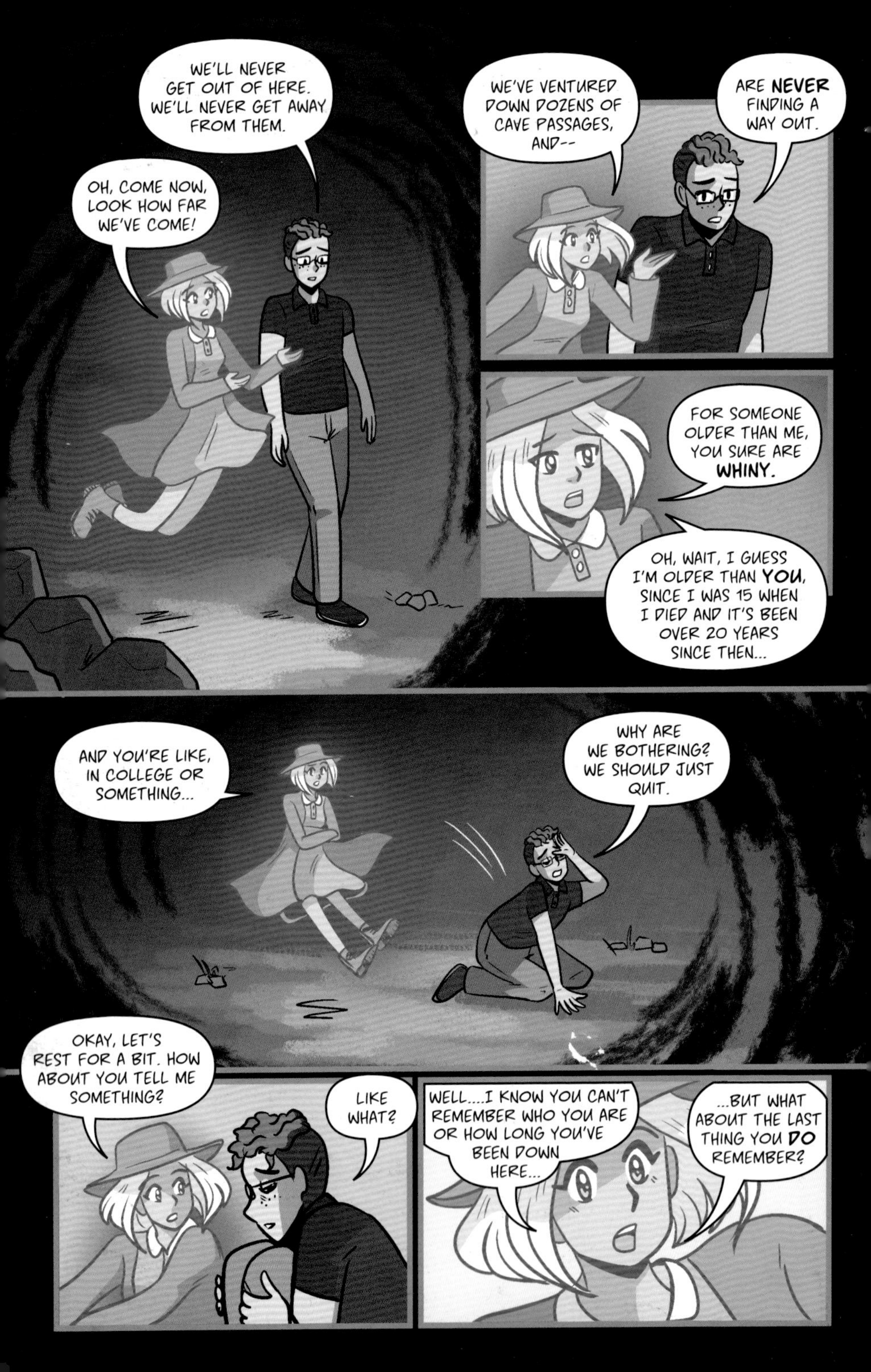

WE'LL NEVER GET OUT OF HERE. WE'LL NEVER GET AWAY FROM THEM.
OH, COME NOW, LOOK HOW FAR WE'VE COME!
WE'VE VENTURED DOWN DOZENS OF CAVE PASSAGES, AND--
ARE **NEVER** FINDING A WAY OUT.
FOR SOMEONE OLDER THAN ME, YOU SURE ARE **WHINY.**
OH, WAIT, I GUESS I'M OLDER THAN **YOU**, SINCE I WAS 15 WHEN I DIED AND IT'S BEEN OVER 20 YEARS SINCE THEN...
AND YOU'RE LIKE, IN COLLEGE OR SOMETHING...
WHY ARE WE BOTHERING? WE SHOULD JUST QUIT.
OKAY, LET'S REST FOR A BIT. HOW ABOUT YOU TELL ME SOMETHING?
LIKE WHAT?
WELL....I KNOW YOU CAN'T REMEMBER WHO YOU ARE OR HOW LONG YOU'VE BEEN DOWN HERE...
...BUT WHAT ABOUT THE LAST THING YOU **DO** REMEMBER?

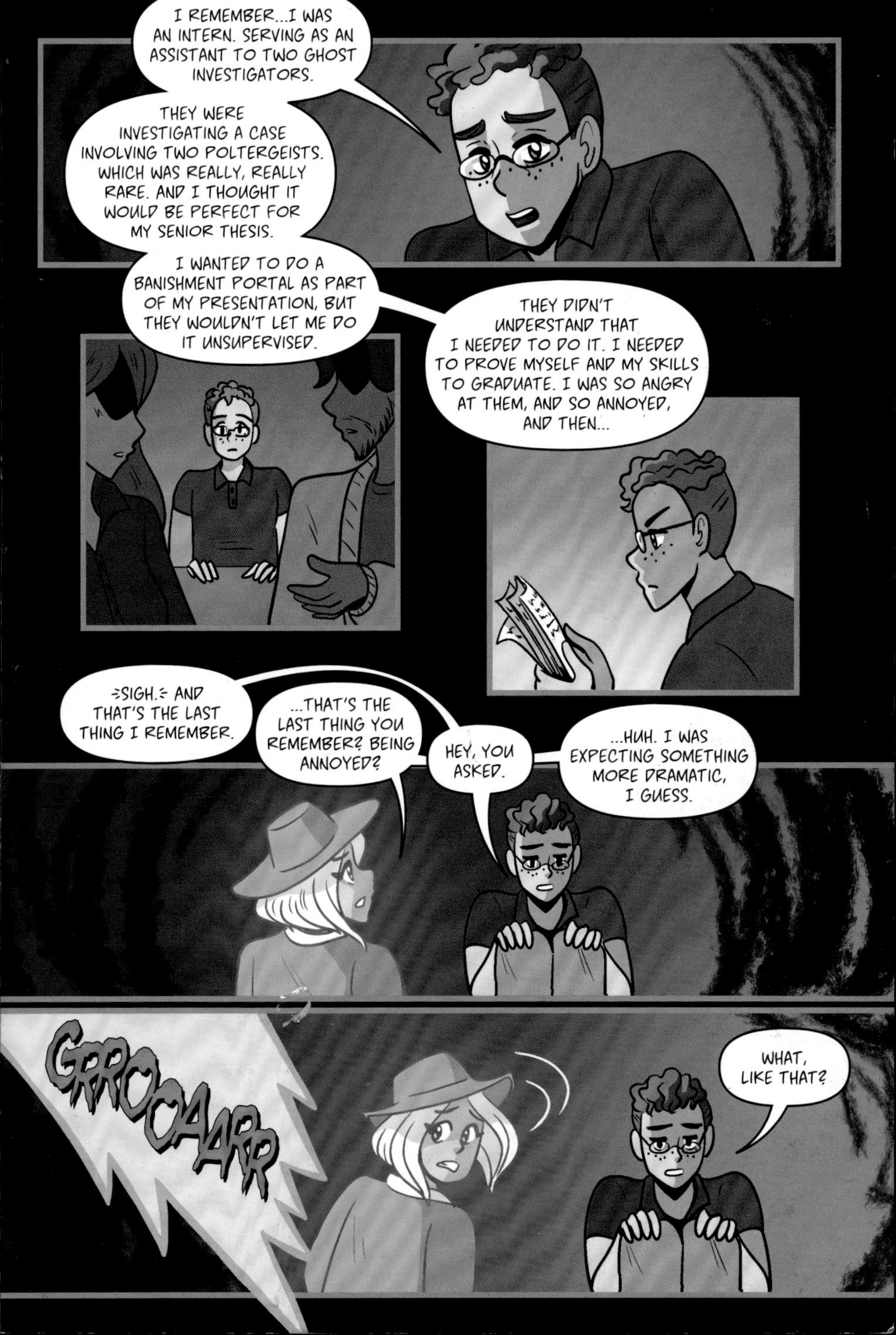
I REMEMBER...I WAS AN INTERN. SERVING AS AN ASSISTANT TO TWO GHOST INVESTIGATORS.
THEY WERE INVESTIGATING A CASE INVOLVING TWO POLTERGEISTS. WHICH WAS REALLY, REALLY RARE. AND I THOUGHT IT WOULD BE PERFECT FOR MY SENIOR THESIS.
I WANTED TO DO A BANISHMENT PORTAL AS PART OF MY PRESENTATION, BUT THEY WOULDN'T LET ME DO IT UNSUPERVISED.
THEY DIDN'T UNDERSTAND THAT I NEEDED TO DO IT. I NEEDED TO PROVE MYSELF AND MY SKILLS TO GRADUATE. I WAS SO ANGRY AT THEM, AND SO ANNOYED, AND THEN...
SIGH. AND THAT'S THE LAST THING I REMEMBER.
...THAT'S THE LAST THING YOU REMEMBER? BEING ANNOYED?
HEY, YOU ASKED.
...HUH. I WAS EXPECTING SOMETHING MORE DRAMATIC, I GUESS.
GRROOAARR
WHAT, LIKE THAT?

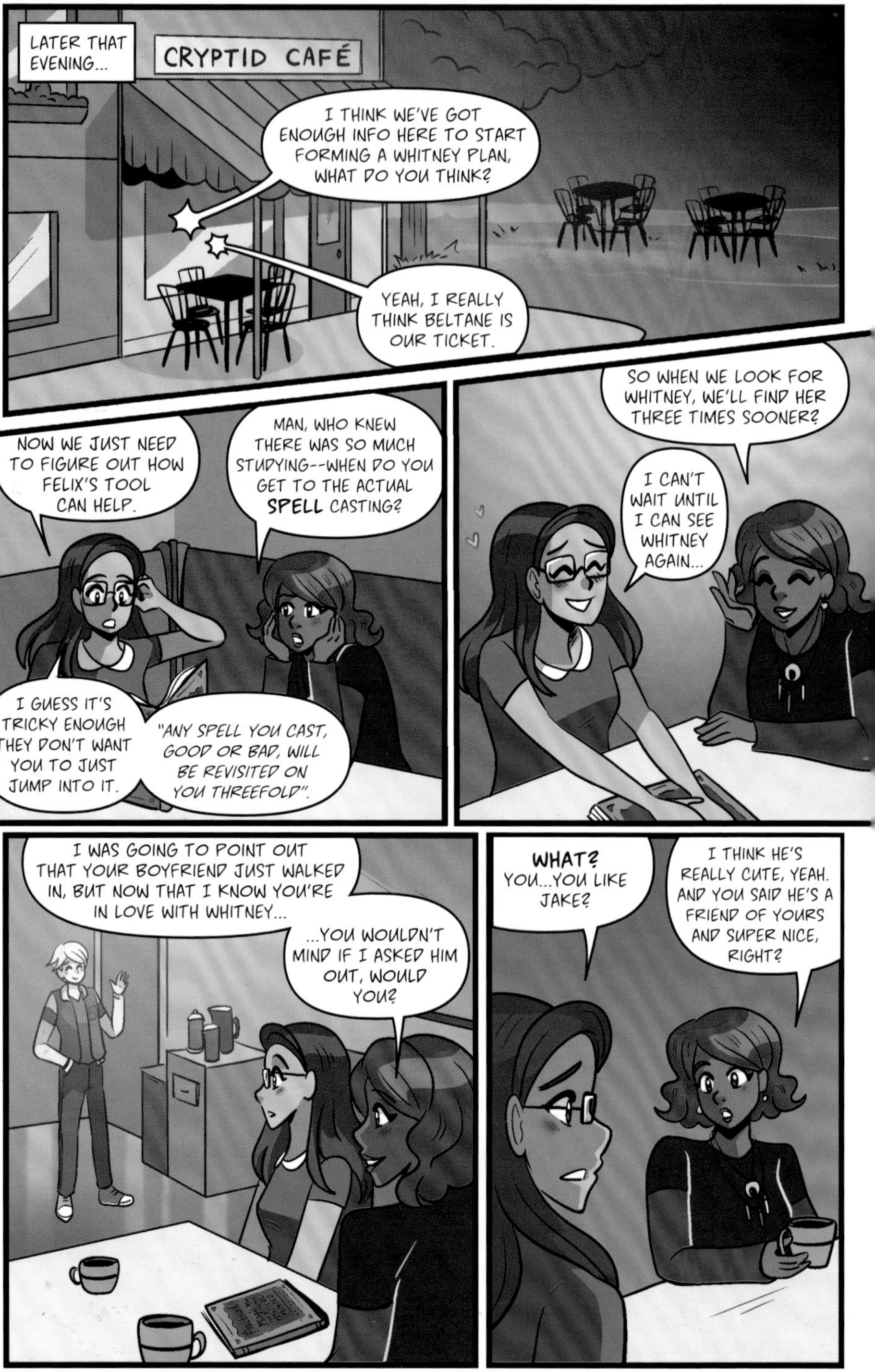
LATER THAT EVENING...
CRYPTID CAFÉ
I THINK WE'VE GOT ENOUGH INFO HERE TO START FORMING A WHITNEY PLAN, WHAT DO YOU THINK?
YEAH, I REALLY THINK BELTANE IS OUR TICKET.
NOW WE JUST NEED TO FIGURE OUT HOW FELIX'S TOOL CAN HELP.
MAN, WHO KNEW THERE WAS SO MUCH STUDYING--WHEN DO YOU GET TO THE ACTUAL **SPELL** CASTING?
I GUESS IT'S TRICKY ENOUGH THEY DON'T WANT YOU TO JUST JUMP INTO IT.
"ANY SPELL YOU CAST, GOOD OR BAD, WILL BE REVISITED ON YOU THREEFOLD".
SO WHEN WE LOOK FOR WHITNEY, WE'LL FIND HER THREE TIMES SOONER?
I CAN'T WAIT UNTIL I CAN SEE WHITNEY AGAIN...
I WAS GOING TO POINT OUT THAT YOUR BOYFRIEND JUST WALKED IN, BUT NOW THAT I KNOW YOU'RE IN LOVE WITH WHITNEY...
...YOU WOULDN'T MIND IF I ASKED HIM OUT, WOULD YOU?
WHAT? YOU...YOU LIKE JAKE?
I THINK HE'S REALLY CUTE, YEAH. AND YOU SAID HE'S A FRIEND OF YOURS AND SUPER NICE, RIGHT?

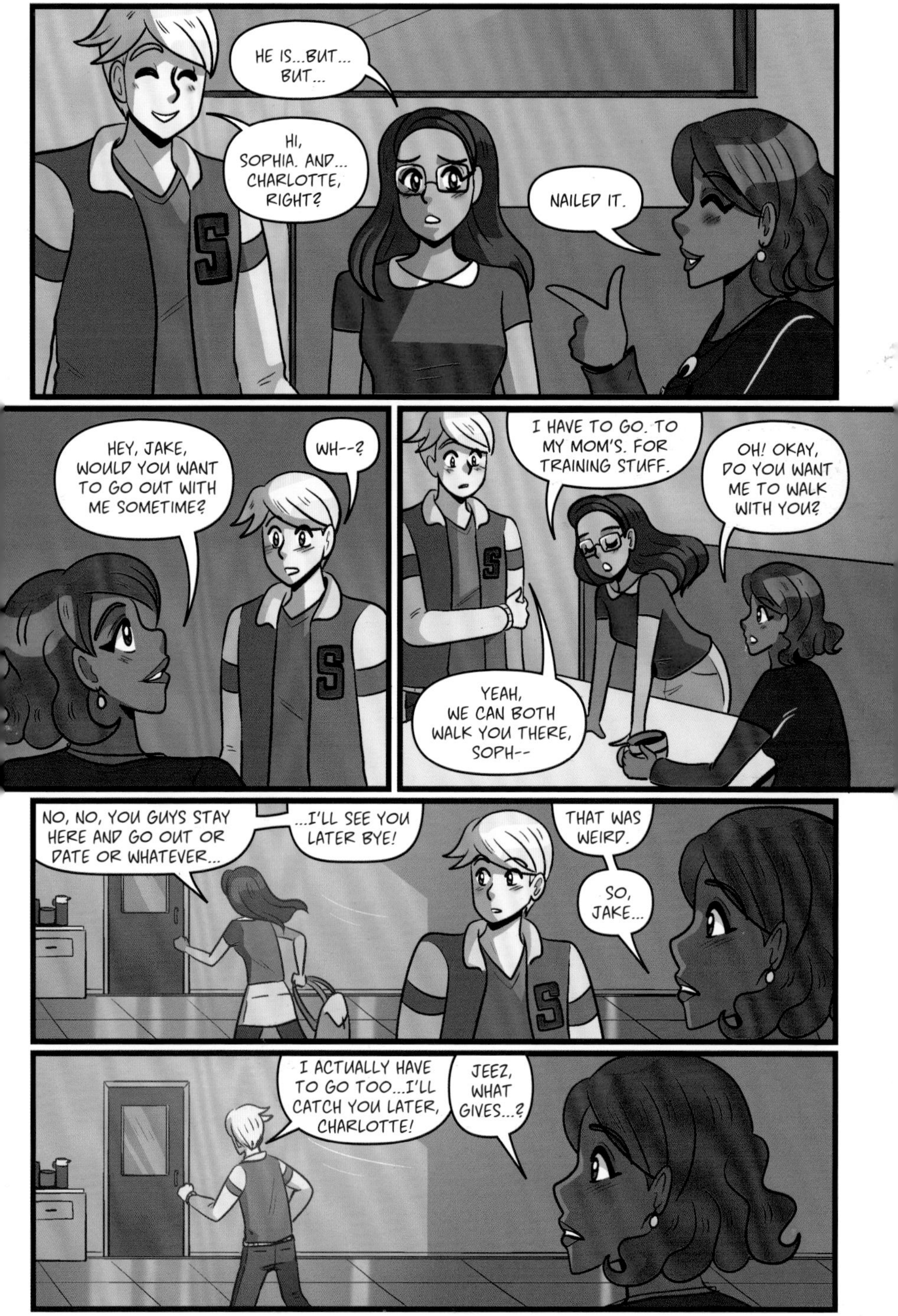
HE IS...BUT...
BUT...
HI, SOPHIA. AND... CHARLOTTE, RIGHT?
NAILED IT.
HEY, JAKE, WOULD YOU WANT TO GO OUT WITH ME SOMETIME?
WH--?
I HAVE TO GO. TO MY MOM'S. FOR TRAINING STUFF.
OH! OKAY, DO YOU WANT ME TO WALK WITH YOU?
YEAH, WE CAN BOTH WALK YOU THERE, SOPH--
NO, NO, YOU GUYS STAY HERE AND GO OUT OR DATE OR WHATEVER...
...I'LL SEE YOU LATER BYE!
THAT WAS WEIRD.
SO, JAKE...
I ACTUALLY HAVE TO GO TOO...I'LL CATCH YOU LATER, CHARLOTTE!
JEEZ, WHAT GIVES...?

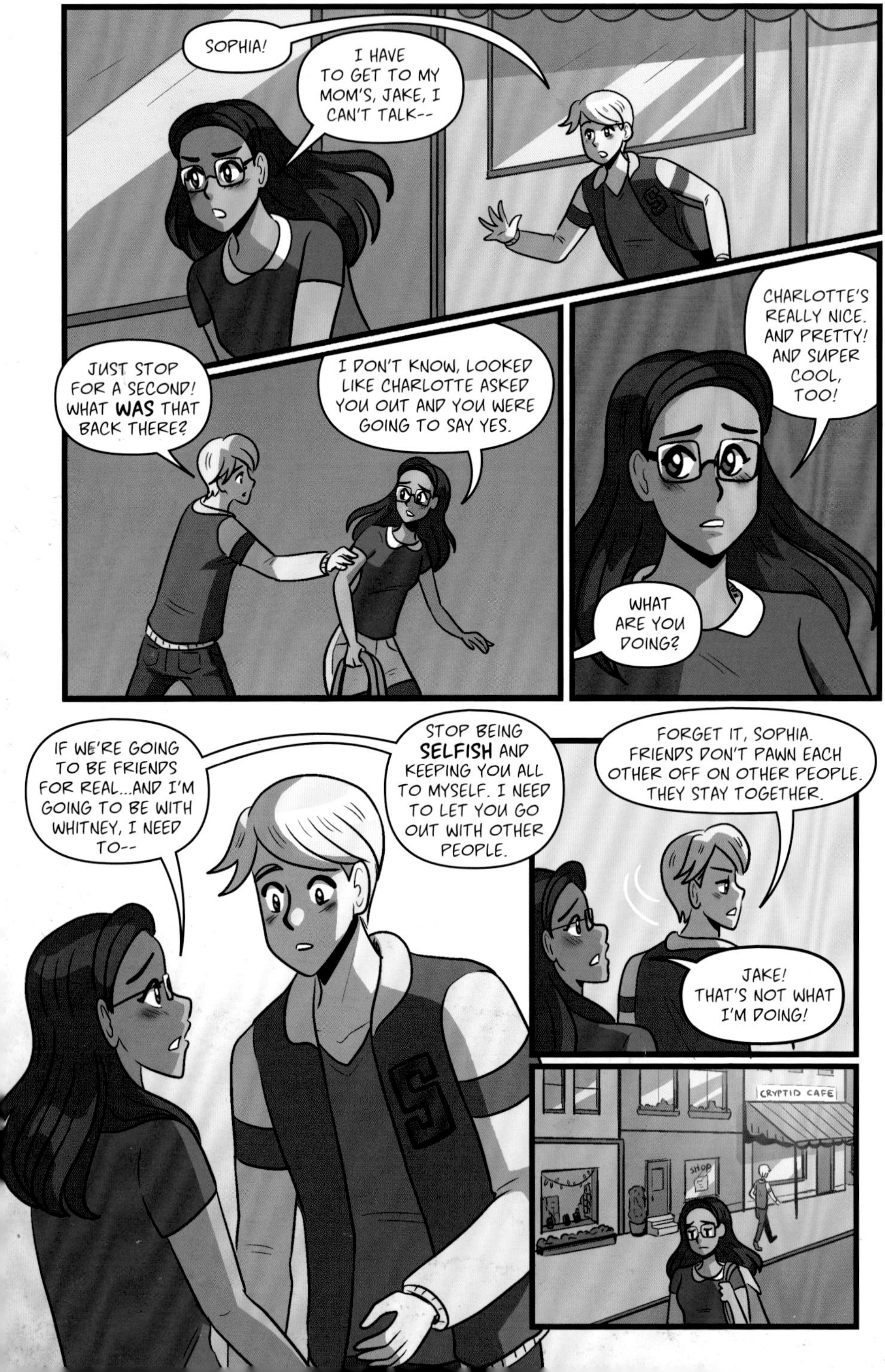
SOPHIA!
I HAVE TO GET TO MY MOM'S, JAKE, I CAN'T TALK--
JUST STOP FOR A SECOND! WHAT WAS THAT BACK THERE?
I DON'T KNOW, LOOKED LIKE CHARLOTTE ASKED YOU OUT AND YOU WERE GOING TO SAY YES.
CHARLOTTE'S REALLY NICE. AND PRETTY! AND SUPER COOL, TOO!
WHAT ARE YOU DOING?
IF WE'RE GOING TO BE FRIENDS FOR REAL...AND I'M GOING TO BE WITH WHITNEY, I NEED TO--
STOP BEING SELFISH AND KEEPING YOU ALL TO MYSELF. I NEED TO LET YOU GO OUT WITH OTHER PEOPLE.
FORGET IT, SOPHIA. FRIENDS DON'T PAWN EACH OTHER OFF ON OTHER PEOPLE. THEY STAY TOGETHER.
JAKE! THAT'S NOT WHAT I'M DOING!
CRYPTID CAFE
SHOP

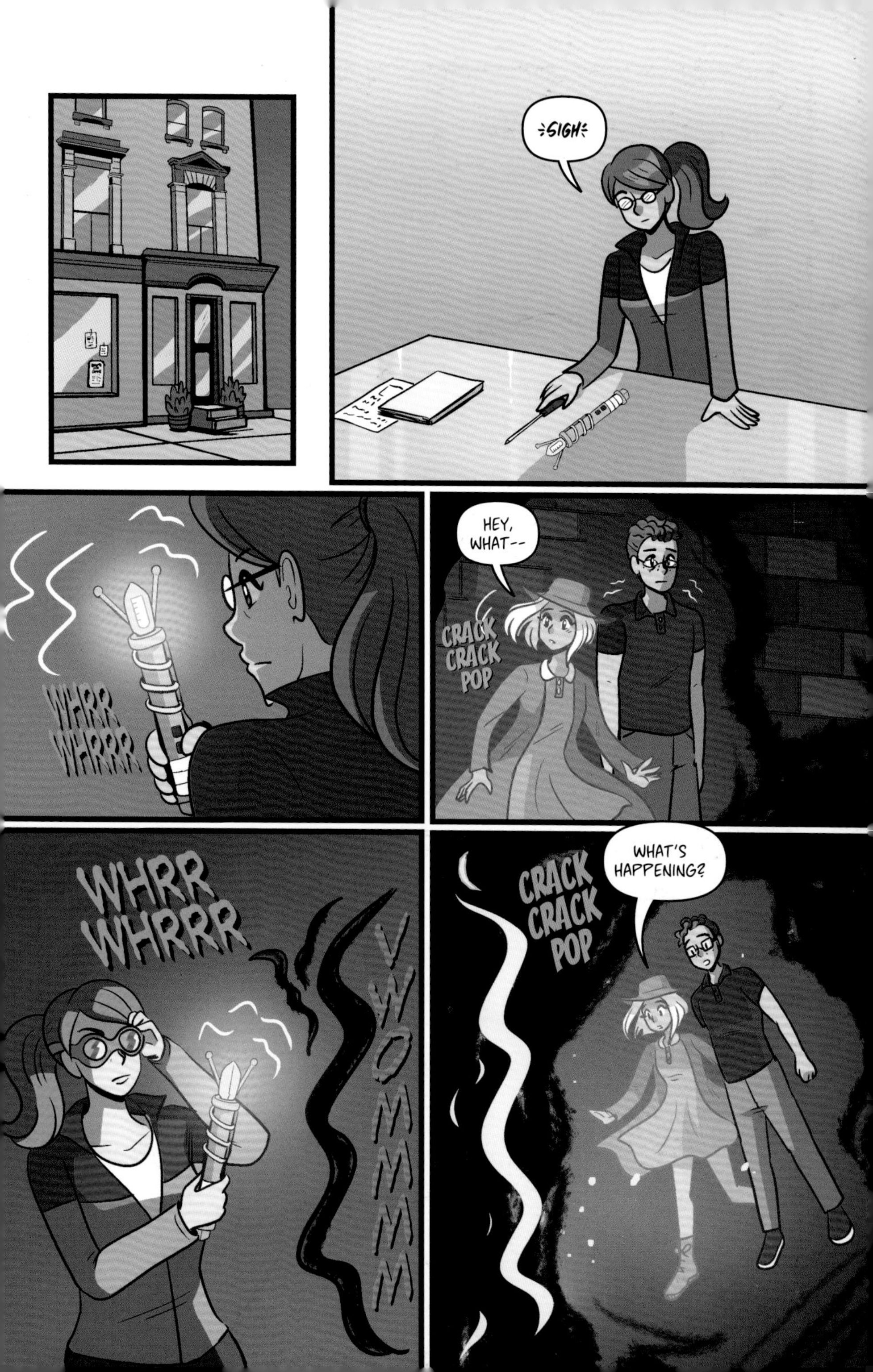

SIGH
WHRR WHRRR
HEY, WHAT--
CRACK CRACK POP
WHRR WHRRR
VWOMMMMM
CRACK CRACK POP
WHAT'S HAPPENING?

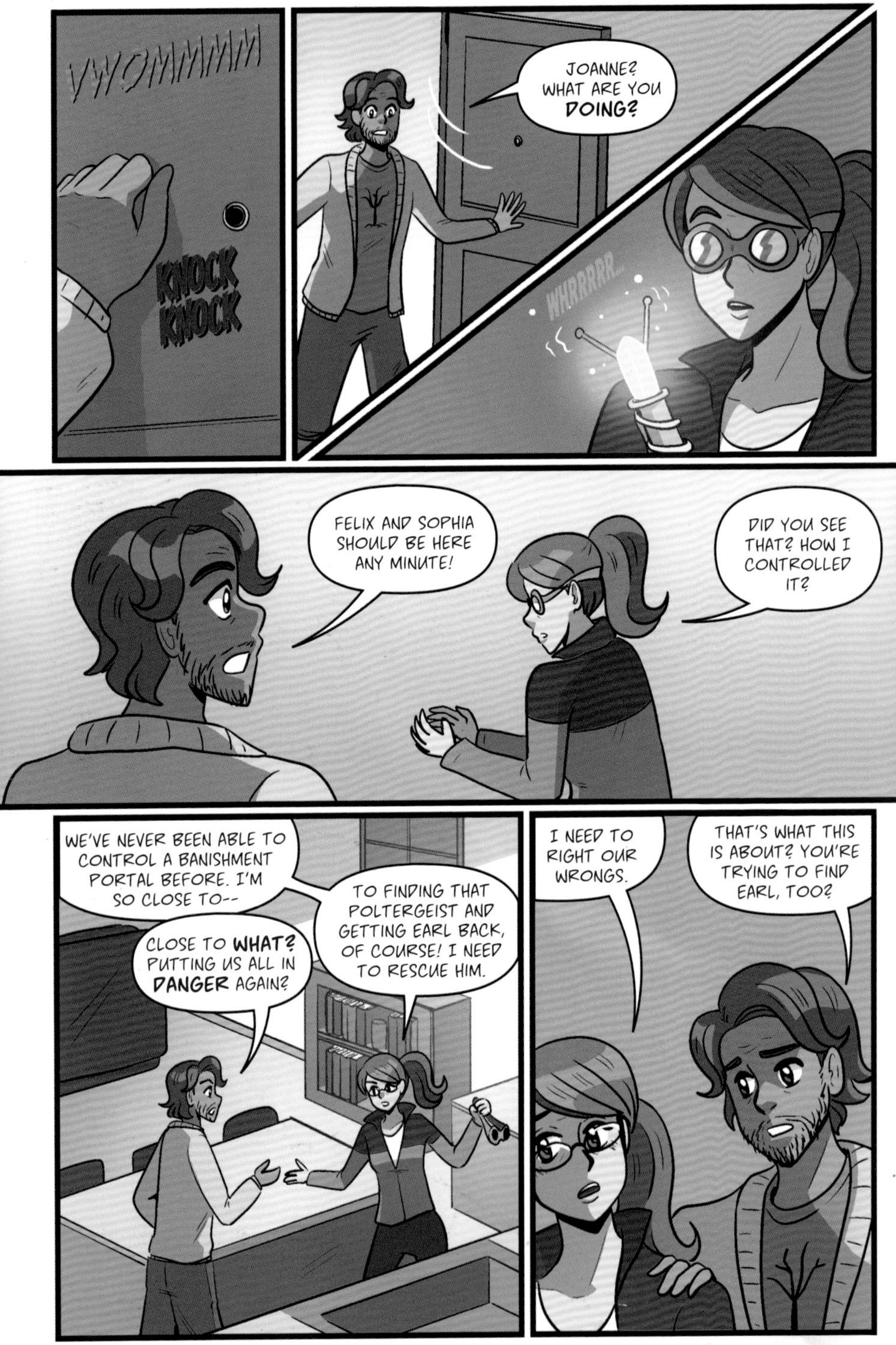
VWOMMMM
KNOCK KNOCK
JOANNE? WHAT ARE YOU DOING?
WHRRRRR...
FELIX AND SOPHIA SHOULD BE HERE ANY MINUTE!
DID YOU SEE THAT? HOW I CONTROLLED IT?
WE'VE NEVER BEEN ABLE TO CONTROL A BANISHMENT PORTAL BEFORE. I'M SO CLOSE TO--
CLOSE TO WHAT? PUTTING US ALL IN DANGER AGAIN?
TO FINDING THAT POLTERGEIST AND GETTING EARL BACK, OF COURSE! I NEED TO RESCUE HIM.
I NEED TO RIGHT OUR WRONGS.
THAT'S WHAT THIS IS ABOUT? YOU'RE TRYING TO FIND EARL, TOO?

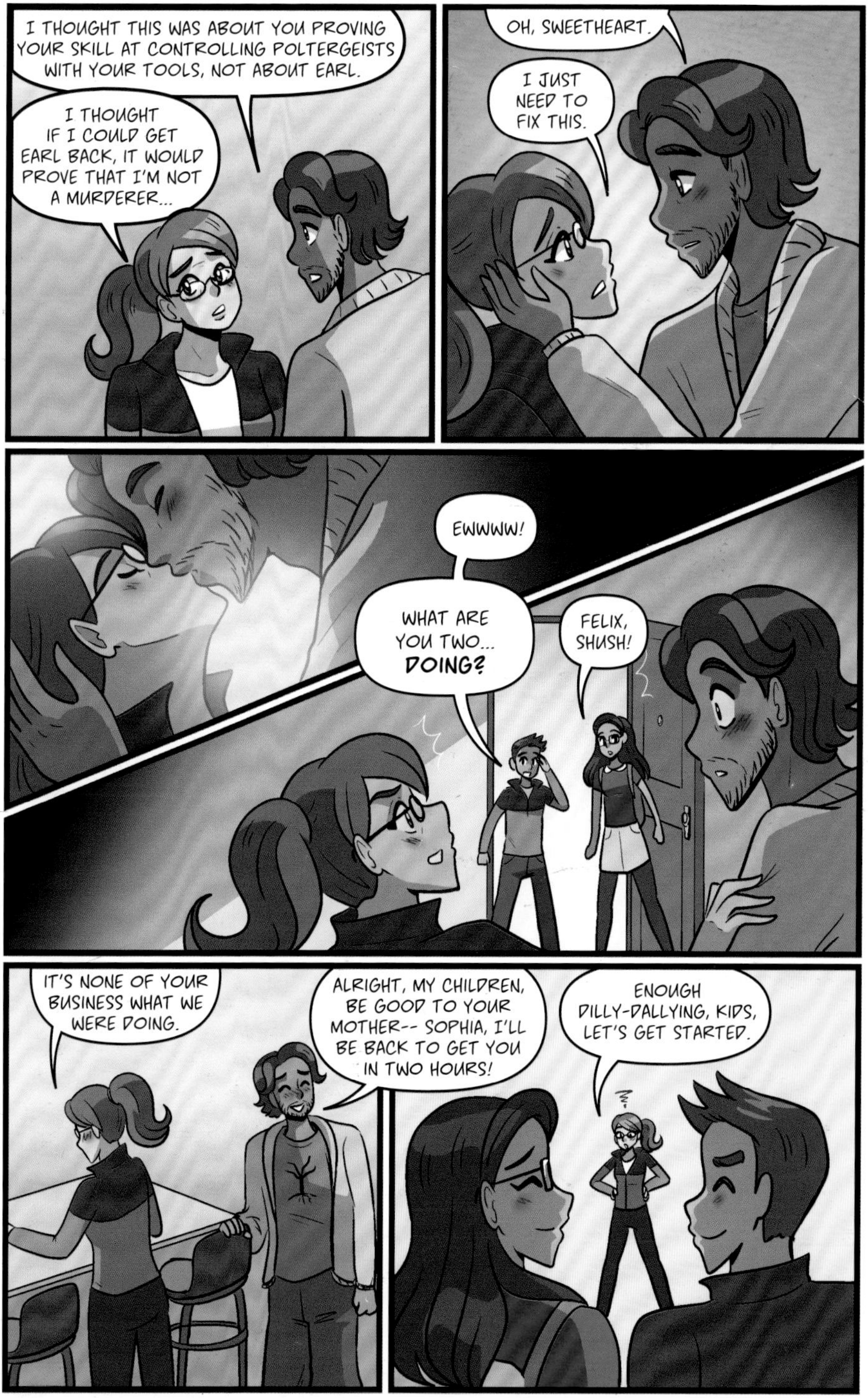
I THOUGHT THIS WAS ABOUT YOU PROVING YOUR SKILL AT CONTROLLING POLTERGEISTS WITH YOUR TOOLS, NOT ABOUT EARL.
I THOUGHT IF I COULD GET EARL BACK, IT WOULD PROVE THAT I'M NOT A MURDERER...
OH, SWEETHEART.
I JUST NEED TO FIX THIS.
EWWWW!
WHAT ARE YOU TWO... DOING?
FELIX, SHUSH!
IT'S NONE OF YOUR BUSINESS WHAT WE WERE DOING.
ALRIGHT, MY CHILDREN, BE GOOD TO YOUR MOTHER-- SOPHIA, I'LL BE BACK TO GET YOU IN TWO HOURS!
ENOUGH DILLY-DALLYING, KIDS, LET'S GET STARTED.

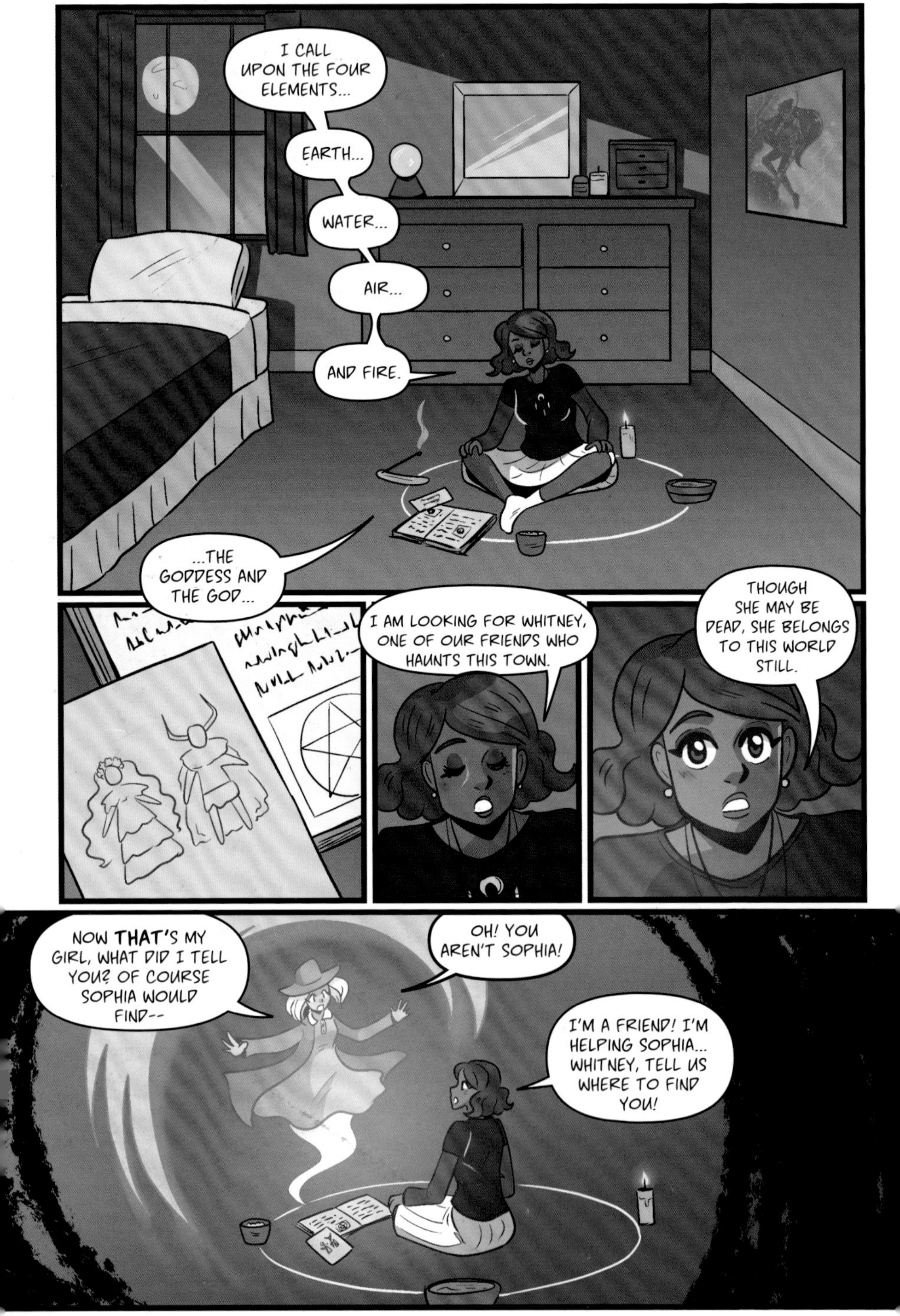
I CALL UPON THE FOUR ELEMENTS...
EARTH...
WATER...
AIR...
AND FIRE.
...THE GODDESS AND THE GOD...
I AM LOOKING FOR WHITNEY, ONE OF OUR FRIENDS WHO HAUNTS THIS TOWN.
THOUGH SHE MAY BE DEAD, SHE BELONGS TO THIS WORLD STILL.
NOW **THAT**'S MY GIRL, WHAT DID I TELL YOU? OF COURSE SOPHIA WOULD FIND--
OH! YOU AREN'T SOPHIA!
I'M A FRIEND! I'M HELPING SOPHIA... WHITNEY, TELL US WHERE TO FIND YOU!

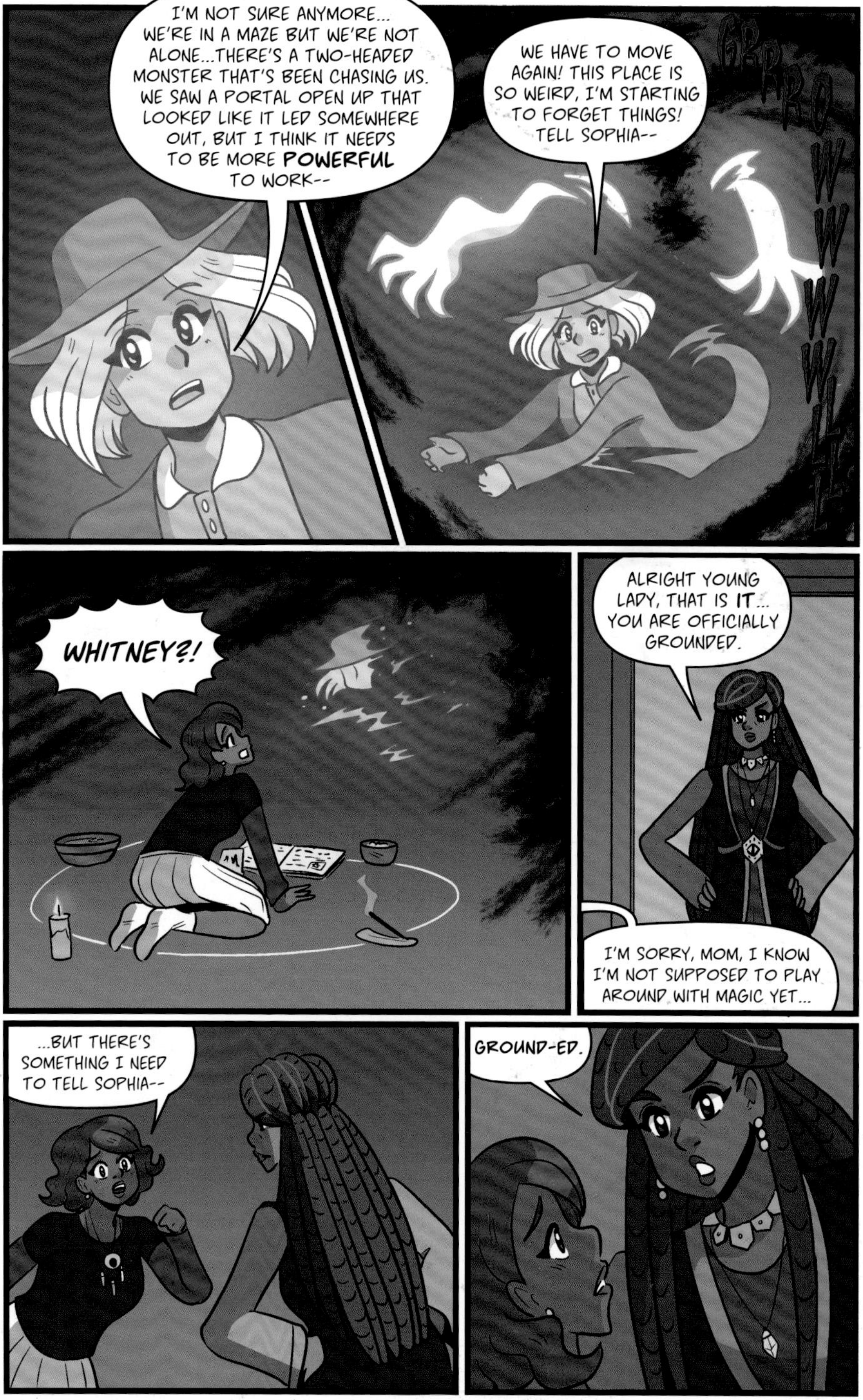
I'M NOT SURE ANYMORE... WE'RE IN A MAZE BUT WE'RE NOT ALONE...THERE'S A TWO-HEADED MONSTER THAT'S BEEN CHASING US. WE SAW A PORTAL OPEN UP THAT LOOKED LIKE IT LED SOMEWHERE OUT, BUT I THINK IT NEEDS TO BE MORE **POWERFUL** TO WORK--
WE HAVE TO MOVE AGAIN! THIS PLACE IS SO WEIRD, I'M STARTING TO FORGET THINGS! TELL SOPHIA--
GRRROWWWWLLL
WHITNEY?!
ALRIGHT YOUNG LADY, THAT IS **IT**... YOU ARE OFFICIALLY GROUNDED.
I'M SORRY, MOM, I KNOW I'M NOT SUPPOSED TO PLAY AROUND WITH MAGIC YET...
...BUT THERE'S SOMETHING I NEED TO TELL SOPHIA--
GROUND-ED.

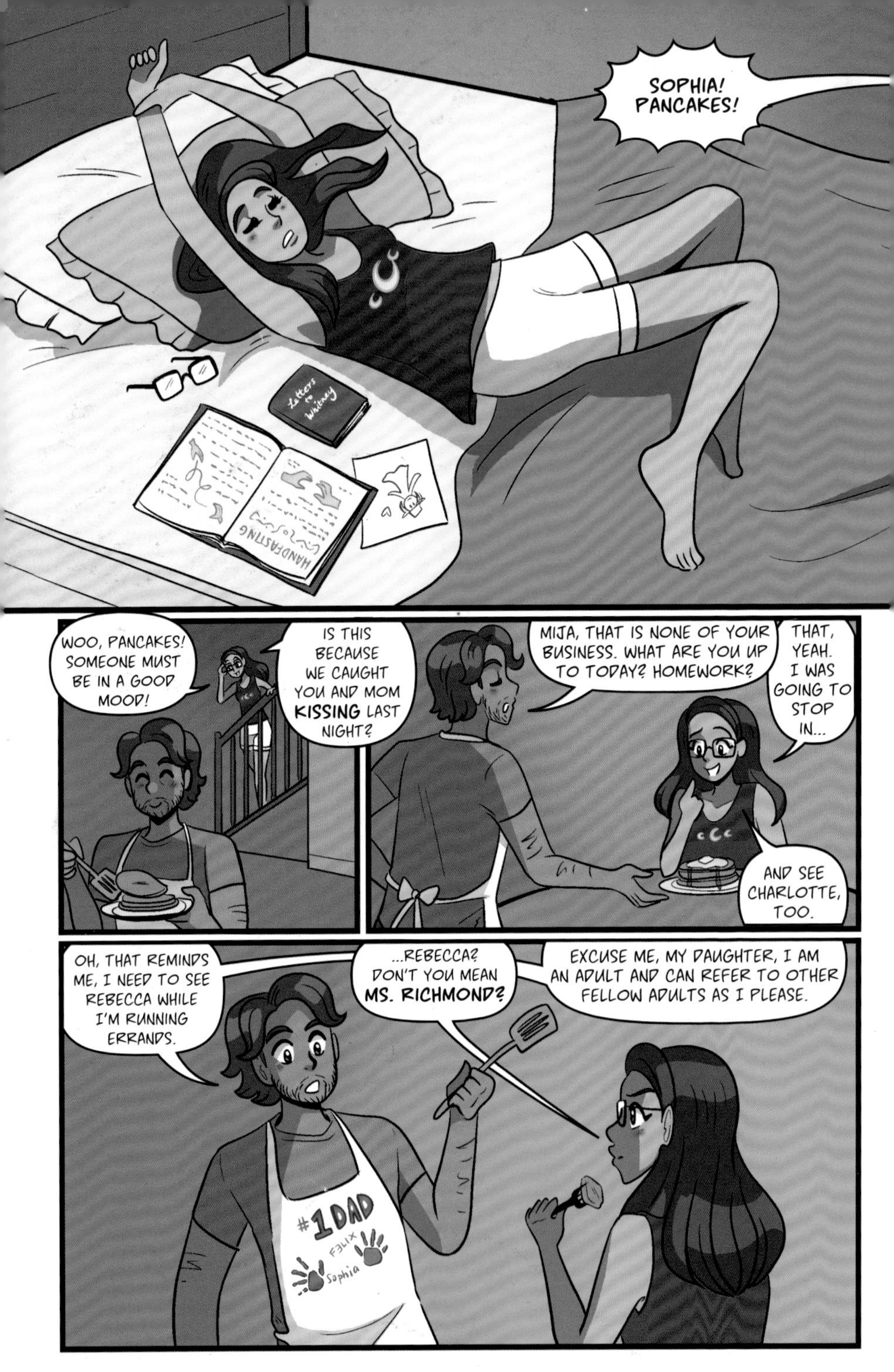
SOPHIA! PANCAKES!
Letters to Whitney
HANDFASTING
WOO, PANCAKES! SOMEONE MUST BE IN A GOOD MOOD!
IS THIS BECAUSE WE CAUGHT YOU AND MOM KISSING LAST NIGHT?
MIJA, THAT IS NONE OF YOUR BUSINESS. WHAT ARE YOU UP TO TODAY? HOMEWORK?
THAT, YEAH. I WAS GOING TO STOP IN...
AND SEE CHARLOTTE, TOO.
OH, THAT REMINDS ME, I NEED TO SEE REBECCA WHILE I'M RUNNING ERRANDS.
...REBECCA? DON'T YOU MEAN MS. RICHMOND?
EXCUSE ME, MY DAUGHTER, I AM AN ADULT AND CAN REFER TO OTHER FELLOW ADULTS AS I PLEASE.
#1 DAD
FELIX
Sophia

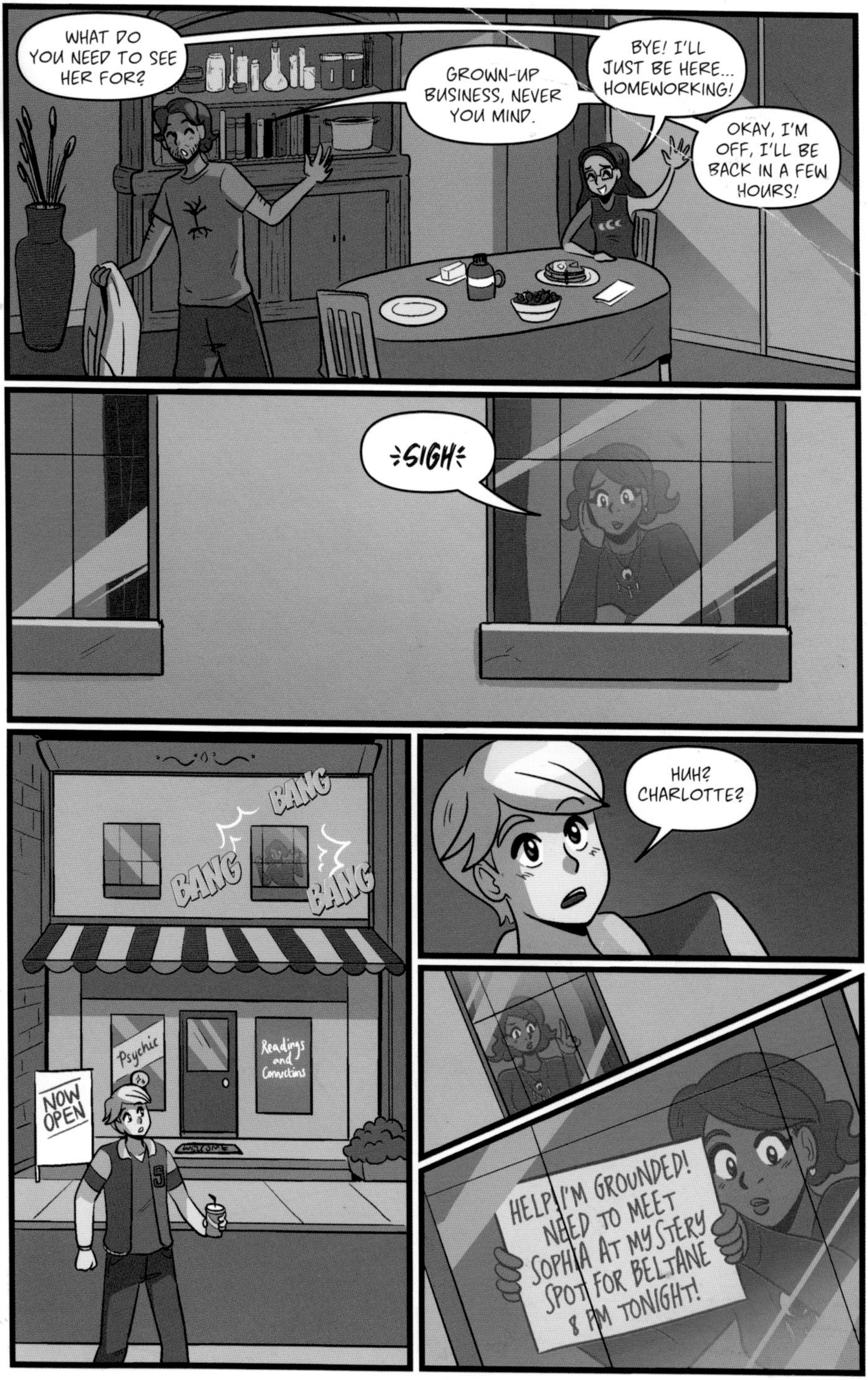
WHAT DO YOU NEED TO SEE HER FOR?
GROWN-UP BUSINESS, NEVER YOU MIND.
BYE! I'LL JUST BE HERE... HOMEWORKING!
OKAY, I'M OFF, I'LL BE BACK IN A FEW HOURS!
SIGH
BANG
BANG
BANG
Psychic
Readings and Connections
NOW OPEN
WELCOME
HUH? CHARLOTTE?
HELP! I'M GROUNDED! NEED TO MEET SOPHIA AT MYSTERY SPOT FOR BELTANE 8 PM TONIGHT!

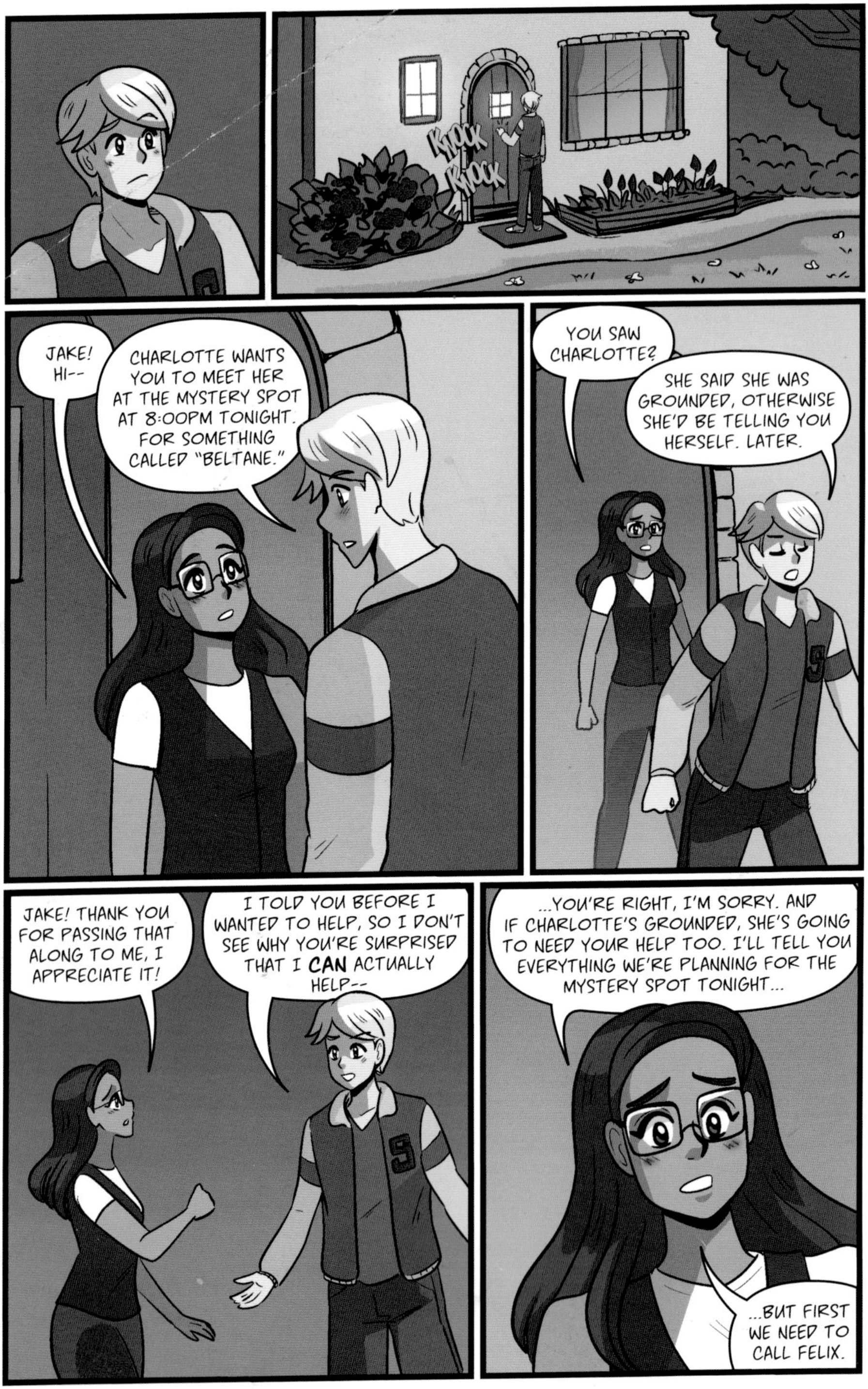
KNOCK KNOCK
JAKE! HI--
CHARLOTTE WANTS YOU TO MEET HER AT THE MYSTERY SPOT AT 8:00PM TONIGHT. FOR SOMETHING CALLED "BELTANE."
YOU SAW CHARLOTTE?
SHE SAID SHE WAS GROUNDED, OTHERWISE SHE'D BE TELLING YOU HERSELF. LATER.
JAKE! THANK YOU FOR PASSING THAT ALONG TO ME, I APPRECIATE IT!
I TOLD YOU BEFORE I WANTED TO HELP, SO I DON'T SEE WHY YOU'RE SURPRISED THAT I **CAN** ACTUALLY HELP--
...YOU'RE RIGHT, I'M SORRY. AND IF CHARLOTTE'S GROUNDED, SHE'S GOING TO NEED YOUR HELP TOO. I'LL TELL YOU EVERYTHING WE'RE PLANNING FOR THE MYSTERY SPOT TONIGHT...
...BUT FIRST WE NEED TO CALL FELIX.

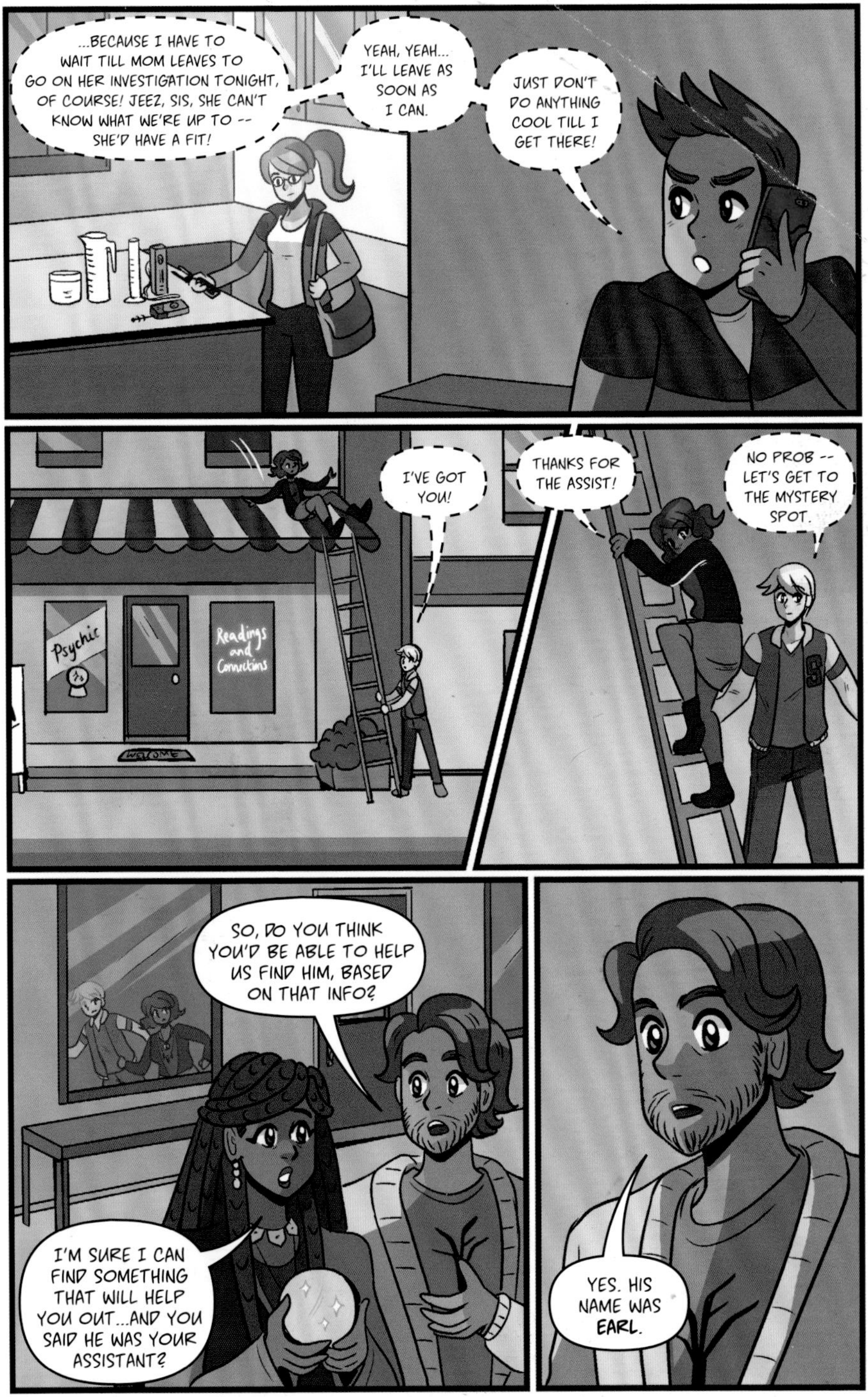
...BECAUSE I HAVE TO WAIT TILL MOM LEAVES TO GO ON HER INVESTIGATION TONIGHT, OF COURSE! JEEZ, SIS, SHE CAN'T KNOW WHAT WE'RE UP TO -- SHE'D HAVE A FIT!
YEAH, YEAH... I'LL LEAVE AS SOON AS I CAN.
JUST DON'T DO ANYTHING COOL TILL I GET THERE!
Psychic
Readings and Connections
WELCOME
I'VE GOT YOU!
THANKS FOR THE ASSIST!
NO PROB -- LET'S GET TO THE MYSTERY SPOT.
SO, DO YOU THINK YOU'D BE ABLE TO HELP US FIND HIM, BASED ON THAT INFO?
I'M SURE I CAN FIND SOMETHING THAT WILL HELP YOU OUT...AND YOU SAID HE WAS YOUR ASSISTANT?
YES. HIS NAME WAS **EARL**.

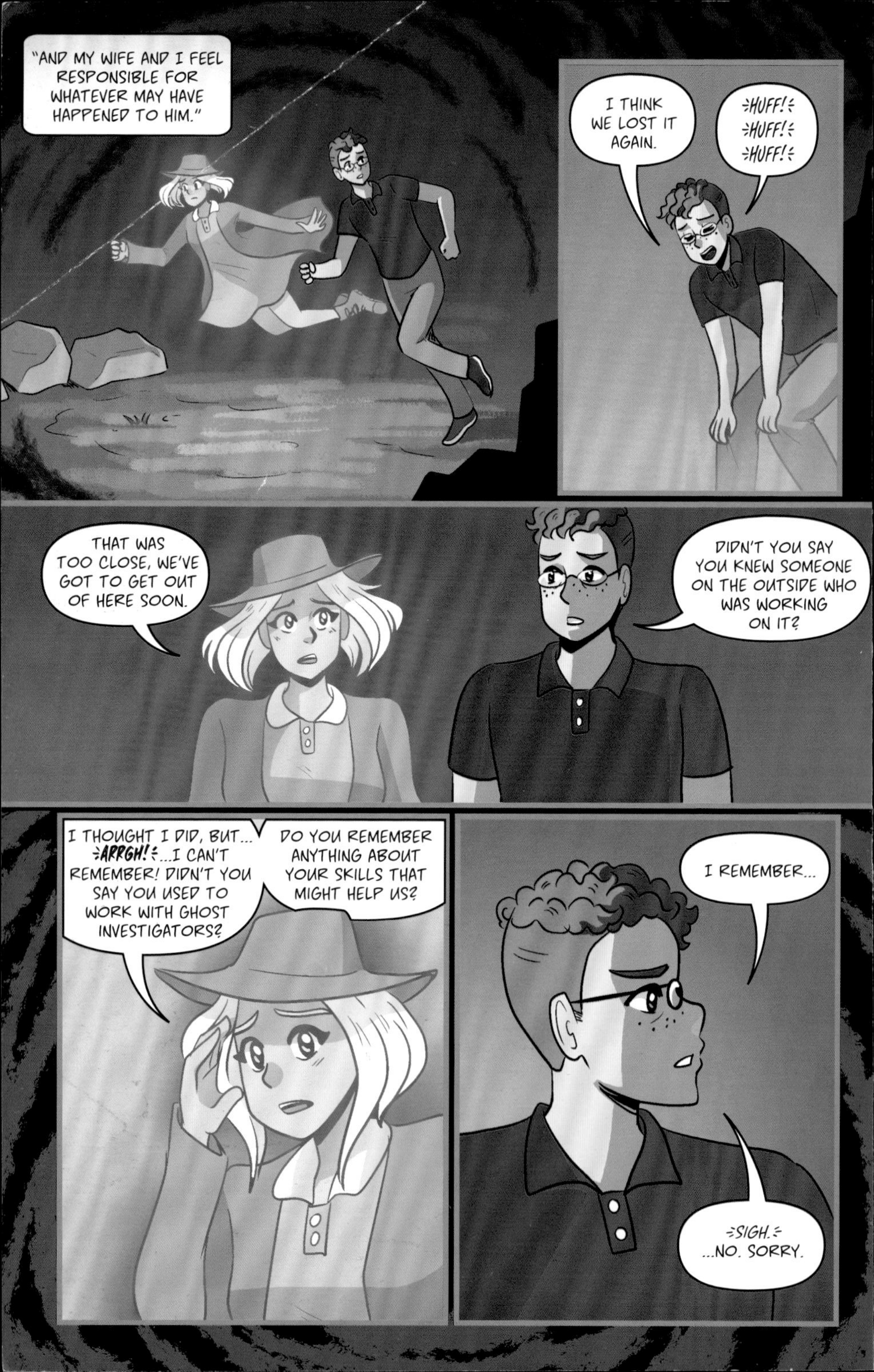
"AND MY WIFE AND I FEEL RESPONSIBLE FOR WHATEVER MAY HAVE HAPPENED TO HIM."
I THINK WE LOST IT AGAIN.
HUFF! HUFF! HUFF!
THAT WAS TOO CLOSE, WE'VE GOT TO GET OUT OF HERE SOON.
DIDN'T YOU SAY YOU KNEW SOMEONE ON THE OUTSIDE WHO WAS WORKING ON IT?
I THOUGHT I DID, BUT... ARRGH! ...I CAN'T REMEMBER! DIDN'T YOU SAY YOU USED TO WORK WITH GHOST INVESTIGATORS?
DO YOU REMEMBER ANYTHING ABOUT YOUR SKILLS THAT MIGHT HELP US?
I REMEMBER...
SIGH. ...NO. SORRY.

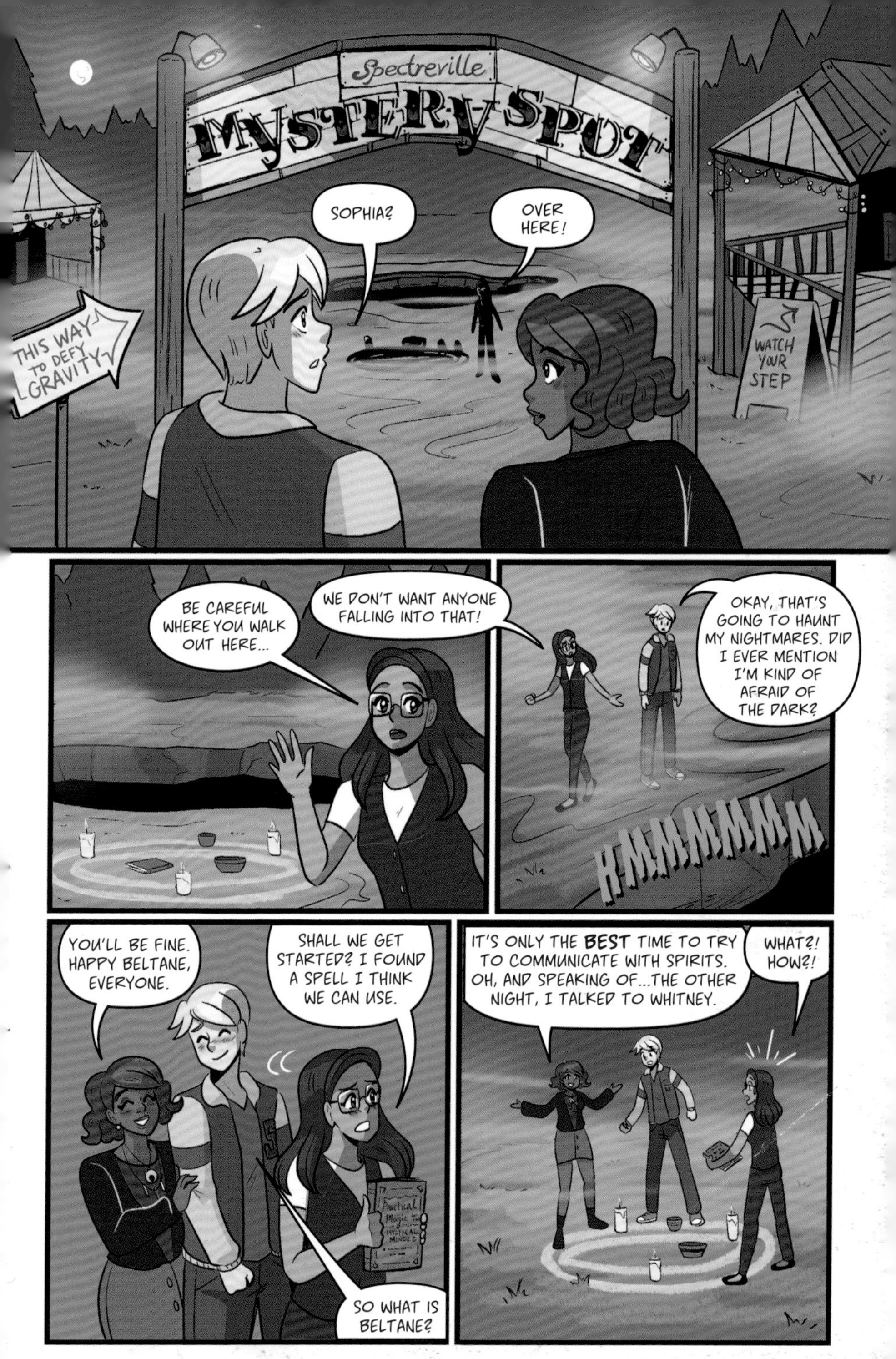
Spectreville
MYSTERY SPOT
THIS WAY TO DEFY GRAVITY
WATCH YOUR STEP
SOPHIA?
OVER HERE!
BE CAREFUL WHERE YOU WALK OUT HERE...
WE DON'T WANT ANYONE FALLING INTO THAT!
OKAY, THAT'S GOING TO HAUNT MY NIGHTMARES. DID I EVER MENTION I'M KIND OF AFRAID OF THE DARK?
HMMMMMMM
YOU'LL BE FINE. HAPPY BELTANE, EVERYONE.
SHALL WE GET STARTED? I FOUND A SPELL I THINK WE CAN USE.
SO WHAT IS BELTANE?
IT'S ONLY THE **BEST** TIME TO TRY TO COMMUNICATE WITH SPIRITS. OH, AND SPEAKING OF...THE OTHER NIGHT, I TALKED TO WHITNEY.
WHAT?! HOW?!

I KNOW, RIGHT? I FOUND HER! SHE WAS ONLY THERE FOR A SECOND, BUT SHE SAID WE NEEDED TO COME SOMEPLACE MORE POWERFUL TO GET HER OUT. AND THEN I REMEMBERED YOUR TOUR...I FIGURED WHAT PLACE IS MORE POWERFUL THAN THE ONE THAT **PULLED** SETTLERS HERE IN THE FIRST PLACE?

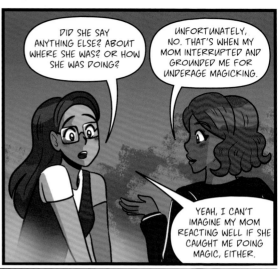

DID SHE SAY ANYTHING ELSE? ABOUT WHERE SHE WAS? OR HOW SHE WAS DOING?

UNFORTUNATELY, NO. THAT'S WHEN MY MOM INTERRUPTED AND GROUNDED ME FOR UNDERAGE MAGICKING.

YEAH, I CAN'T IMAGINE MY MOM REACTING WELL IF SHE CAUGHT ME DOING MAGIC, EITHER.

THAT WAS REALLY BRAVE OF YOU, CHARLOTTE.

LUCKILY MINE COULD PROBABLY CARE LESS.

HAHA, GOOD, SO IF WE GET CAUGHT, WE'LL JUST BOTH HIDE BEHIND JAKE! SO WHAT'S YOUR SPELL?

WELL...IT SAID IT WAS KIND OF ADVANCED, BUT WE BOTH COME FROM STRONG LINES OF WITCHES, RIGHT?

HEH. OR WE **HOPE** WE DO, ANYWAY!

IT'S CALLED "HANDFASTING." IF WE CAN FIND WHITNEY, WE CAN USE IT TO BIND ME TO HER...AND DRAG HER OUT OF WHEREVER SHE IS.

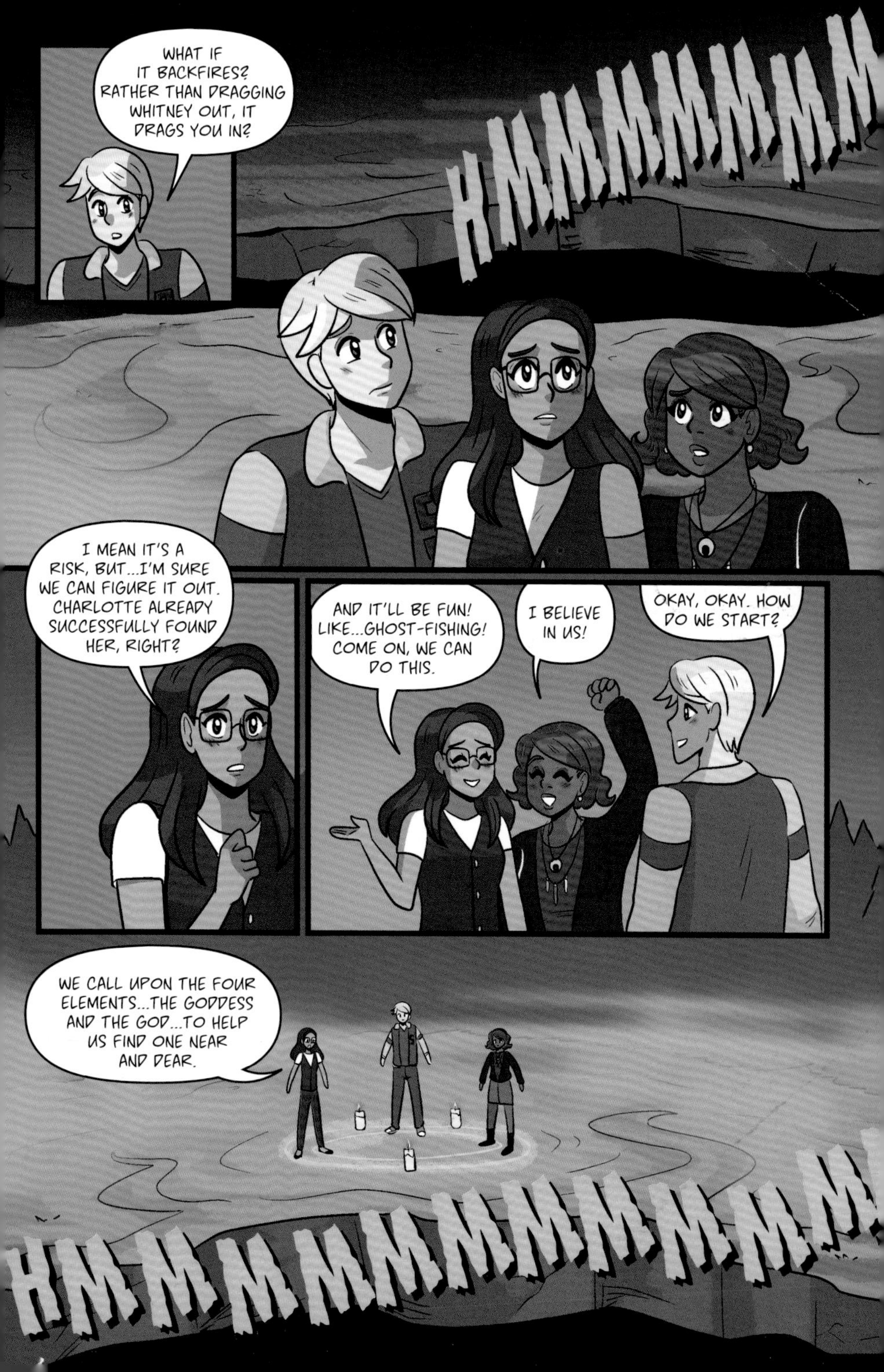
WHAT IF IT BACKFIRES? RATHER THAN DRAGGING WHITNEY OUT, IT DRAGS YOU IN?
HMMMMMMMMM
I MEAN IT'S A RISK, BUT...I'M SURE WE CAN FIGURE IT OUT. CHARLOTTE ALREADY SUCCESSFULLY FOUND HER, RIGHT?
AND IT'LL BE FUN! LIKE...GHOST-FISHING! COME ON, WE CAN DO THIS.
I BELIEVE IN US!
OKAY, OKAY. HOW DO WE START?
WE CALL UPON THE FOUR ELEMENTS...THE GODDESS AND THE GOD...TO HELP US FIND ONE NEAR AND DEAR.
HMMMMMMMMMMMMM

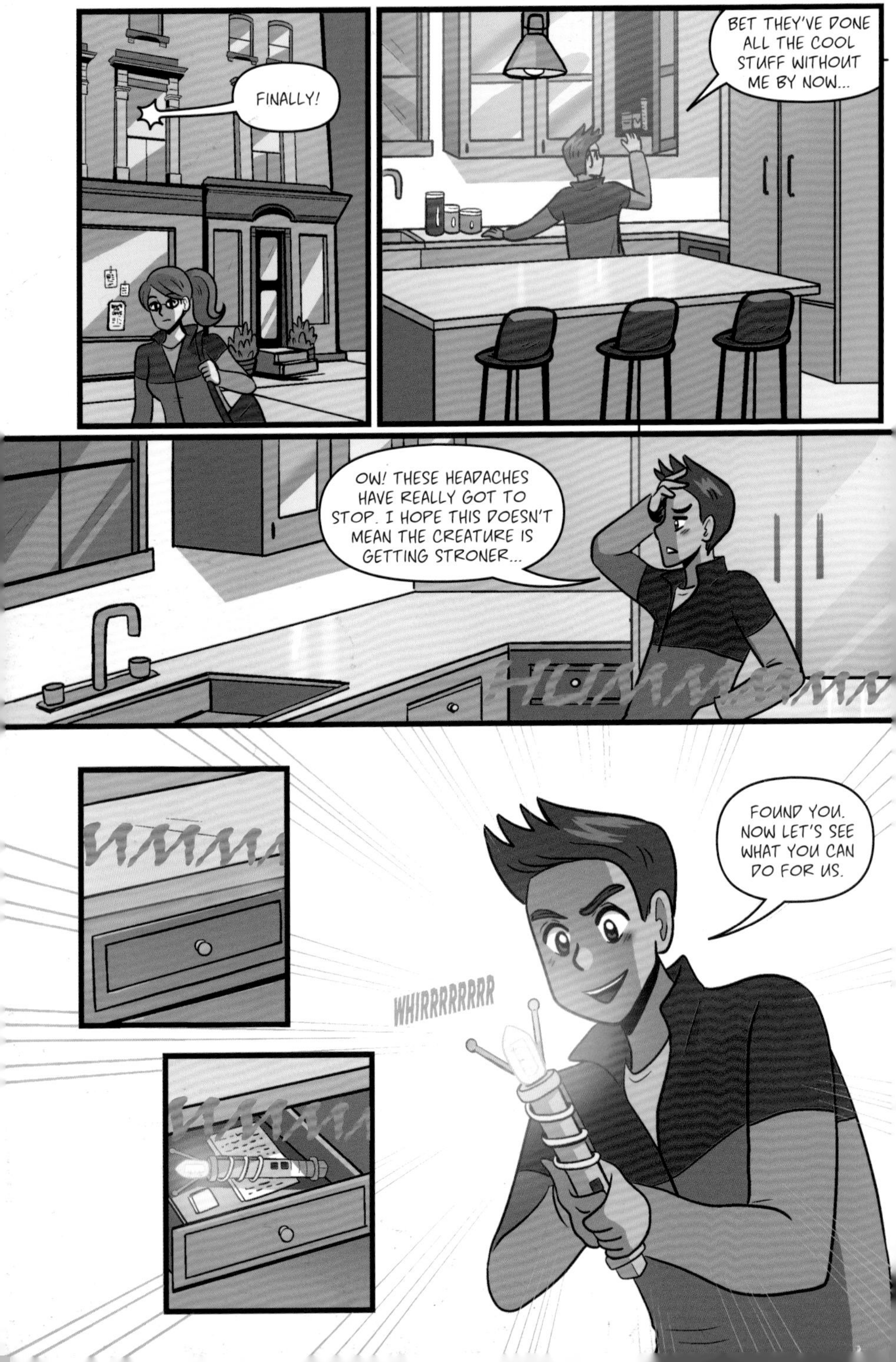
FINALLY!
BET THEY'VE DONE ALL THE COOL STUFF WITHOUT ME BY NOW...
OW! THESE HEADACHES HAVE REALLY GOT TO STOP. I HOPE THIS DOESN'T MEAN THE CREATURE IS GETTING STRONER...
HUMMMMMM
MMMMM
MMMMM
WHIRRRRRRR
FOUND YOU. NOW LET'S SEE WHAT YOU CAN DO FOR US.

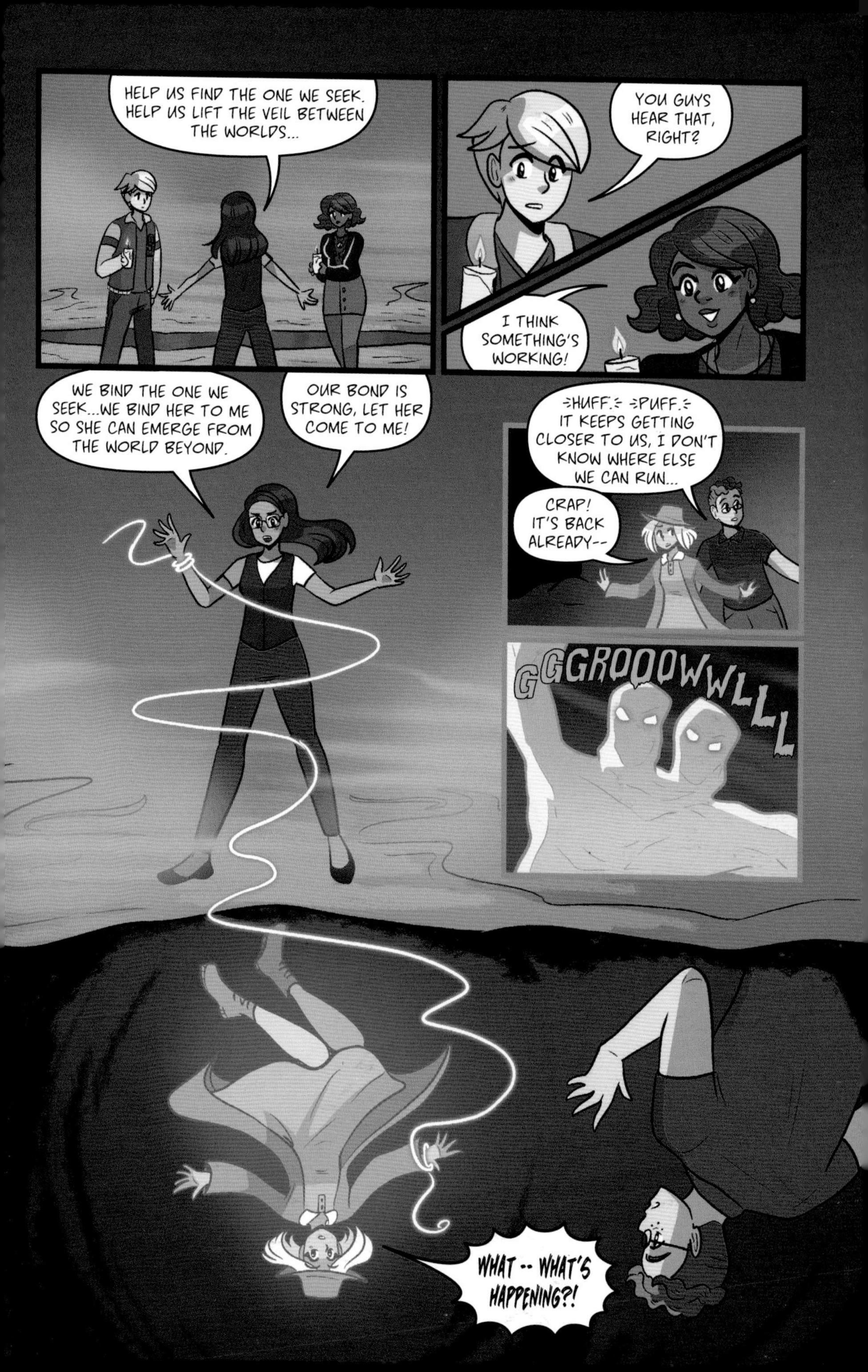
HELP US FIND THE ONE WE SEEK. HELP US LIFT THE VEIL BETWEEN THE WORLDS...
YOU GUYS HEAR THAT, RIGHT?
I THINK SOMETHING'S WORKING!
WE BIND THE ONE WE SEEK...WE BIND HER TO ME SO SHE CAN EMERGE FROM THE WORLD BEYOND.
OUR BOND IS STRONG, LET HER COME TO ME!
HUFF PUFF IT KEEPS GETTING CLOSER TO US, I DON'T KNOW WHERE ELSE WE CAN RUN...
CRAP! IT'S BACK ALREADY--
GGGROOOWWLLL
WHAT -- WHAT'S HAPPENING?!

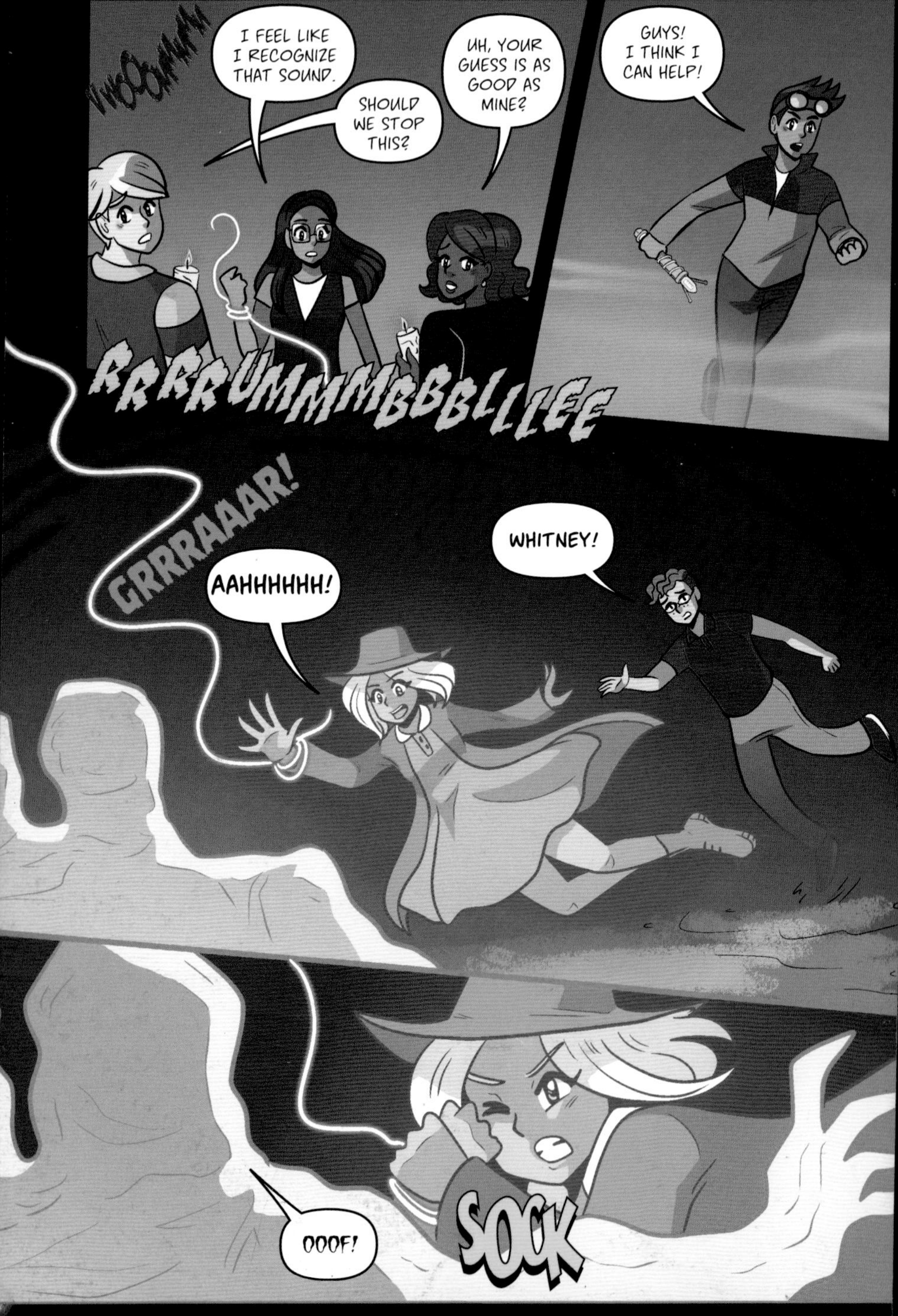
VWOOMMM
I FEEL LIKE I RECOGNIZE THAT SOUND.
SHOULD WE STOP THIS?
UH, YOUR GUESS IS AS GOOD AS MINE?
GUYS! I THINK I CAN HELP!
RRRRUMMMMBBBLLLEE
GRRRAAAR!
WHITNEY!
AAHHHHHH!
OOOF!
SOCK

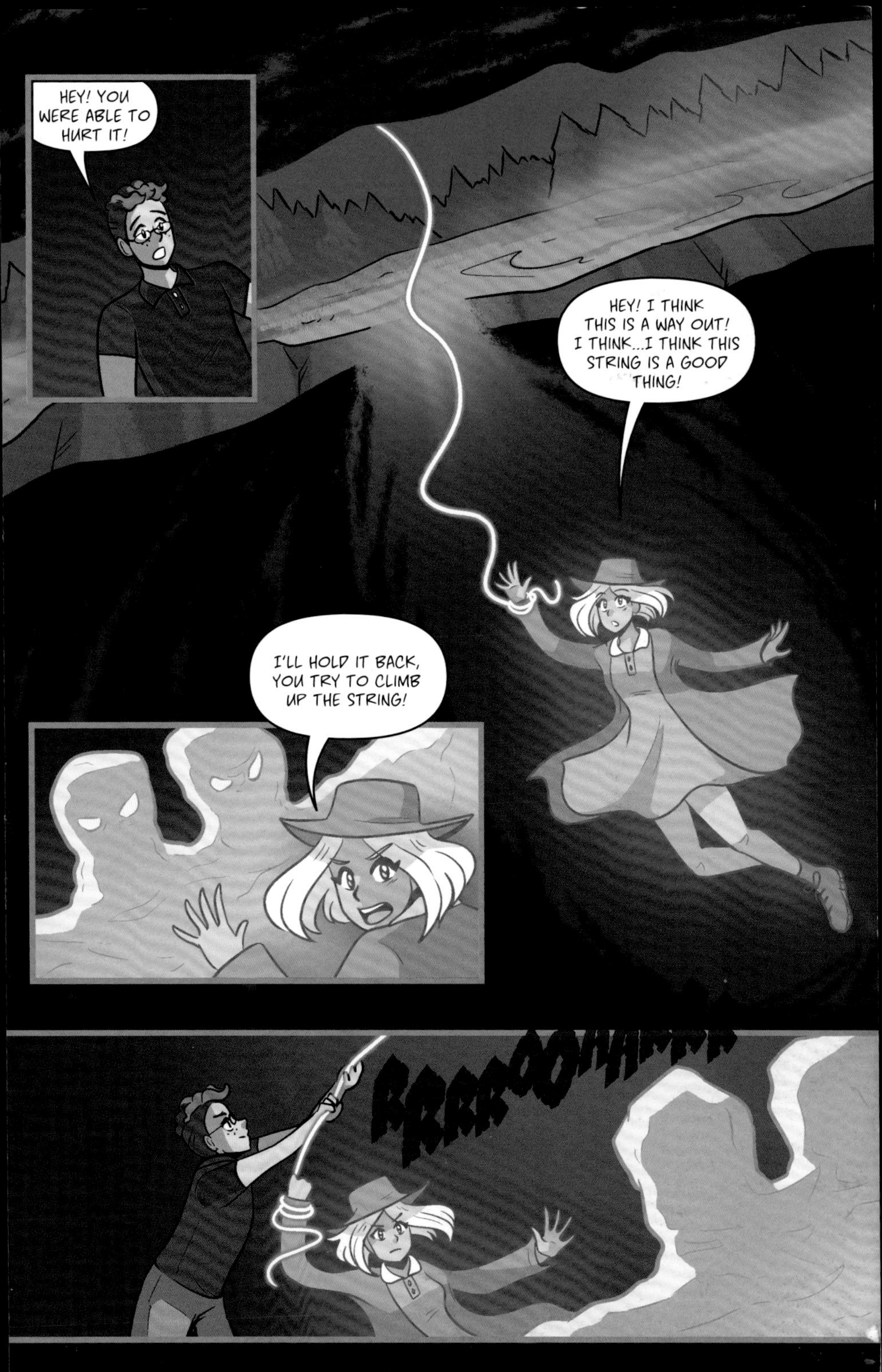

HEY! YOU WERE ABLE TO HURT IT!
HEY! I THINK THIS IS A WAY OUT! I THINK...I THINK THIS STRING IS A GOOD THING!
I'LL HOLD IT BACK, YOU TRY TO CLIMB UP THE STRING!
RRRROOHHMMM

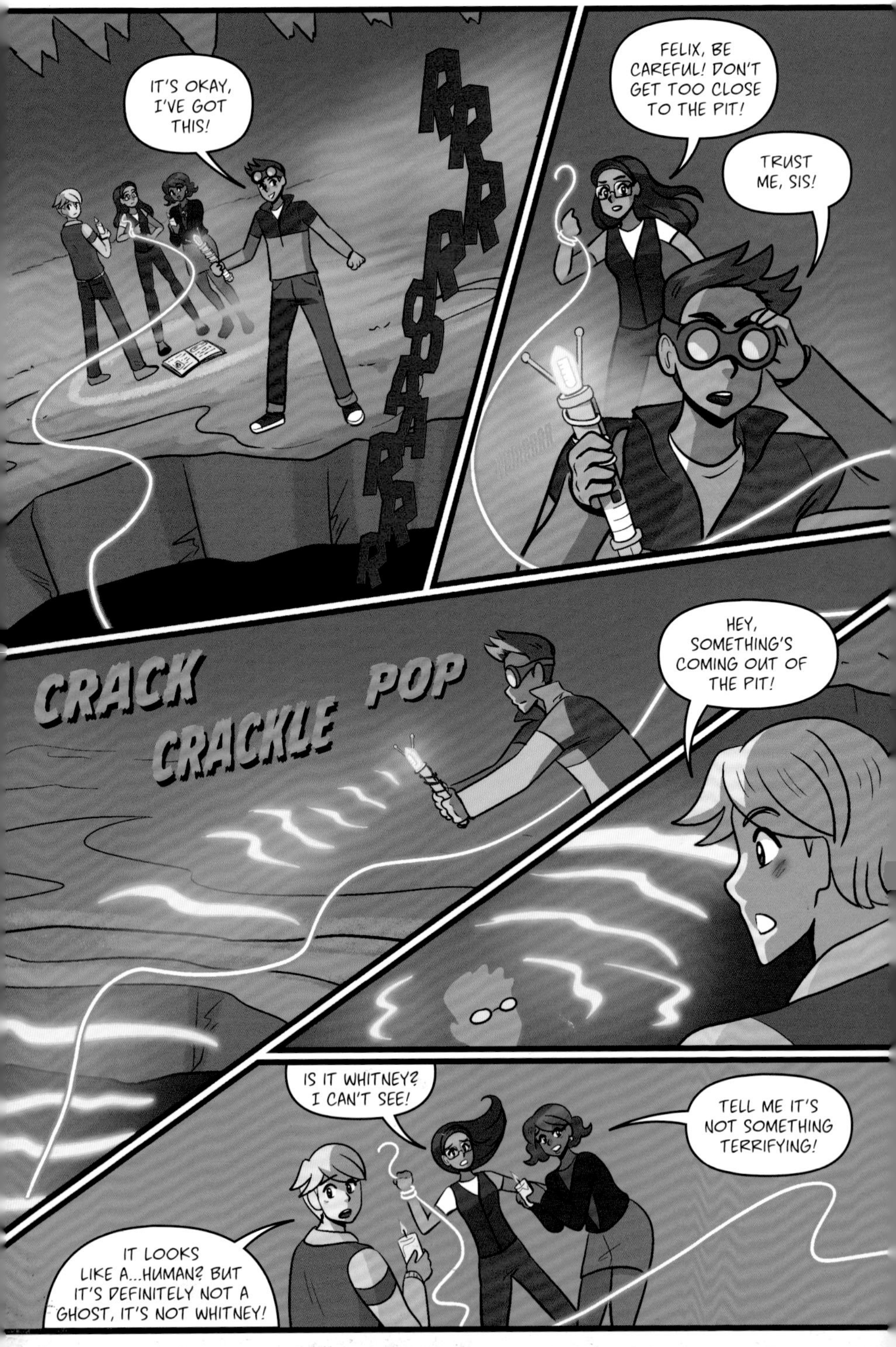

IT'S OKAY, I'VE GOT THIS!
RRRRROAARRR
FELIX, BE CAREFUL! DON'T GET TOO CLOSE TO THE PIT!
TRUST ME, SIS!
CRACK
CRACKLE
POP
HEY, SOMETHING'S COMING OUT OF THE PIT!
IS IT WHITNEY? I CAN'T SEE!
TELL ME IT'S NOT SOMETHING TERRIFYING!
IT LOOKS LIKE A...HUMAN? BUT IT'S DEFINITELY NOT A GHOST, IT'S NOT WHITNEY!

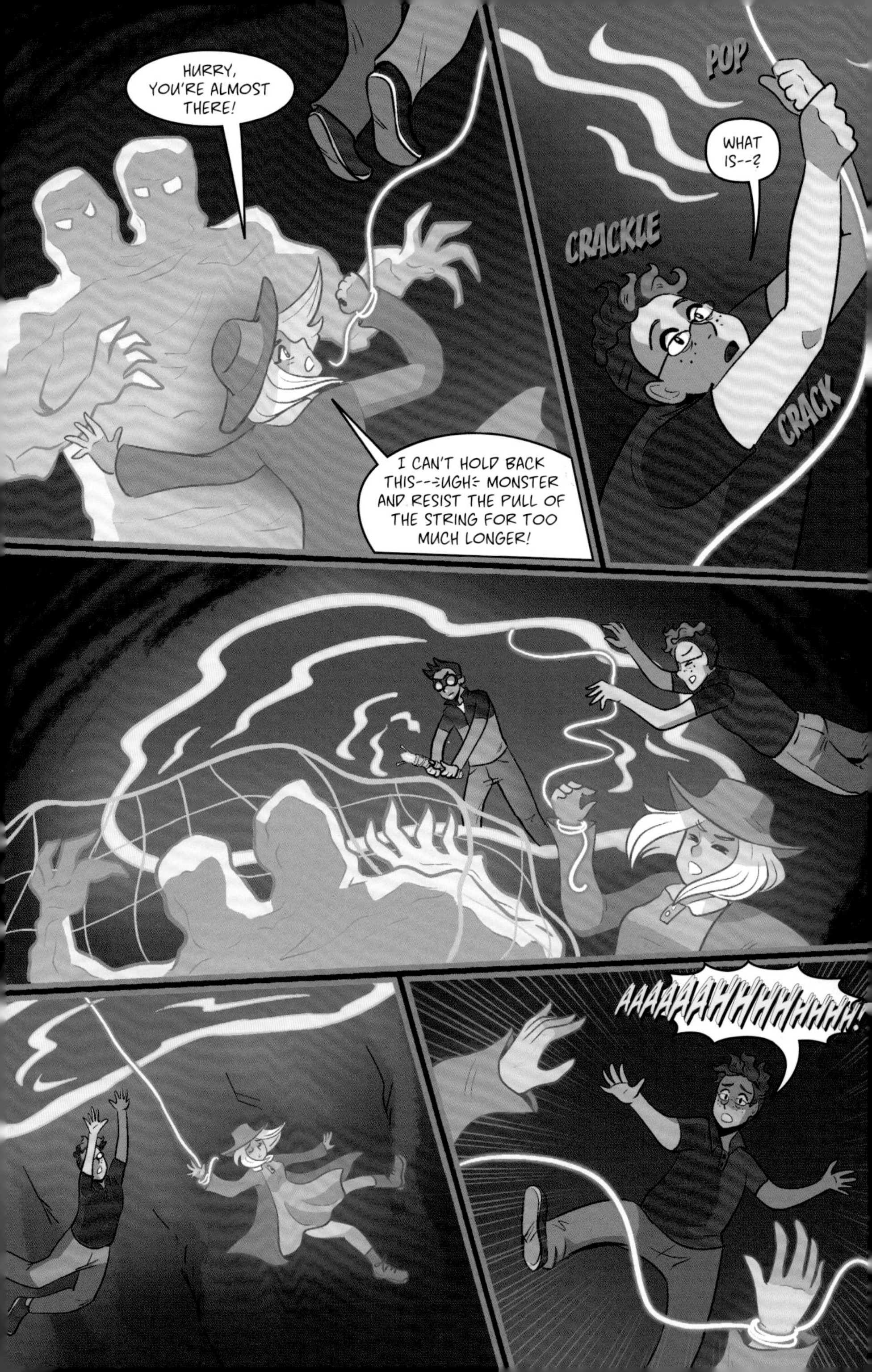
HURRY, YOU'RE ALMOST THERE!
I CAN'T HOLD BACK THIS--=UGH= MONSTER AND RESIST THE PULL OF THE STRING FOR TOO MUCH LONGER!
POP
WHAT IS--?
CRACKLE
CRACK
AAAAAAAHHHHHHHHH!

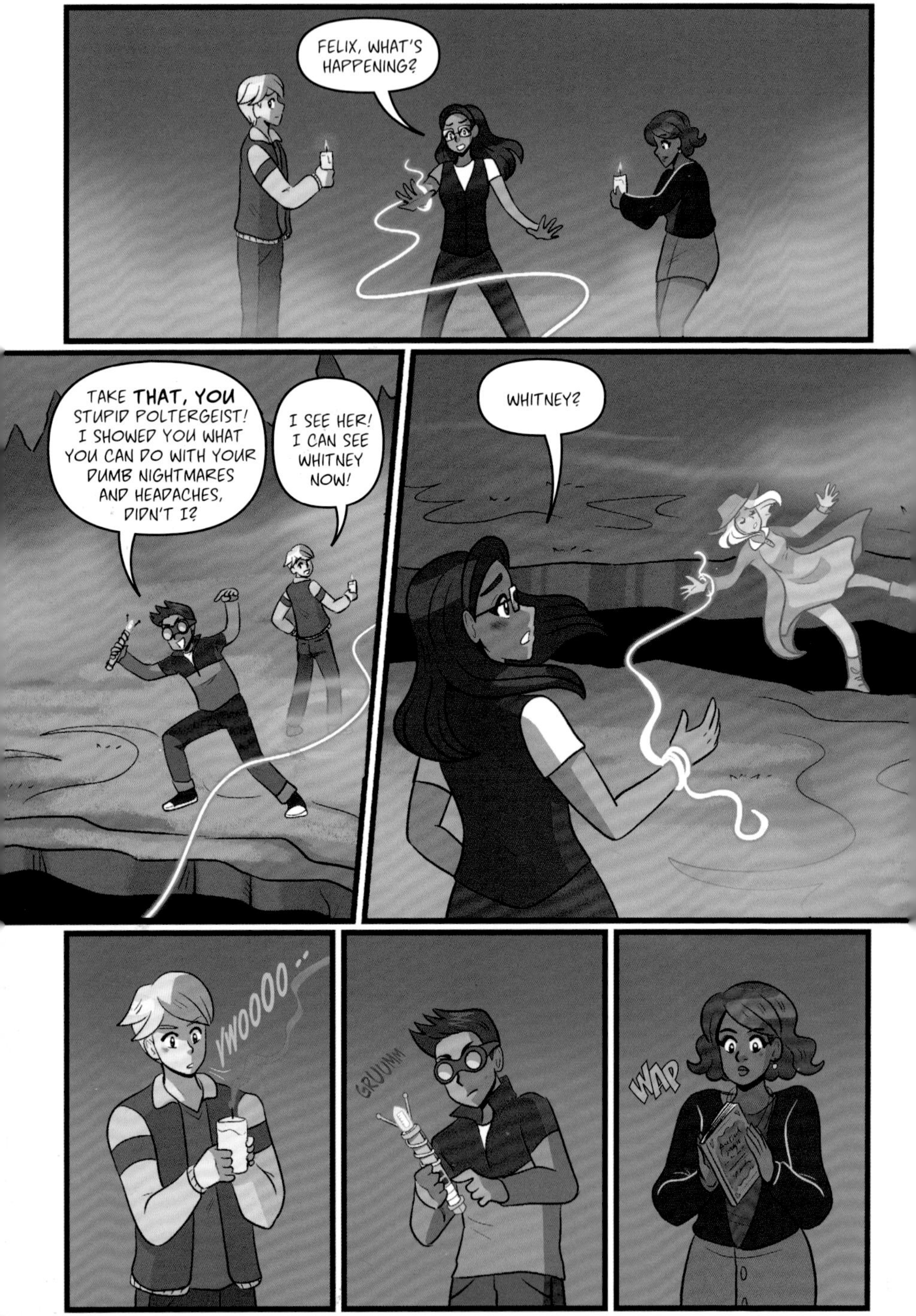
FELIX, WHAT'S HAPPENING?
TAKE **THAT, YOU** STUPID POLTERGEIST! I SHOWED YOU WHAT YOU CAN DO WITH YOUR DUMB NIGHTMARES AND HEADACHES, DIDN'T I?
I SEE HER! I CAN SEE WHITNEY NOW!
WHITNEY?
VWOOOO--
GRUUMM
WAP

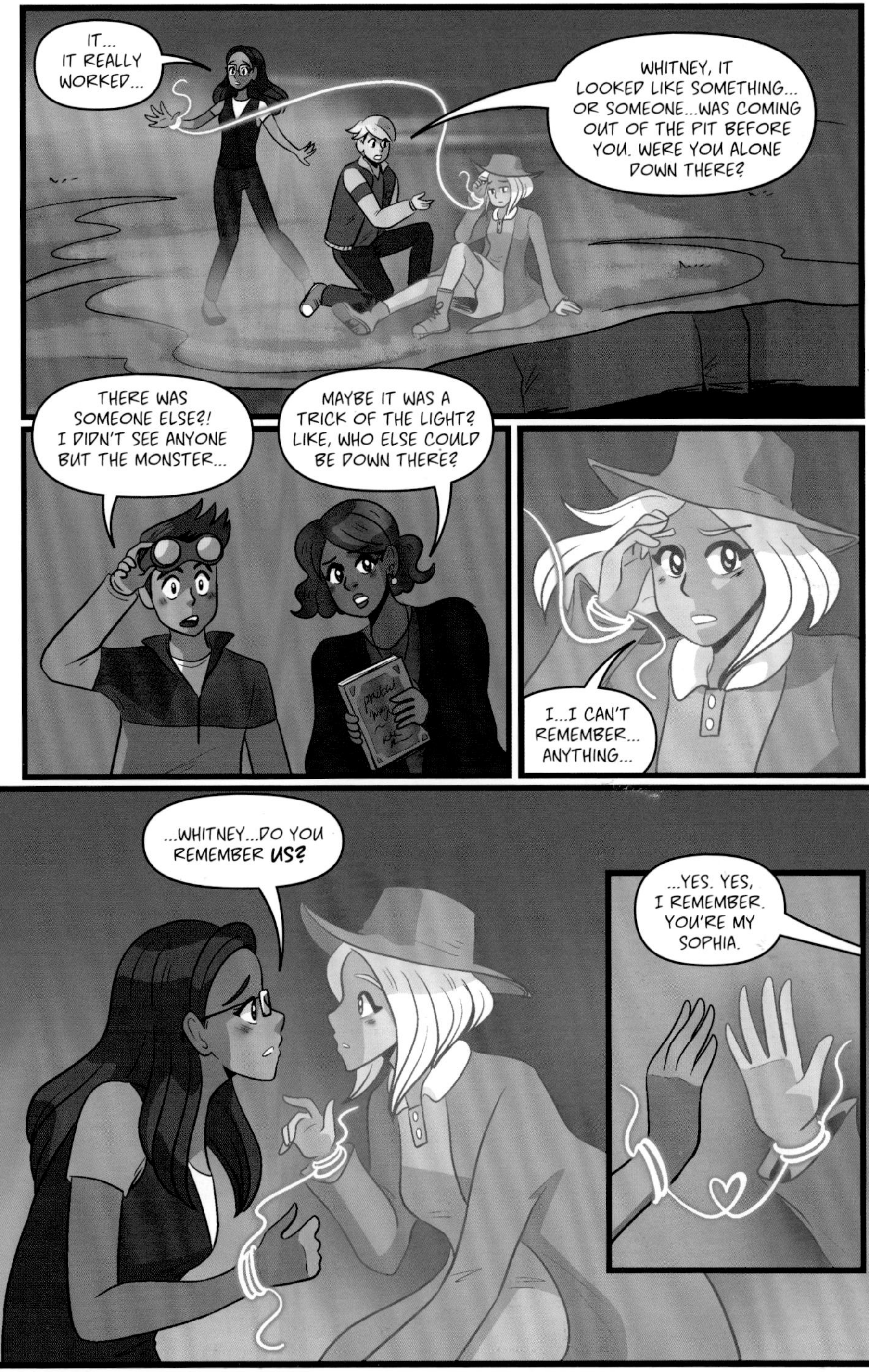
IT... IT REALLY WORKED...
WHITNEY, IT LOOKED LIKE SOMETHING... OR SOMEONE...WAS COMING OUT OF THE PIT BEFORE YOU. WERE YOU ALONE DOWN THERE?
THERE WAS SOMEONE ELSE?! I DIDN'T SEE ANYONE BUT THE MONSTER...
MAYBE IT WAS A TRICK OF THE LIGHT? LIKE, WHO ELSE COULD BE DOWN THERE?
I...I CAN'T REMEMBER... ANYTHING...
...WHITNEY...DO YOU REMEMBER **US?**
...YES. YES, I REMEMBER. YOU'RE MY SOPHIA.

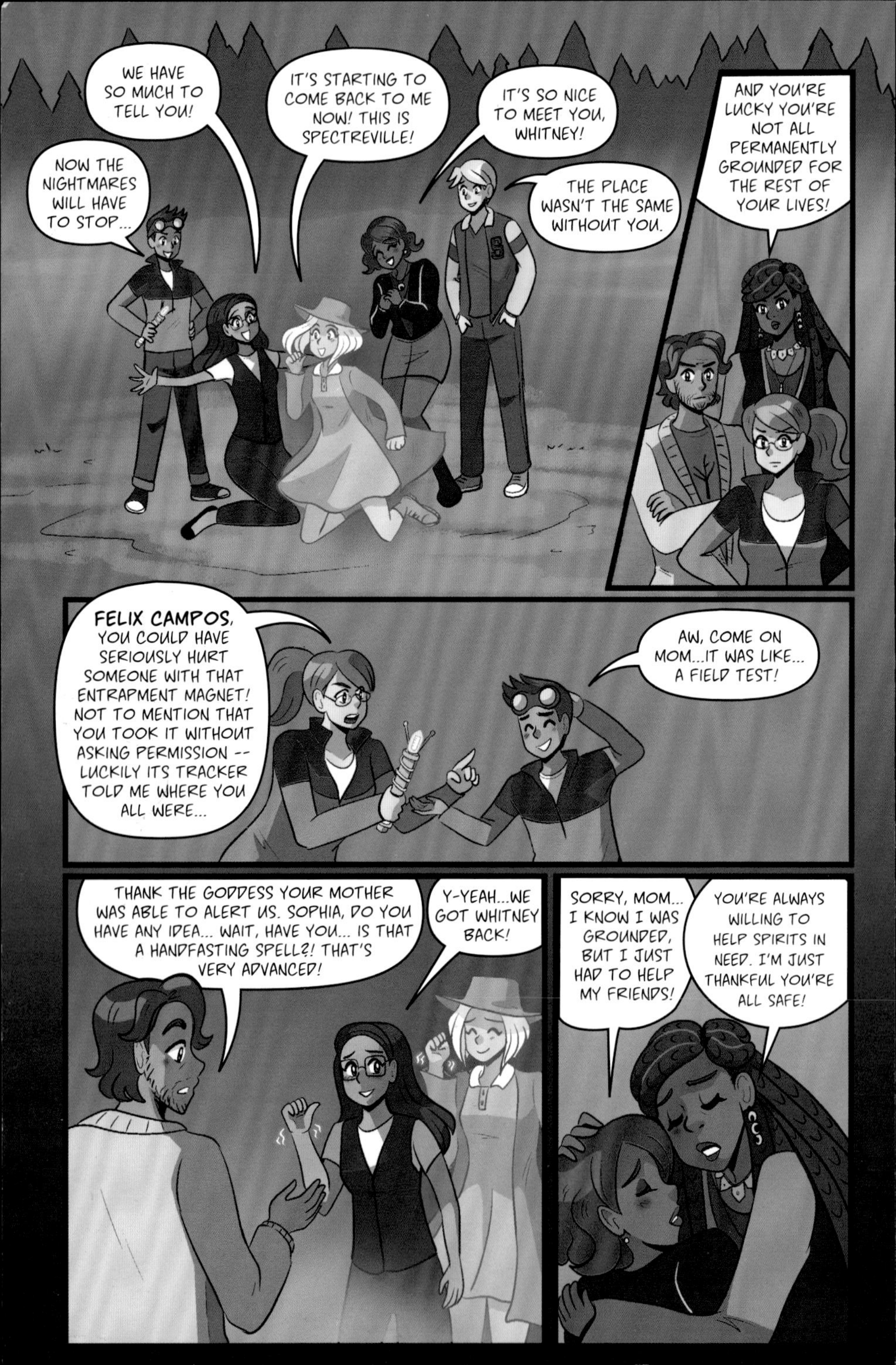
NOW THE NIGHTMARES WILL HAVE TO STOP...
WE HAVE SO MUCH TO TELL YOU!
IT'S STARTING TO COME BACK TO ME NOW! THIS IS SPECTREVILLE!
IT'S SO NICE TO MEET YOU, WHITNEY!
THE PLACE WASN'T THE SAME WITHOUT YOU.
AND YOU'RE LUCKY YOU'RE NOT ALL PERMANENTLY GROUNDED FOR THE REST OF YOUR LIVES!
FELIX CAMPOS, YOU COULD HAVE SERIOUSLY HURT SOMEONE WITH THAT ENTRAPMENT MAGNET! NOT TO MENTION THAT YOU TOOK IT WITHOUT ASKING PERMISSION -- LUCKILY ITS TRACKER TOLD ME WHERE YOU ALL WERE...
AW, COME ON MOM...IT WAS LIKE... A FIELD TEST!
THANK THE GODDESS YOUR MOTHER WAS ABLE TO ALERT US. SOPHIA, DO YOU HAVE ANY IDEA... WAIT, HAVE YOU... IS THAT A HANDFASTING SPELL?! THAT'S VERY ADVANCED!
Y-YEAH...WE GOT WHITNEY BACK!
SORRY, MOM... I KNOW I WAS GROUNDED, BUT I JUST HAD TO HELP MY FRIENDS!
YOU'RE ALWAYS WILLING TO HELP SPIRITS IN NEED. I'M JUST THANKFUL YOU'RE ALL SAFE!

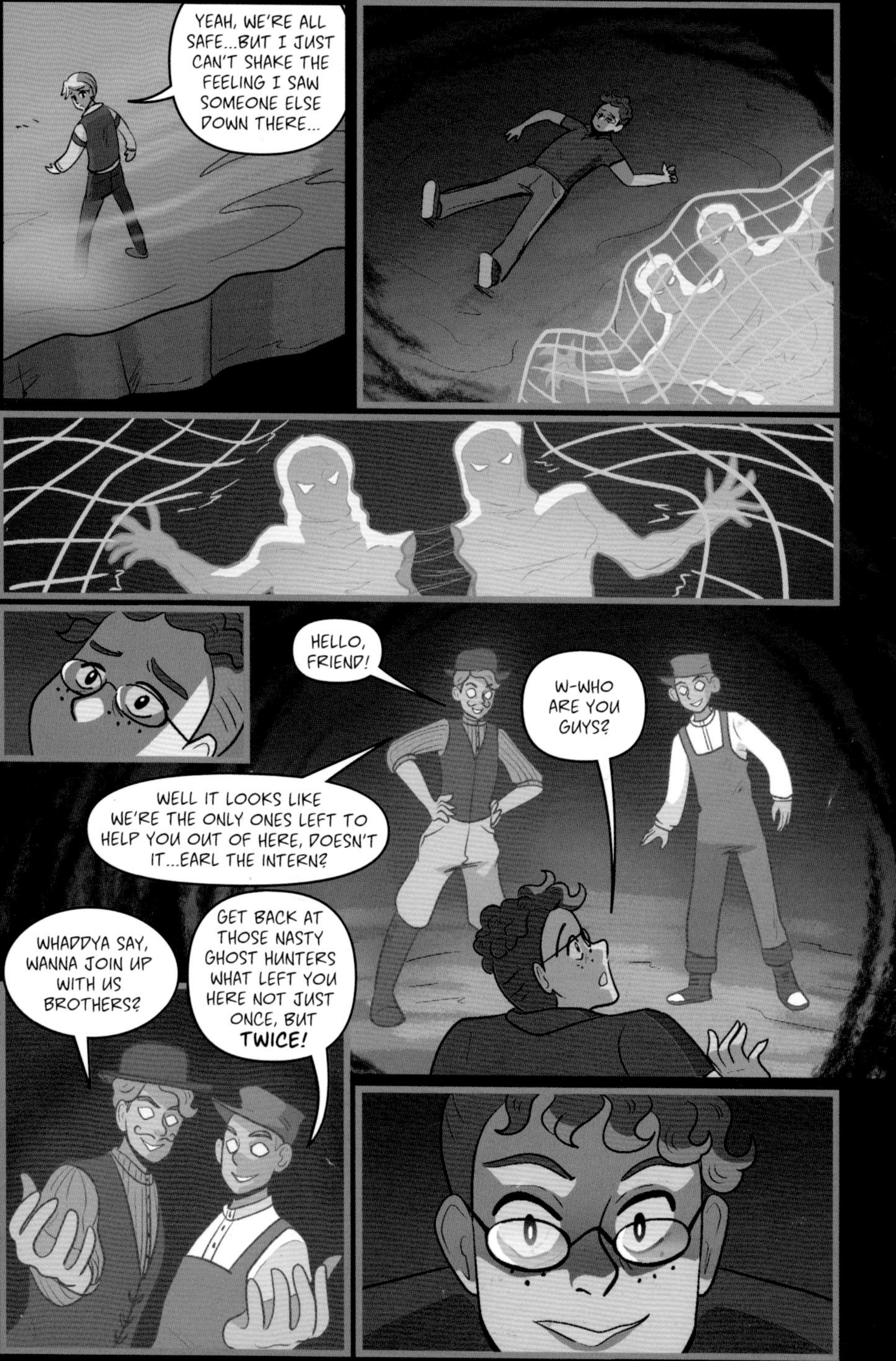
YEAH, WE'RE ALL SAFE...BUT I JUST CAN'T SHAKE THE FEELING I SAW SOMEONE ELSE DOWN THERE...
HELLO, FRIEND!
W-WHO ARE YOU GUYS?
WELL IT LOOKS LIKE WE'RE THE ONLY ONES LEFT TO HELP YOU OUT OF HERE, DOESN'T IT...EARL THE INTERN?
WHADDYA SAY, WANNA JOIN UP WITH US BROTHERS?
GET BACK AT THOSE NASTY GHOST HUNTERS WHAT LEFT YOU HERE NOT JUST ONCE, BUT **TWICE!**

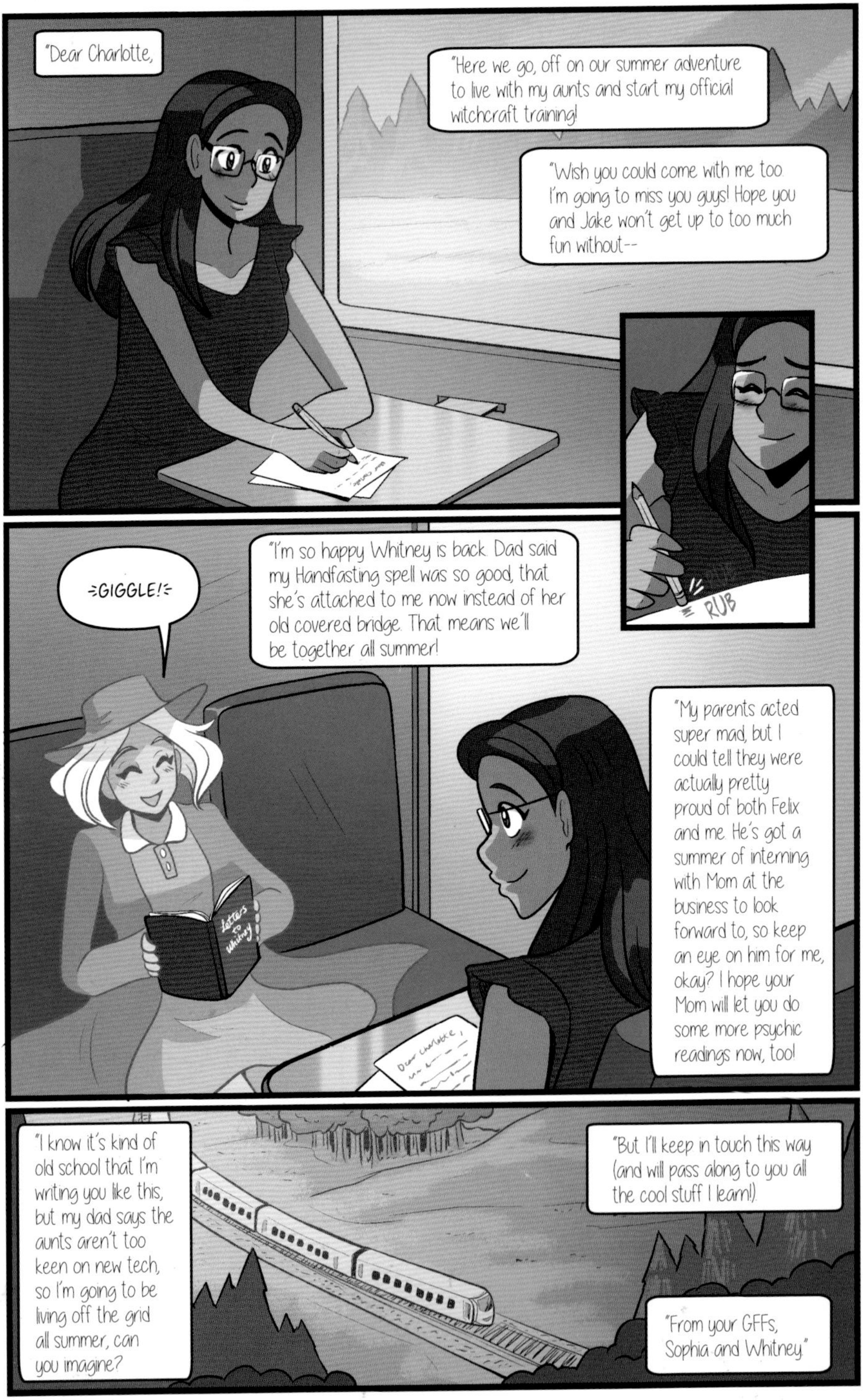

"Dear Charlotte,
"Here we go, off on our summer adventure to live with my aunts and start my official witchcraft training!
"Wish you could come with me too. I'm going to miss you guys! Hope you and Jake won't get up to too much fun without--
RUB
=GIGGLE!=
"I'm so happy Whitney is back. Dad said my Handfasting spell was so good, that she's attached to me now instead of her old covered bridge. That means we'll be together all summer!
"My parents acted super mad, but I could tell they were actually pretty proud of both Felix and me. He's got a summer of interning with Mom at the business to look forward to, so keep an eye on him for me, okay? I hope your Mom will let you do some more psychic readings now, too!
Letters to Whitney
"I know it's kind of old school that I'm writing you like this, but my dad says the aunts aren't too keen on new tech, so I'm going to be living off the grid all summer, can you imagine?
"But I'll keep in touch this way (and will pass along to you all the cool stuff I learn!).
"From your GFFs, Sophia and Whitney."

charmzchat

Monica Gallagher is the writer and co-creator of GFFs. She has over ten years experience making comics and illustrations with a positive feminist spin. She has worked for Oni Press, Vertigo, and Valiant, as well as self-published several of her own comics at her website, eatyour-lipstick.com. Her latest webcomic is Assassin Roommate, updated weekly on Webtoons.

Kata Kane is the artist and co-creator of GFFs. She is also the artist on ANA AND THE COSMIC RACE from Charmz, the creator of Altar Girl, and she loves to draw comics for all ages and young adults. She loves watching anime and reading manga such as Sailor Moon. You can find more of her comicbooks and artwork at kata-kane.com.

We asked our Charmz creators a few questions about GFFs and present their answers here...

How did the two of you come up with the idea for GFFs?

Kata Kane: Monica had the really cool story idea of a spooky old tourist town where ghosts and spirits were the norm, so that was how we founded the town of Spectreville. I added some character ideas for a family that could be investigators in the town: a sister and brother duo who didn't always get along and had very different methods of how to deal with their work. We knew we needed a ghost character that could be Sophia's first solo job... but Whitney was much more and we knew from the beginning she would become the love interest for Sophia!

Monica Gallagher: Spectreville is a

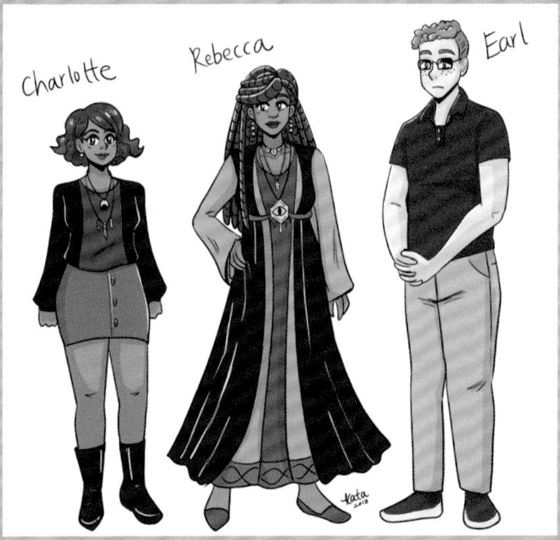
Charlotte
Rebecca
Earl
Kata 2018

Monica Gallagher: I find all the scientific tools really fun and fascinating, but since ghosts and the paranormal aren't logical and clear cut, it makes sense to me that the methods of investigating them wouldn't be either! Overall I think it has to be a blended approach, but I also get really into the fun of the more out there mystical techniques.

Do you have any advice for those who want to create their own comics?

shout-out to my love of the ghost tours that have been springing up in small towns throughout this country. I've always wanted to do a story involving ghost characters, so I thought it'd be a nice change to put them in a place that had already accepted (and was enthusiastic about!) ghosts and the paranormal in general. I was also interested in ideas involving romance when it involved not gender, but the person you fall in love with. And Kata was a terrific collaborator with bouncing ideas off of and fleshing out all the characters.

If you were a Paranormal Investigator like Sophia and Felix's family, would you use "scientific tools" or "magical witchcraft"?

Kata Kane: I think it is all pretty magical in Spectreville to be able to see ghosts, but I would probably try to use research like Felix and his mom Joanne do to figure out the best methods for dealing with the spirits. I really like that Sophia and her dad Oscar are good at communicating with ghosts and understanding what the ghosts need emotionally too.

Kata Kane: Start writing and drawing now! Even if you think it won't be perfect. It's okay to make mistakes and to learn from them. The more you practice creating comics for yourself, the better you'll get. Sometimes I just start with a character idea, and the story gets built around them. You should always create something that makes you happy!

Monica Gallagher: Definitely just keep doing it! Don't be afraid to put stuff out there, and to keep putting stuff out there. Plus it's really important to finish something, not put off doing something because what you have in mind is a giant story. None of us who create are ever 100% satisfied and happy with what we put out there, but the fun of it is seeing what you come up with and watching your own style grow and improve!

Thanks Monica and Kata! If you have a question for either Monica or Kata or both, send it to us at salicrup@papercutz.com.

And now a special sneak peek at AMY'S DIARY #1 "Space Alien…Almost?"

SEPTEMBER
The End of the World

-Tuesday, September 13th-

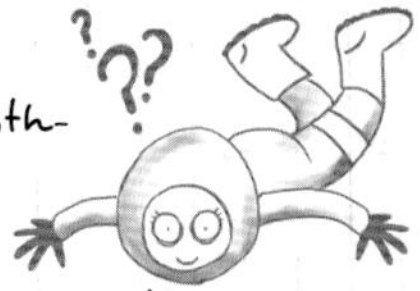

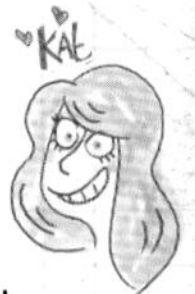
Kat

7:05pm:
Sometimes I feel alone in the universe. I don't get along with anybody, except for my best friend, Kat, but ever since we got into an argument over something stupid, we're not talking anymore. There's my mom, of course, (she's downstairs in the kitchen making some spaghetti sauce and it smells soooooo good), but I can't really tell her everything and she gets on my nerves sometimes. Like right now.

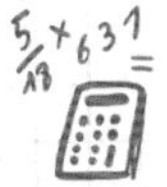

7:10pm: My mom's calling me to tell me dinner's ready.

7:12pm: Okay, I'll go downstairs and eat...But first, I've got to point out that I'm being punished, because I made a little, let's say, "behavior mistake" at school. Honestly, I don't deserve my punishment. I just played a little joke on the math teacher (who, let me point out, has been a real pain since the beginning of the year). She shouted in class: "You must follow the process or you'll miss the train for your diploma!" And I answered: "We'll catch a boat..." and then found myself in the principal's office:

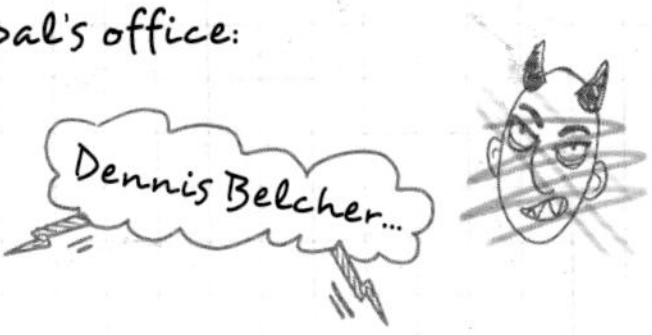
Dennis Belcher...

7:16pm: Okay, I've got to go have dinner.

8:35pm: Great...My mom's decided my punishment would be not getting to watch "One Tree Hill." That sucks! What's more, she told me the principal wanted to see her tomorrow to talk about my grades. Tssk! I was just starting to hate him when she said: "He's cute."

Cute handsome? Or cute nice? Argh!

Does she have a crush on him or something?!

10:00pm: My mom came into to my room and saw me crying. She told me she didn't know "One Tree Hill" was that important to me and let me watch it on my computer. But I wasn't crying about that. I was crying because I was thinking about my dad, who's not here anymore...

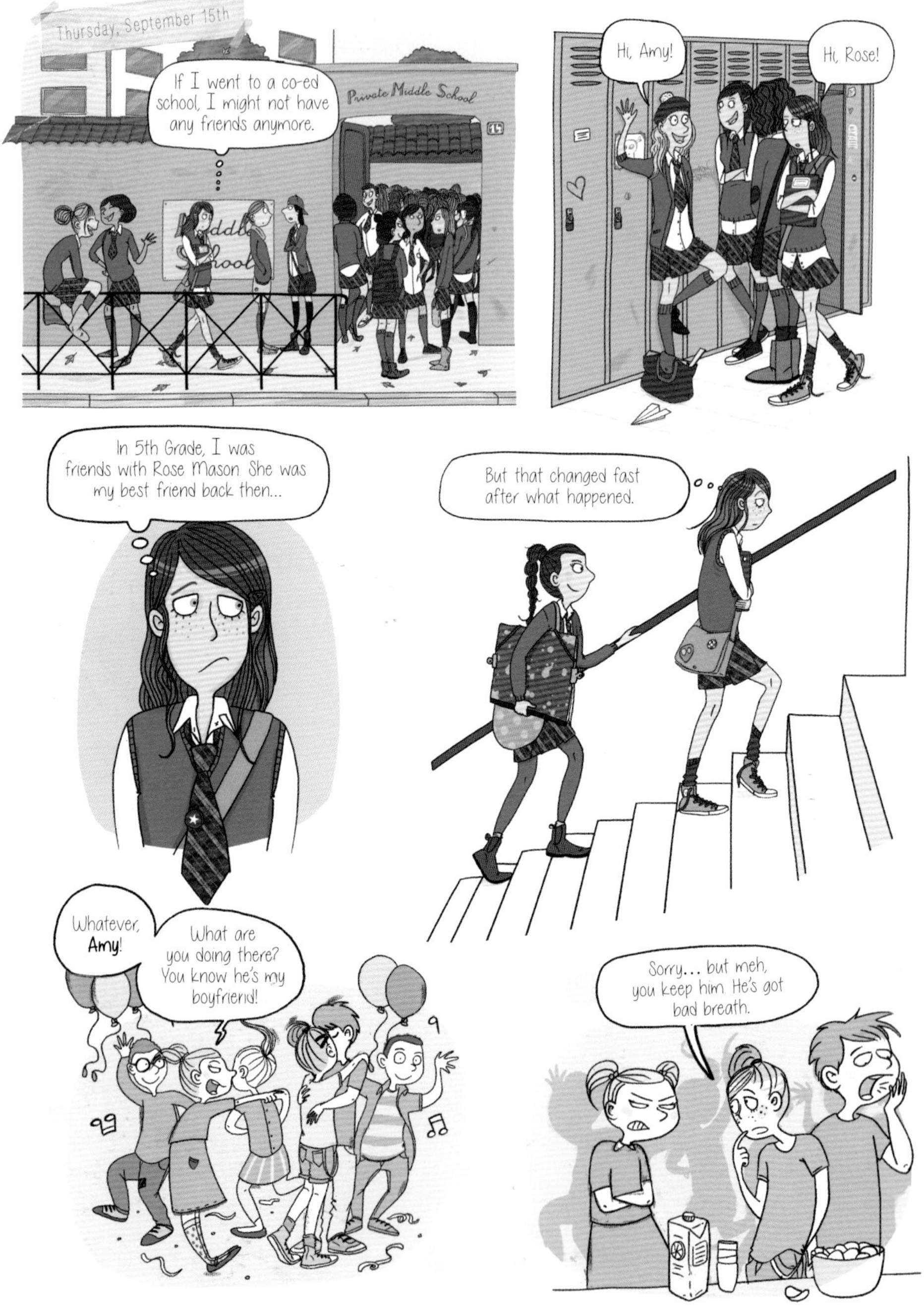
Thursday, September 15th
Private Middle School
Middle School
If I went to a co-ed school, I might not have any friends anymore.
Hi, Amy!
Hi, Rose!
In 5th Grade, I was friends with Rose Mason. She was my best friend back then...
But that changed fast after what happened.
Whatever, Amy!
What are you doing there? You know he's my boyfriend!
Sorry... but meh, you keep him. He's got bad breath.

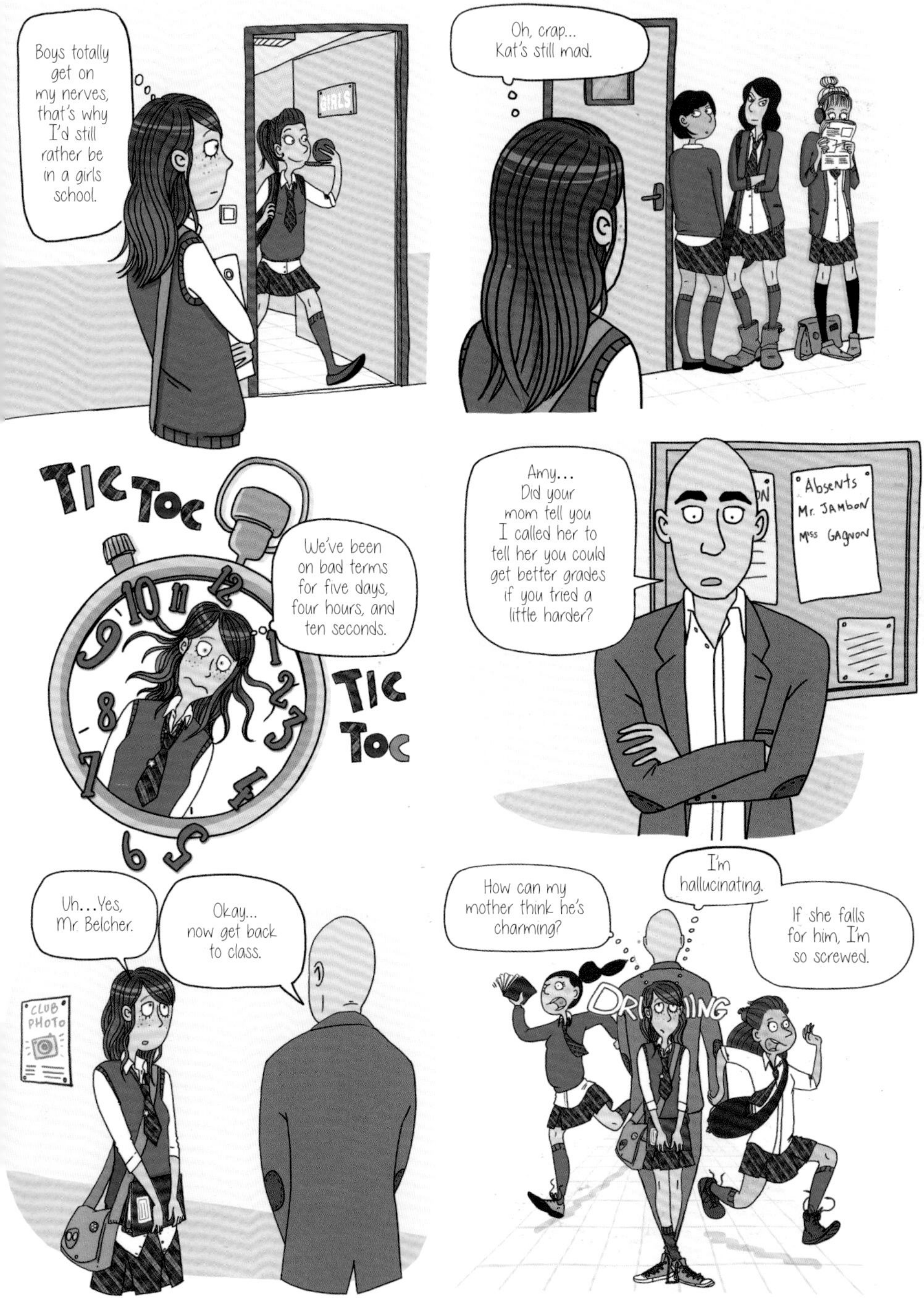

Boys totally get on my nerves, that's why I'd still rather be in a girls school.
GIRLS
Oh, crap... Kat's still mad.
TIC TOC
We've been on bad terms for five days, four hours, and ten seconds.
TIC TOC
Amy... Did your mom tell you I called her to tell her you could get better grades if you tried a little harder?
Absents
Mr. JAMBON
Miss GAGNON
Uh...Yes, Mr. Belcher.
Okay... now get back to class.
CLUB PHOTO
How can my mother think he's charming?
I'm hallucinating.
If she falls for him, I'm so screwed.

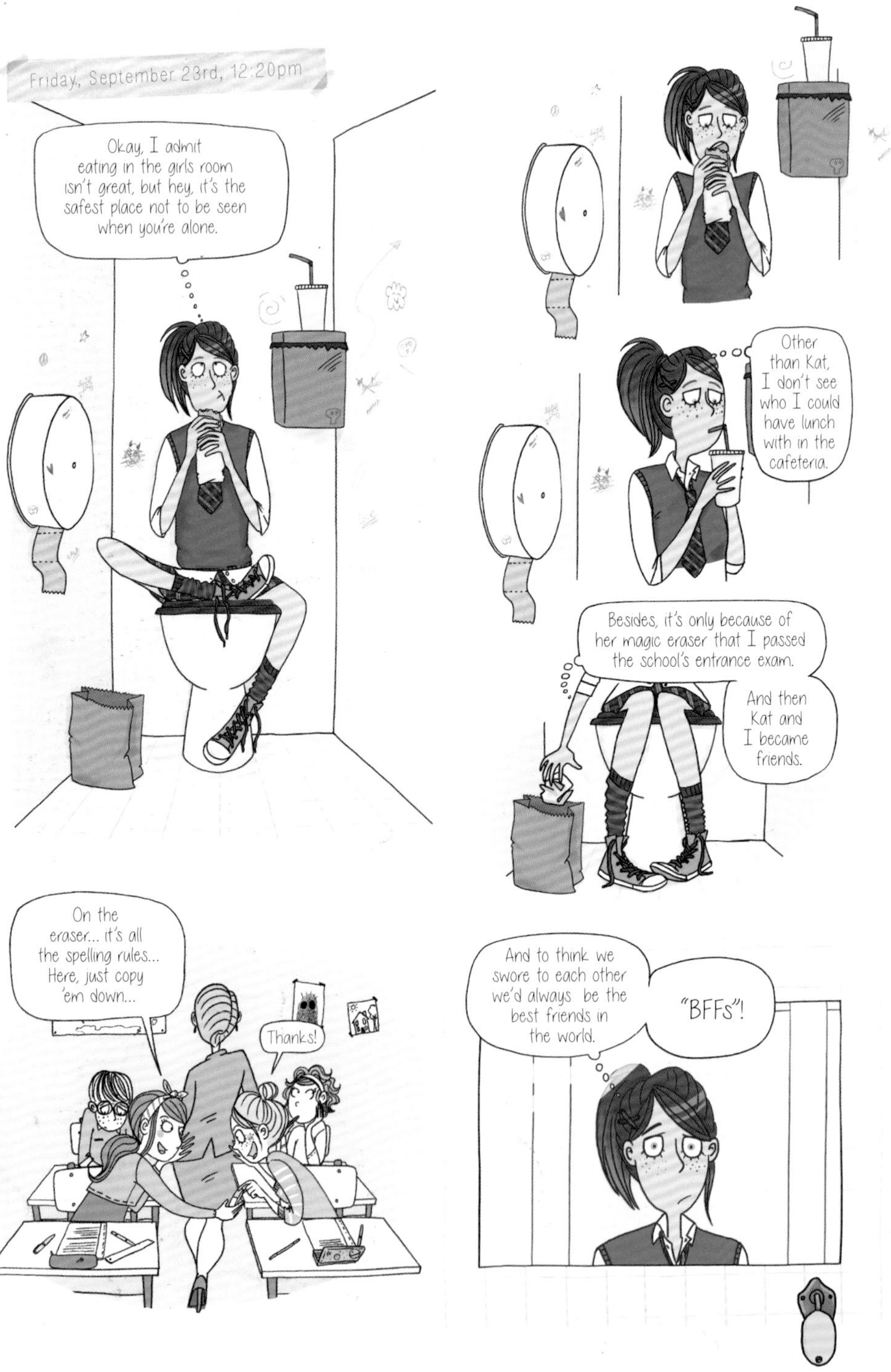
Friday, September 23rd, 12:20pm
Okay, I admit eating in the girls room isn't great, but hey, it's the safest place not to be seen when you're alone.
Other than Kat, I don't see who I could have lunch with in the cafeteria.
Besides, it's only because of her magic eraser that I passed the school's entrance exam.
And then Kat and I became friends.
On the eraser... it's all the spelling rules... Here, just copy 'em down...
Thanks!
And to think we swore to each other we'd always be the best friends in the world.
"BFFs"!

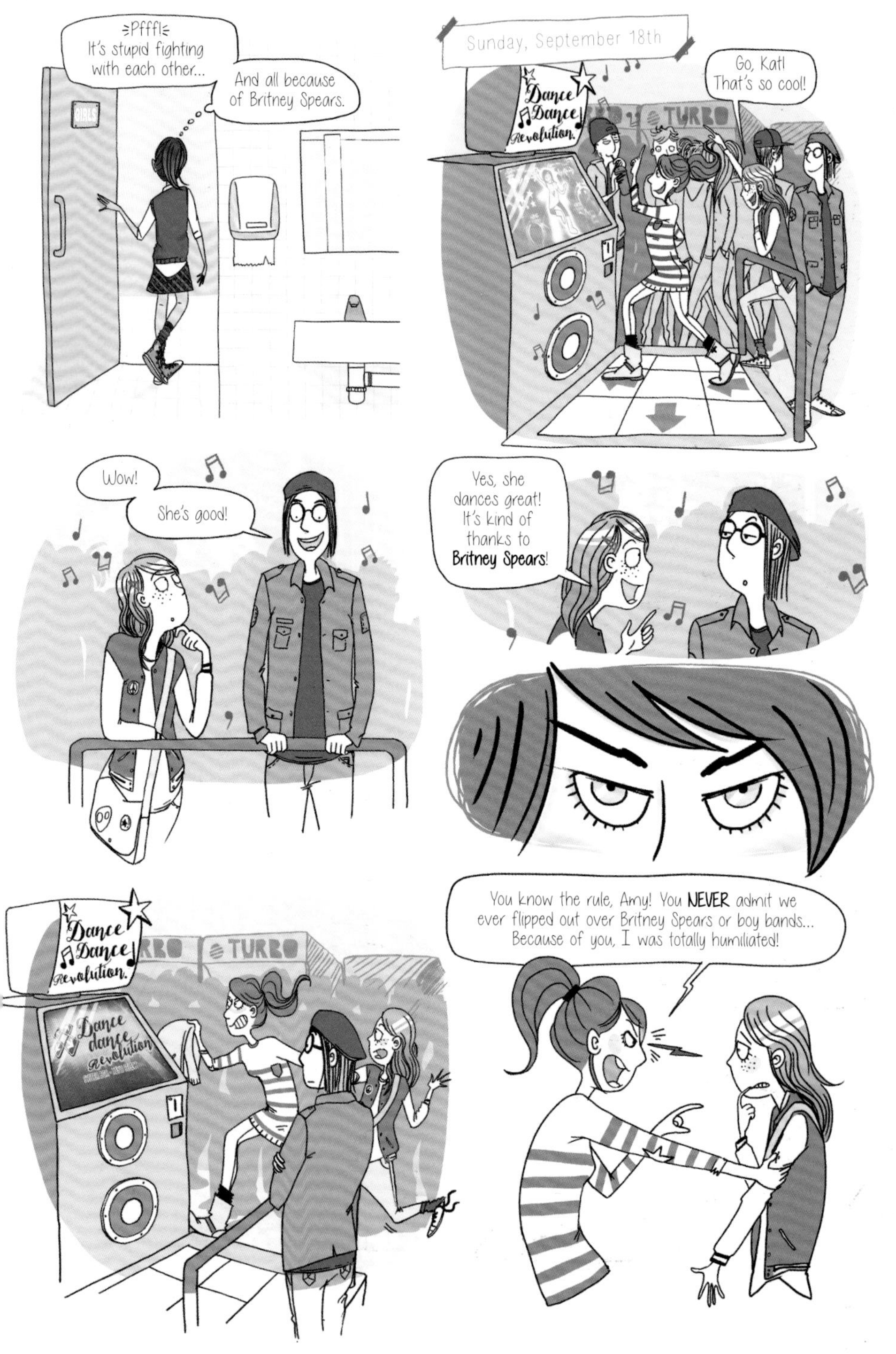

≡Pfff!≡
It's stupid fighting with each other...
And all because of Britney Spears.
GIRLS
Sunday, September 18th
Dance Dance Revolution
Go, Kat! That's so cool!
TURBO
Wow!
She's good!
Yes, she dances great! It's kind of thanks to Britney Spears!
Dance Dance Revolution
TURBO
You know the rule, Amy! You NEVER admit we ever flipped out over Britney Spears or boy bands... Because of you, I was totally humiliated!

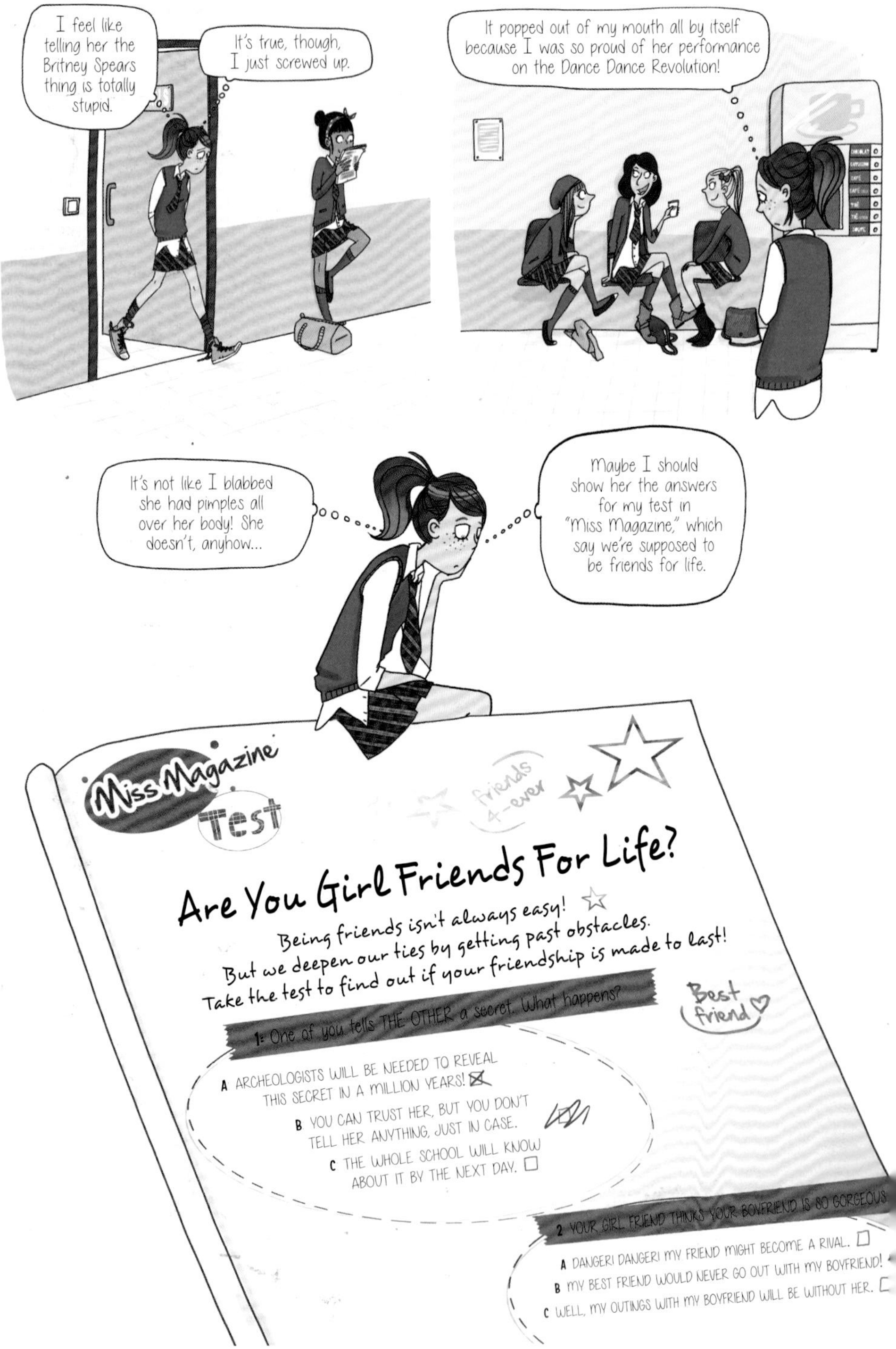
I feel like telling her the Britney Spears thing is totally stupid.
It's true, though, I just screwed up.
It popped out of my mouth all by itself because I was so proud of her performance on the Dance Dance Revolution!
It's not like I blabbed she had pimples all over her body! She doesn't, anyhow...
Maybe I should show her the answers for my test in "Miss Magazine," which say we're supposed to be friends for life.
Miss Magazine
Test
friends 4-ever
Are You Girl Friends For Life?
Being friends isn't always easy!
But we deepen our ties by getting past obstacles.
Take the test to find out if your friendship is made to last!
Best friend
1: One of you tells THE OTHER a secret. What happens?
A ARCHEOLOGISTS WILL BE NEEDED TO REVEAL THIS SECRET IN A MILLION YEARS!
B YOU CAN TRUST HER, BUT YOU DON'T TELL HER ANYTHING, JUST IN CASE.
C THE WHOLE SCHOOL WILL KNOW ABOUT IT BY THE NEXT DAY.
2 YOUR GIRL FRIEND THINKS YOUR BOYFRIEND IS SO GORGEOUS
A DANGER! DANGER! MY FRIEND MIGHT BECOME A RIVAL.
B MY BEST FRIEND WOULD NEVER GO OUT WITH MY BOYFRIEND!
C WELL, MY OUTINGS WITH MY BOYFRIEND WILL BE WITHOUT HER.

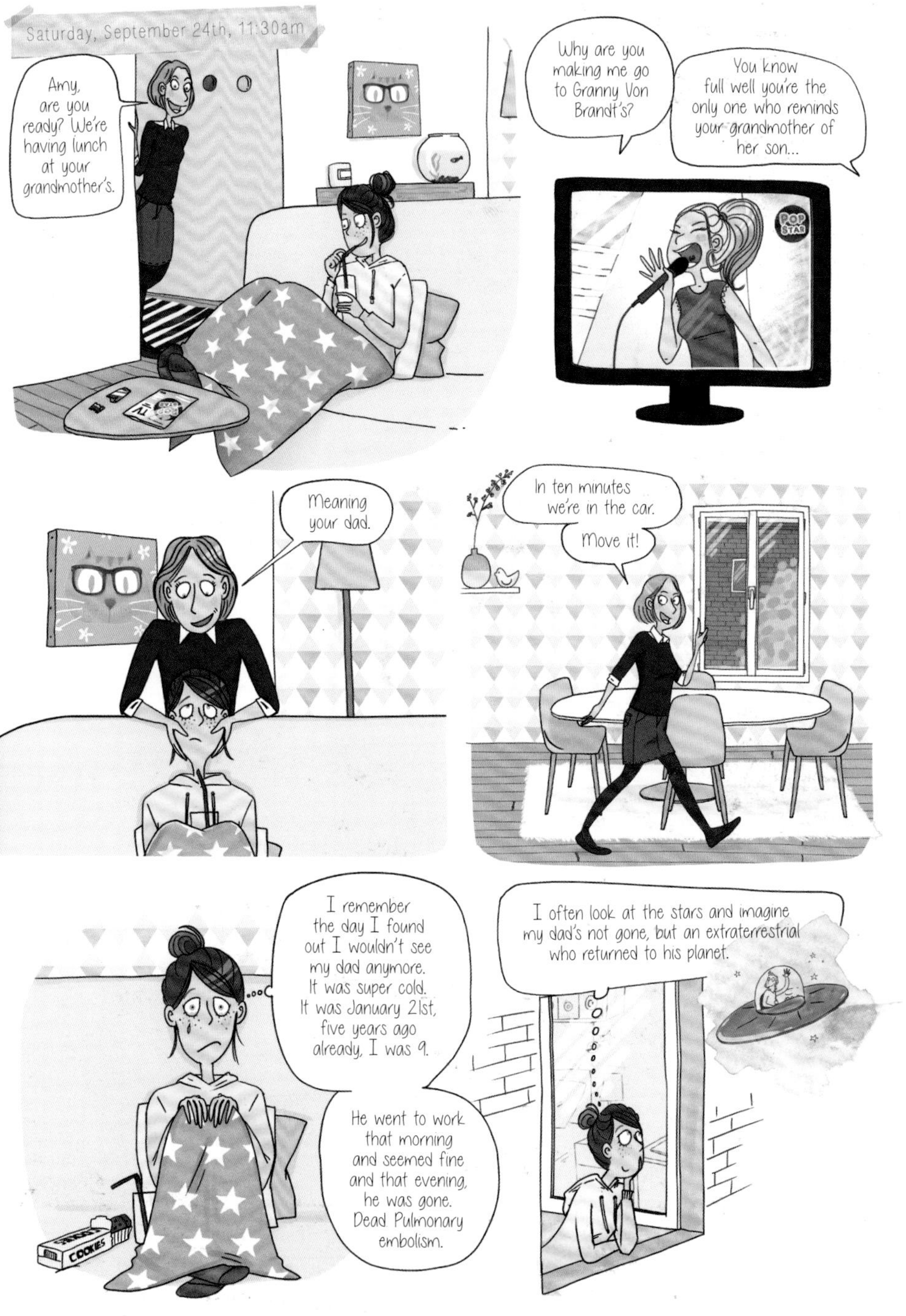
Saturday, September 24th, 11:30am
Amy, are you ready? We're having lunch at your grandmother's.
Why are you making me go to Granny Von Brandt's?
You know full well you're the only one who reminds your grandmother of her son...
POP STAR
Meaning your dad.
In ten minutes we're in the car.
Move it!
I remember the day I found out I wouldn't see my dad anymore. It was super cold. It was January 21st, five years ago already, I was 9.
He went to work that morning and seemed fine and that evening, he was gone. Dead. Pulmonary embolism.
COOKIES
I often look at the stars and imagine my dad's not gone, but an extraterrestrial who returned to his planet.

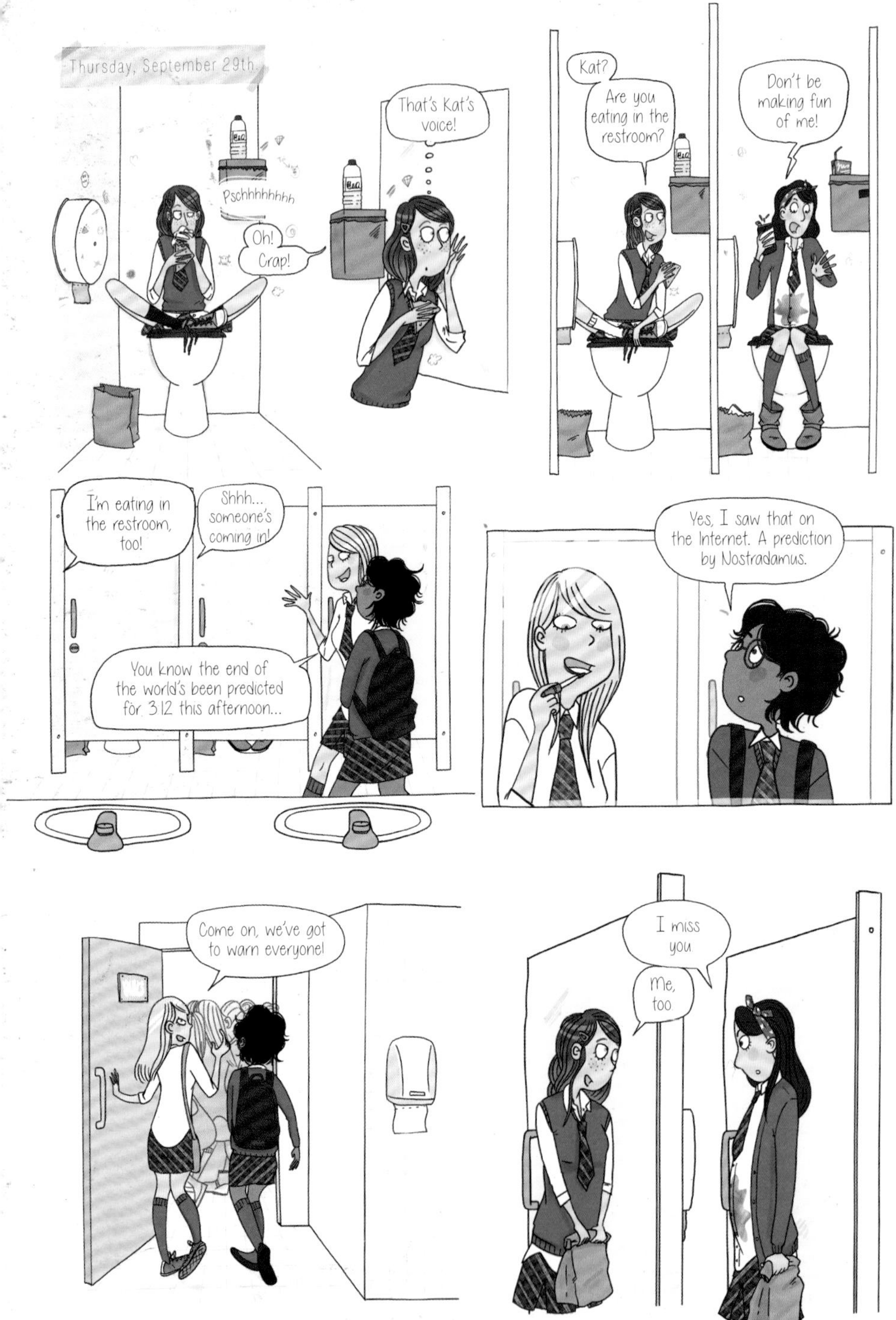
Thursday, September 29th.
Pschhhhhhhh
Oh! Crap!
That's Kat's voice!
Kat?
Are you eating in the restroom?
Don't be making fun of me!
I'm eating in the restroom, too!
Shhh... someone's coming in!
You know the end of the world's been predicted for 3:12 this afternoon...
Yes, I saw that on the Internet. A prediction by Nostradamus.
Come on, we've got to warn everyone!
I miss you.
Me, too.

Don't miss AMY'S DIARY #1 coming Winter 2019!

Now, check in with Crimson the patchwork girl in STITCHED #2...

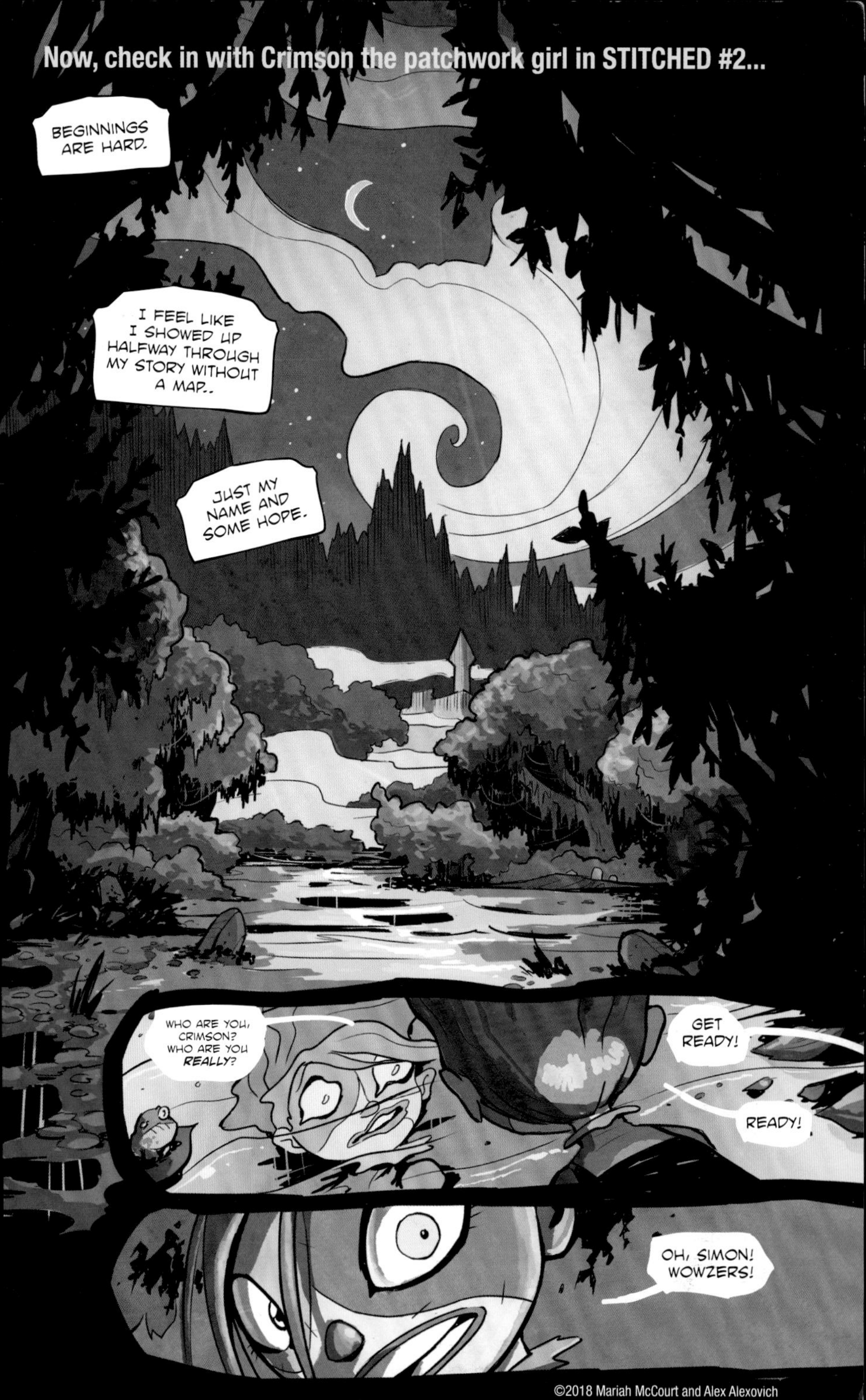
BEGINNINGS ARE HARD.
I FEEL LIKE I SHOWED UP HALFWAY THROUGH MY STORY WITHOUT A MAP..
JUST MY NAME AND SOME HOPE.
WHO ARE YOU, CRIMSON? WHO ARE YOU REALLY?
GET READY!
READY!
OH, SIMON! WOWZERS!

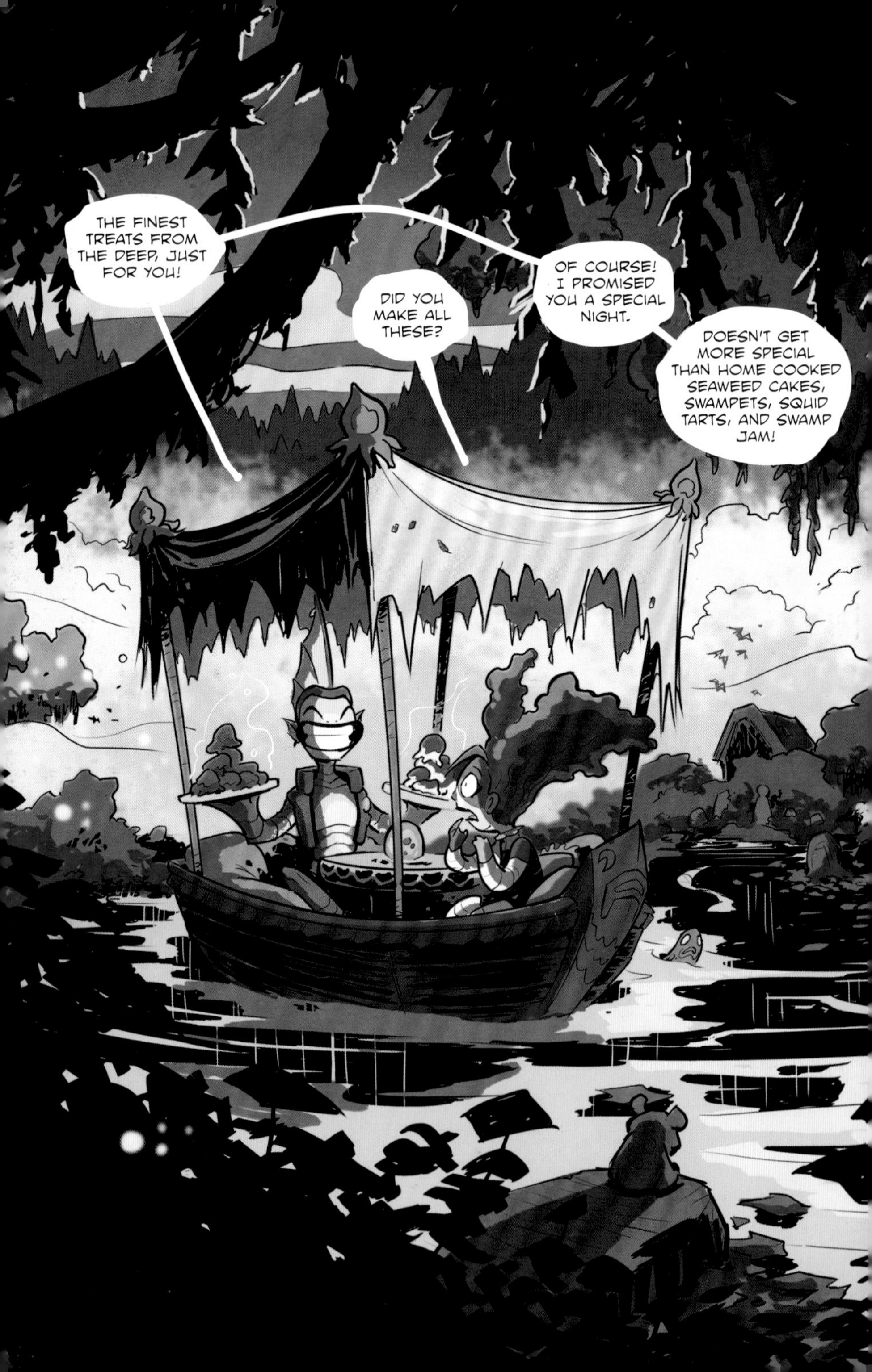
THE FINEST TREATS FROM THE DEEP, JUST FOR YOU!
DID YOU MAKE ALL THESE?
OF COURSE! I PROMISED YOU A SPECIAL NIGHT.
DOESN'T GET MORE SPECIAL THAN HOME COOKED SEAWEED CAKES, SWAMPETS, SQUID TARTS, AND SWAMP JAM!

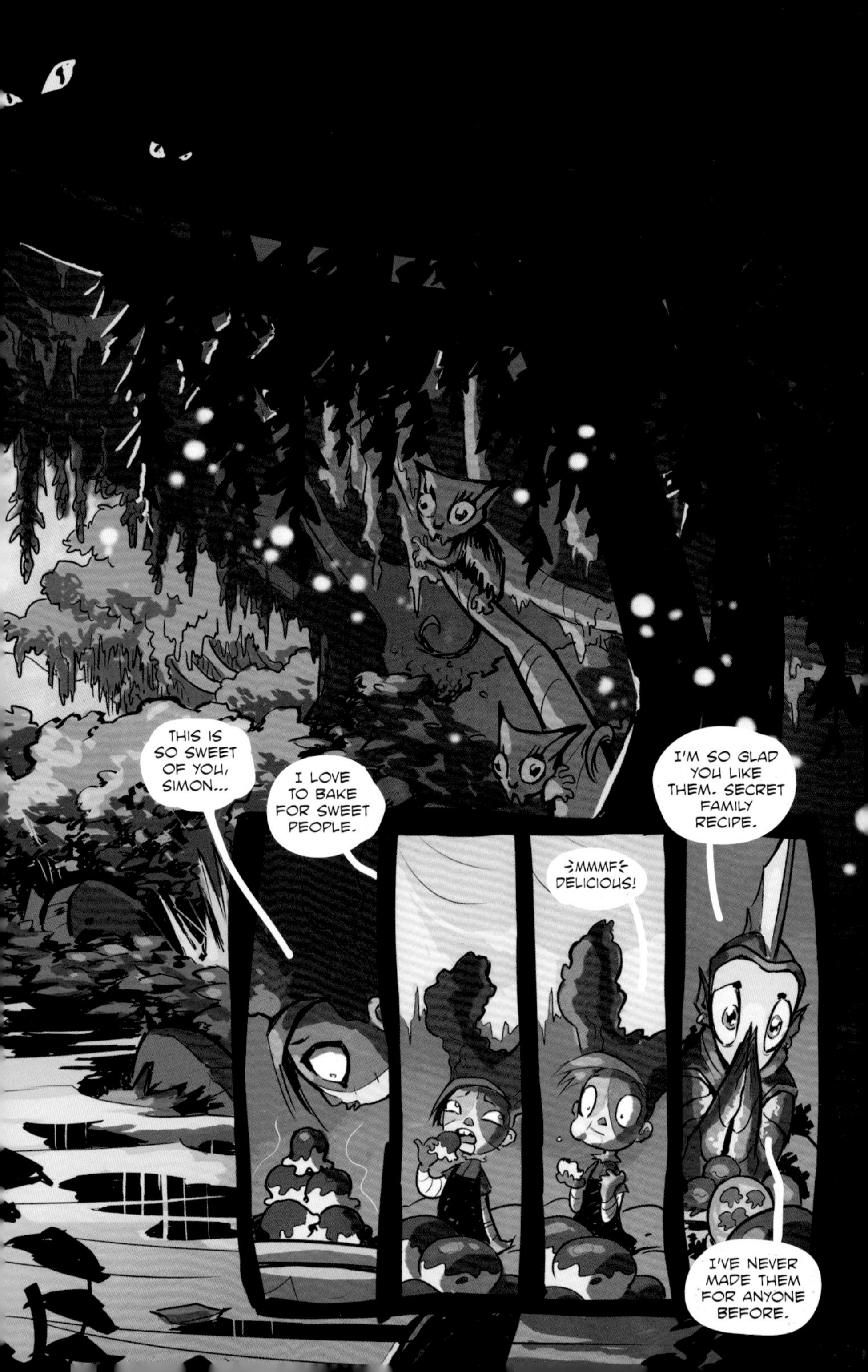
THIS IS SO SWEET OF YOU, SIMON...
I LOVE TO BAKE FOR SWEET PEOPLE.
MMMF DELICIOUS!
I'M SO GLAD YOU LIKE THEM. SECRET FAMILY RECIPE.
I'VE NEVER MADE THEM FOR ANYONE BEFORE.

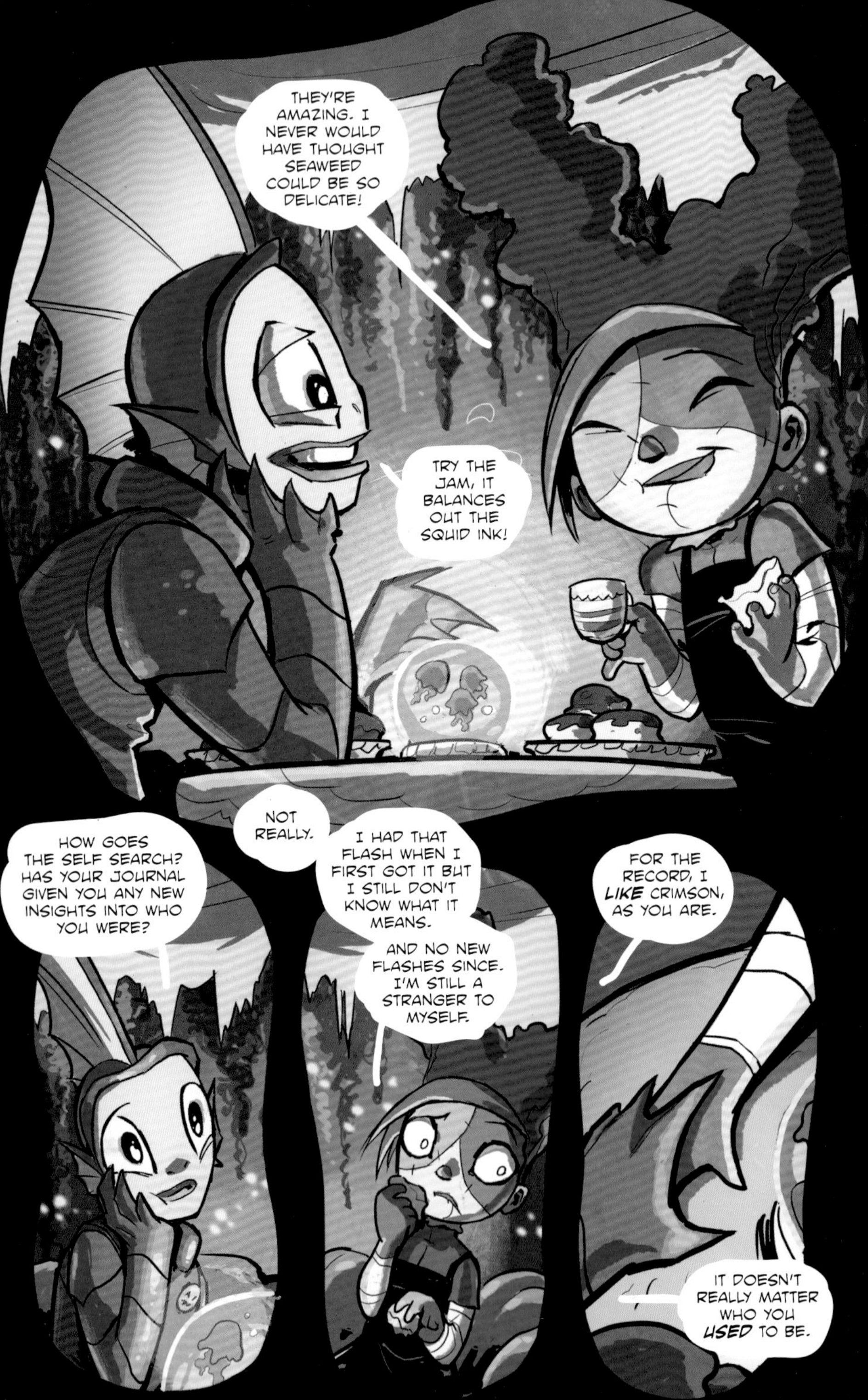
THEY'RE AMAZING. I NEVER WOULD HAVE THOUGHT SEAWEED COULD BE SO DELICATE!
TRY THE JAM, IT BALANCES OUT THE SQUID INK!
HOW GOES THE SELF SEARCH? HAS YOUR JOURNAL GIVEN YOU ANY NEW INSIGHTS INTO WHO YOU WERE?
NOT REALLY.
I HAD THAT FLASH WHEN I FIRST GOT IT BUT I STILL DON'T KNOW WHAT IT MEANS.
AND NO NEW FLASHES SINCE. I'M STILL A STRANGER TO MYSELF.
FOR THE RECORD, I LIKE CRIMSON, AS YOU ARE.
IT DOESN'T REALLY MATTER WHO YOU USED TO BE.

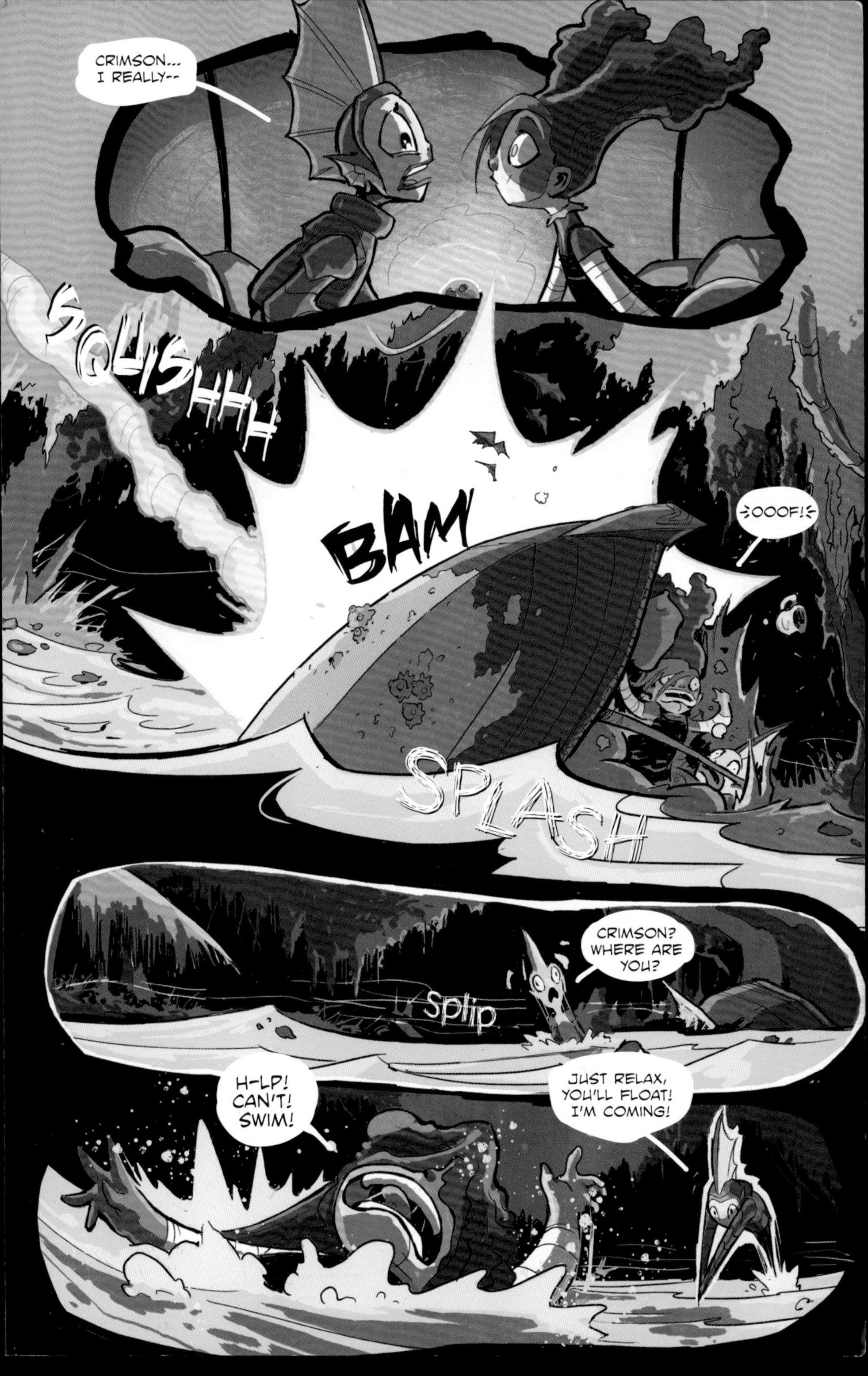
CRIMSON... I REALLY--
SQUISHHH
BAM
OOOF!
SPLASH
CRIMSON? WHERE ARE YOU?
Splip
H-LP! CAN'T! SWIM!
JUST RELAX, YOU'LL FLOAT! I'M COMING!

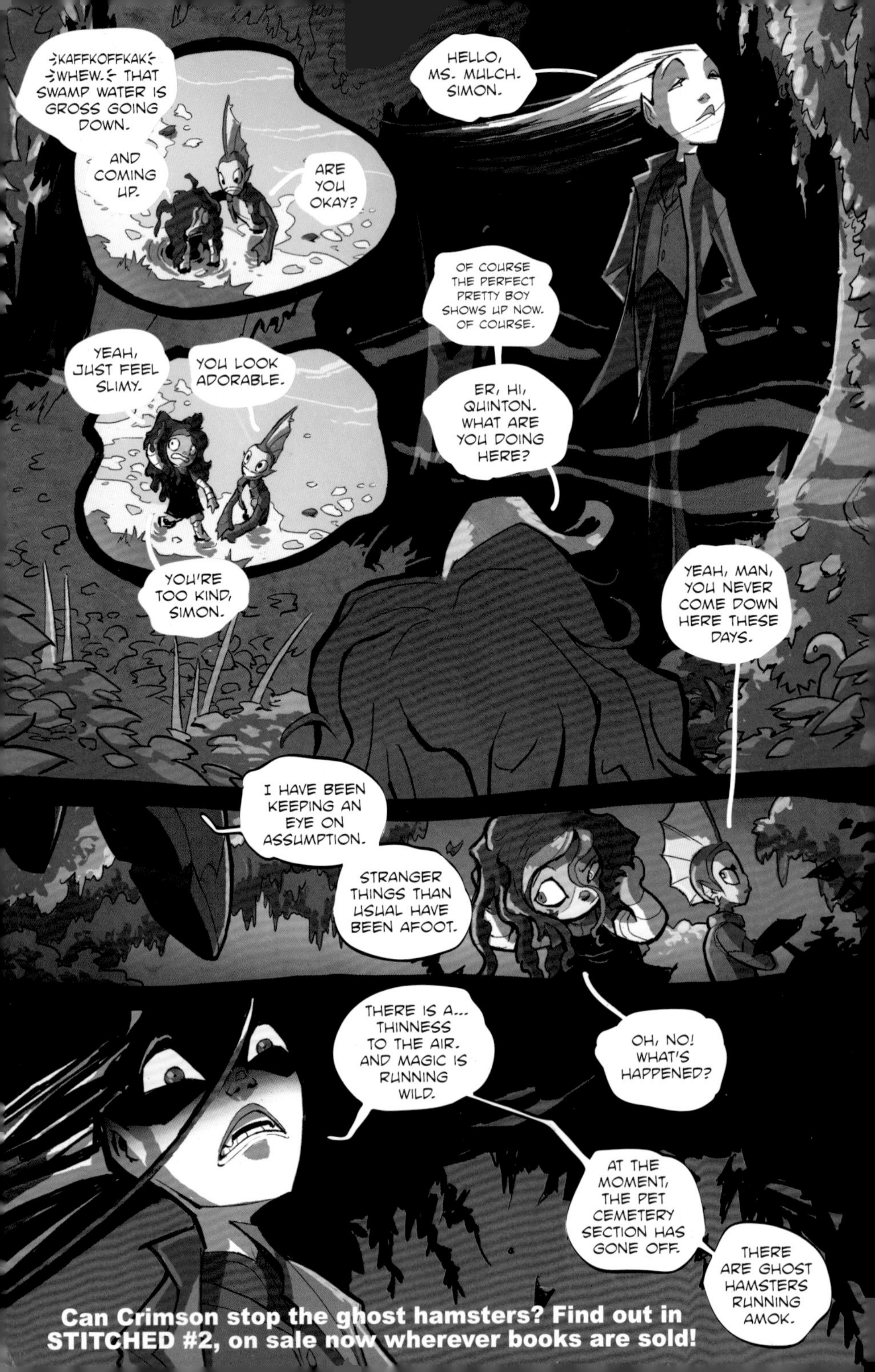

KAFFKOFFKAK
WHEW. THAT SWAMP WATER IS GROSS GOING DOWN.
AND COMING UP.
ARE YOU OKAY?
HELLO, MS. MULCH. SIMON.
YEAH, JUST FEEL SLIMY.
YOU LOOK ADORABLE.
YOU'RE TOO KIND, SIMON.
OF COURSE THE PERFECT PRETTY BOY SHOWS UP NOW. OF COURSE.
ER, HI, QUINTON. WHAT ARE YOU DOING HERE?
YEAH, MAN, YOU NEVER COME DOWN HERE THESE DAYS.
I HAVE BEEN KEEPING AN EYE ON ASSUMPTION.
STRANGER THINGS THAN USUAL HAVE BEEN AFOOT.
OH, NO! WHAT'S HAPPENED?
THERE IS A... THINNESS TO THE AIR. AND MAGIC IS RUNNING WILD.
AT THE MOMENT, THE PET CEMETERY SECTION HAS GONE OFF.
THERE ARE GHOST HAMSTERS RUNNING AMOK.

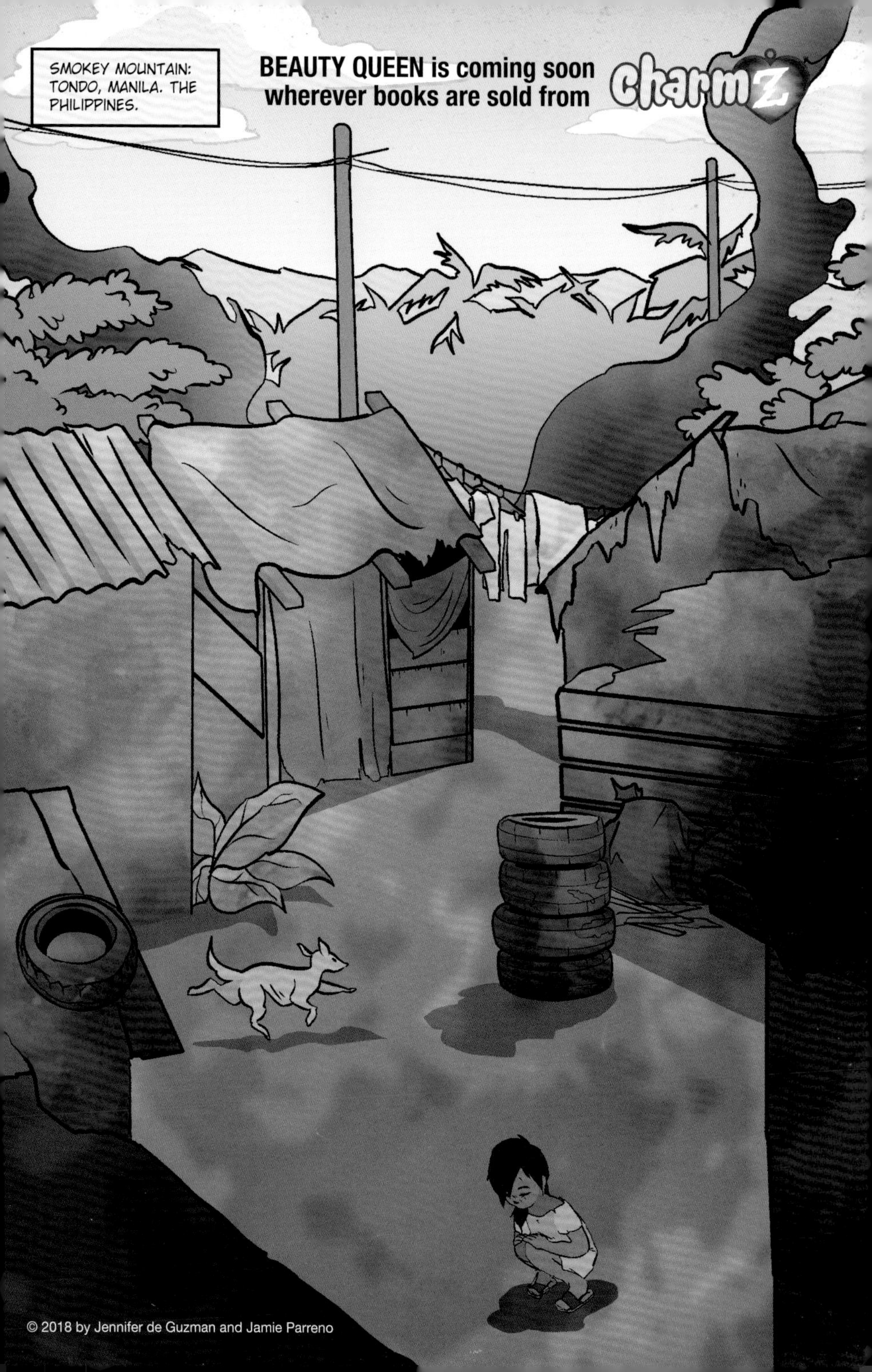
SMOKEY MOUNTAIN: TONDO, MANILA. THE PHILIPPINES.
BEAUTY QUEEN is coming soon wherever books are sold from
Charmz

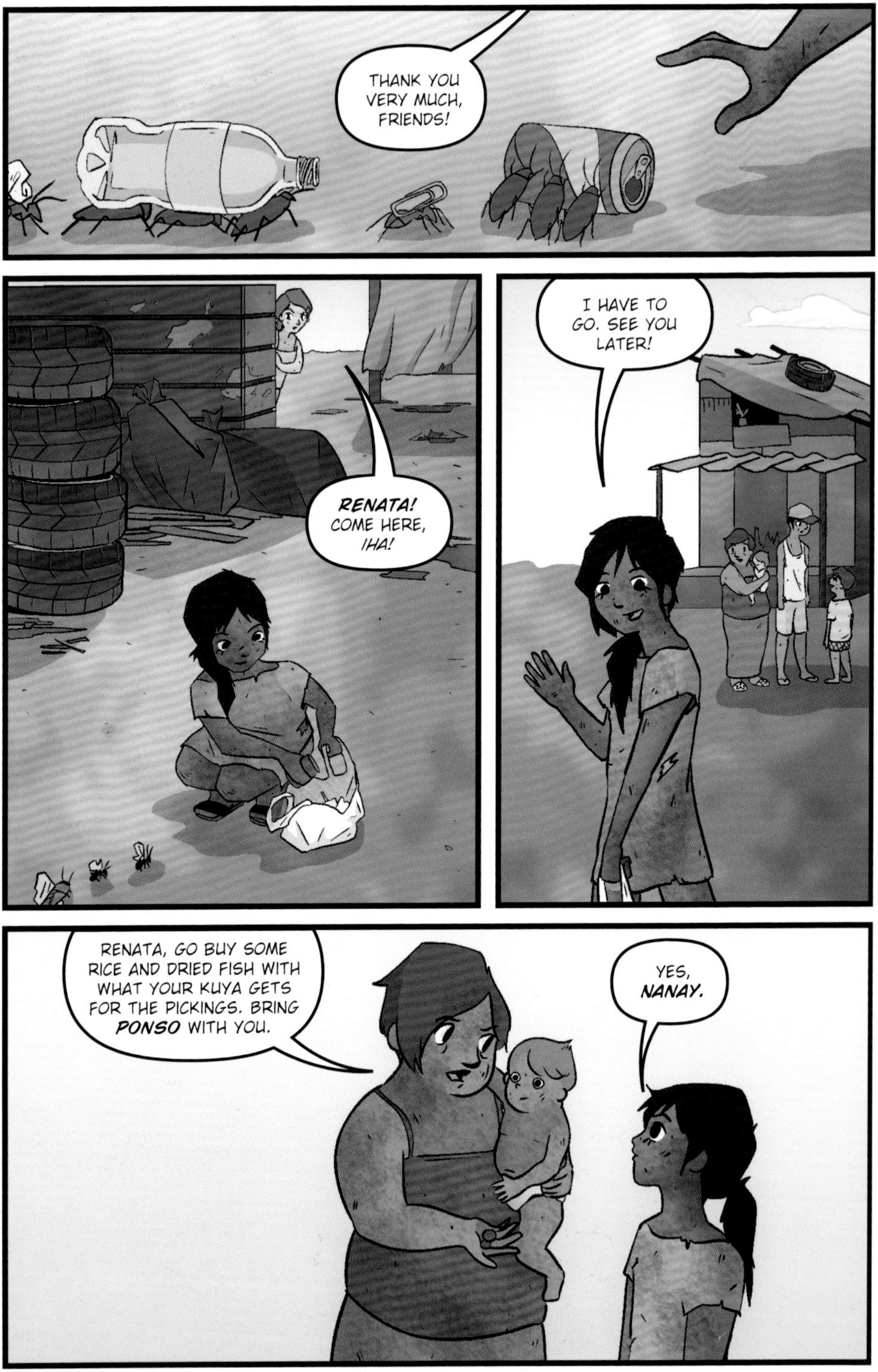
THANK YOU VERY MUCH, FRIENDS!
RENATA! COME HERE, IHA!
I HAVE TO GO. SEE YOU LATER!
RENATA, GO BUY SOME RICE AND DRIED FISH WITH WHAT YOUR KUYA GETS FOR THE PICKINGS. BRING PONSO WITH YOU.
YES, NANAY.

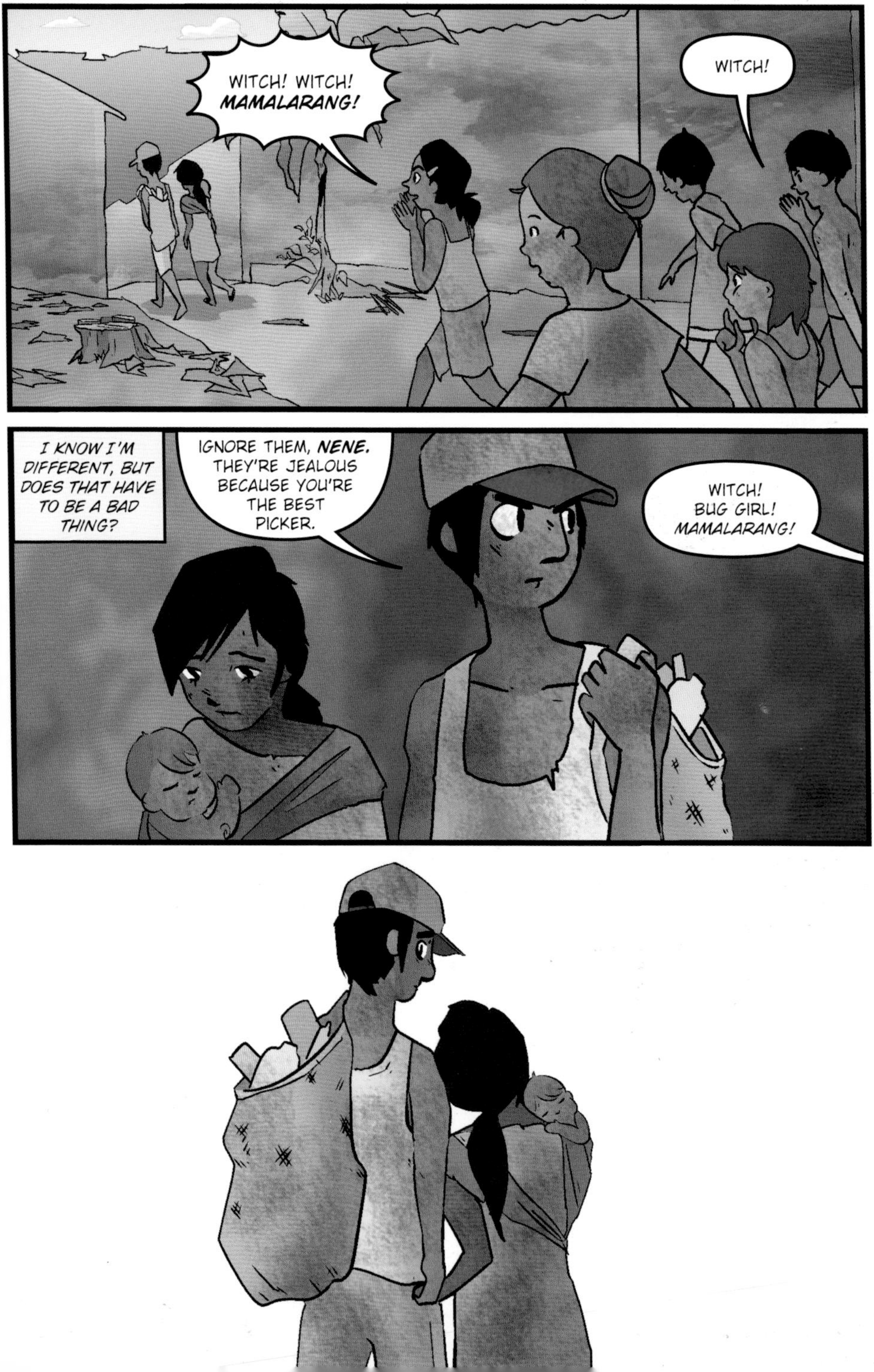
WITCH! WITCH! MAMALARANG!
WITCH!
I KNOW I'M DIFFERENT, BUT DOES THAT HAVE TO BE A BAD THING?
IGNORE THEM, NENE. THEY'RE JEALOUS BECAUSE YOU'RE THE BEST PICKER.
WITCH! BUG GIRL! MAMALARANG!

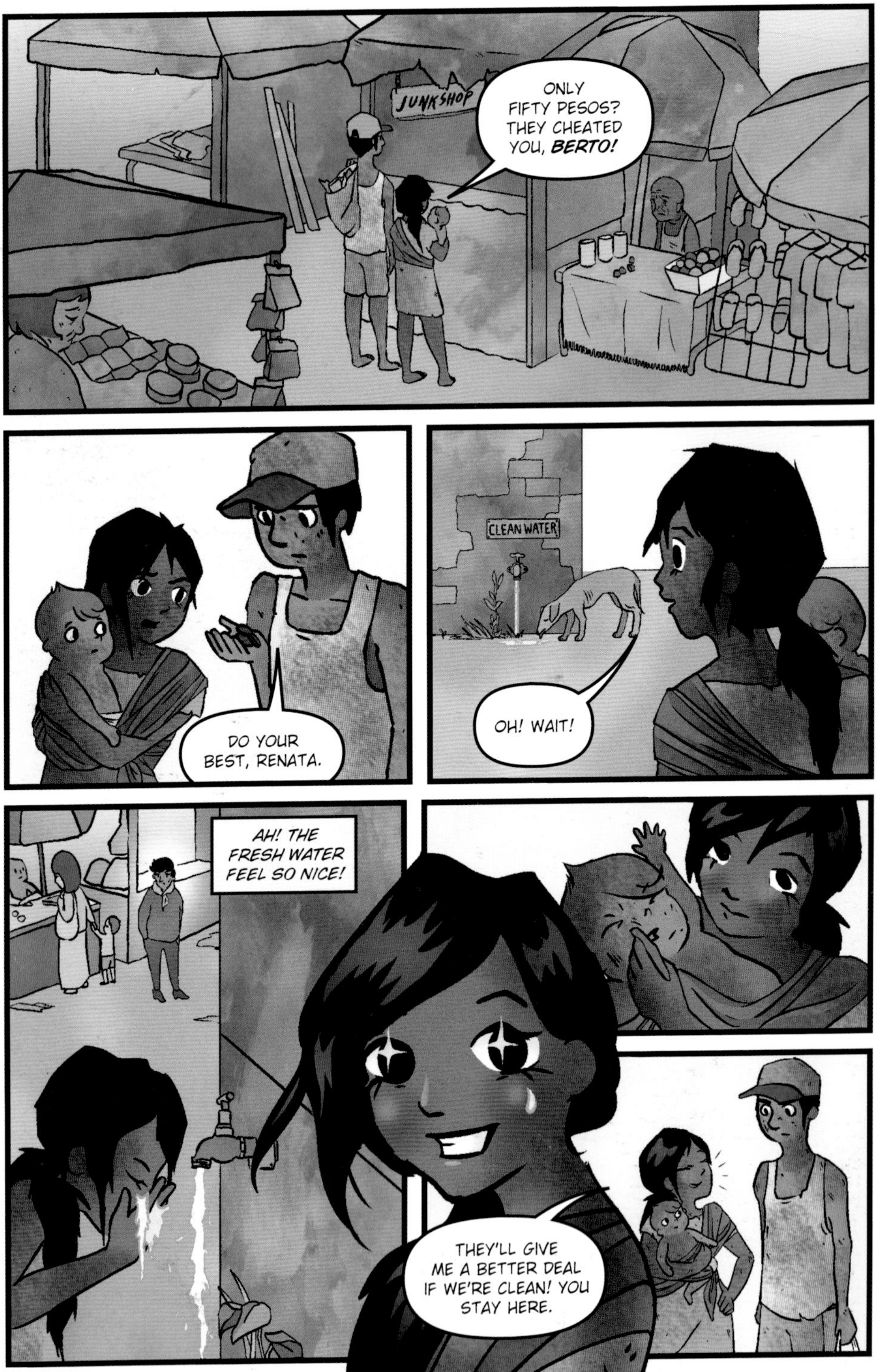
JUNKSHOP
ONLY FIFTY PESOS? THEY CHEATED YOU, **BERTO!**
DO YOUR BEST, RENATA.
CLEAN WATER
OH! WAIT!
AH! THE FRESH WATER FEEL SO NICE!
THEY'LL GIVE ME A BETTER DEAL IF WE'RE CLEAN! YOU STAY HERE.

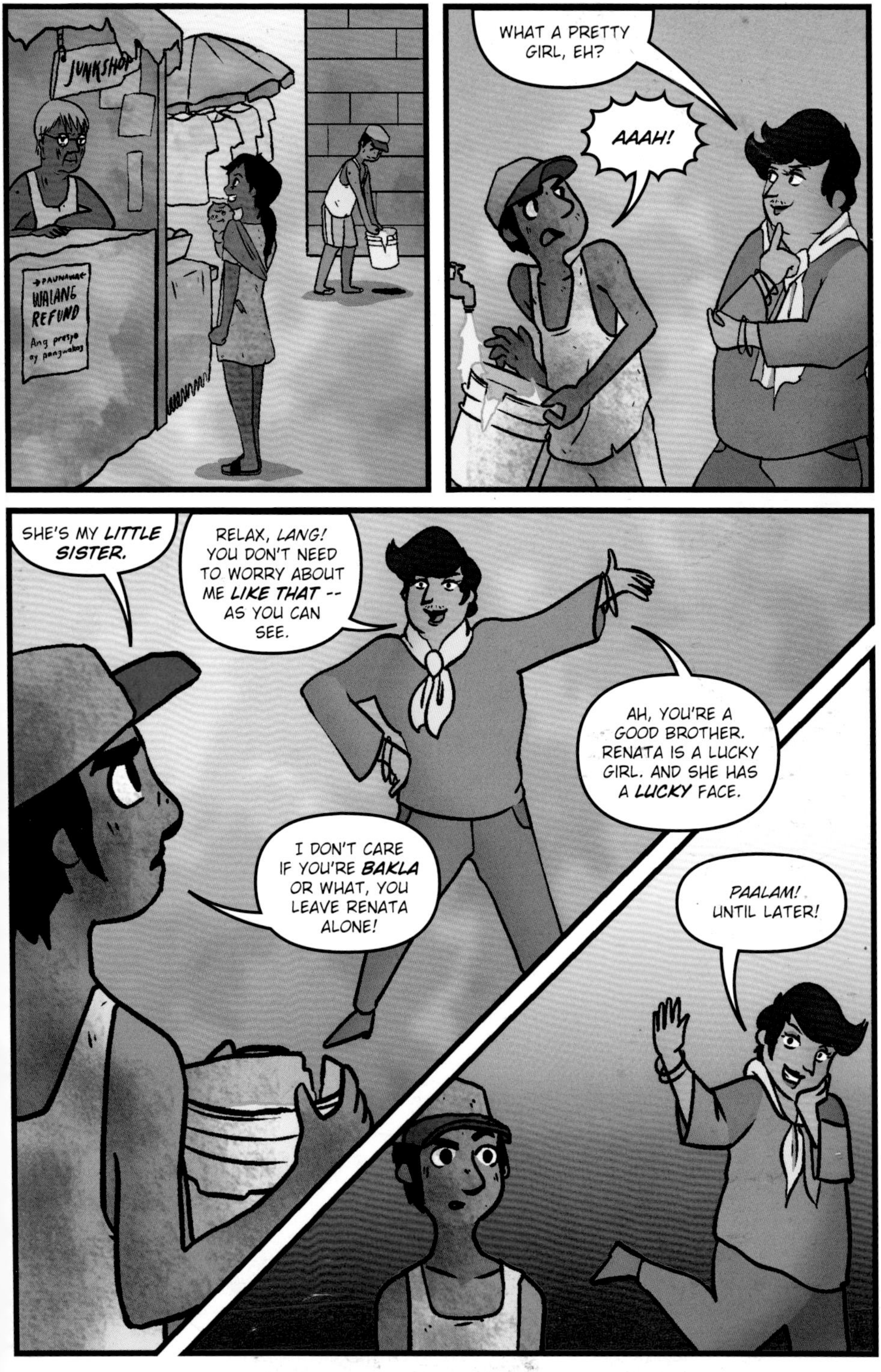

JUNKSHOP
PAUNAWA
WALANG REFUND
Ang presyo ay pangwakas
WHAT A PRETTY GIRL, EH?
AAAH!
SHE'S MY **LITTLE SISTER.**
RELAX, *LANG!* YOU DON'T NEED TO WORRY ABOUT ME **LIKE THAT** -- AS YOU CAN SEE.
I DON'T CARE IF YOU'RE **BAKLA** OR WHAT, YOU LEAVE RENATA ALONE!
AH, YOU'RE A GOOD BROTHER. RENATA IS A LUCKY GIRL. AND SHE HAS A **LUCKY** FACE.
PAALAM! UNTIL LATER!

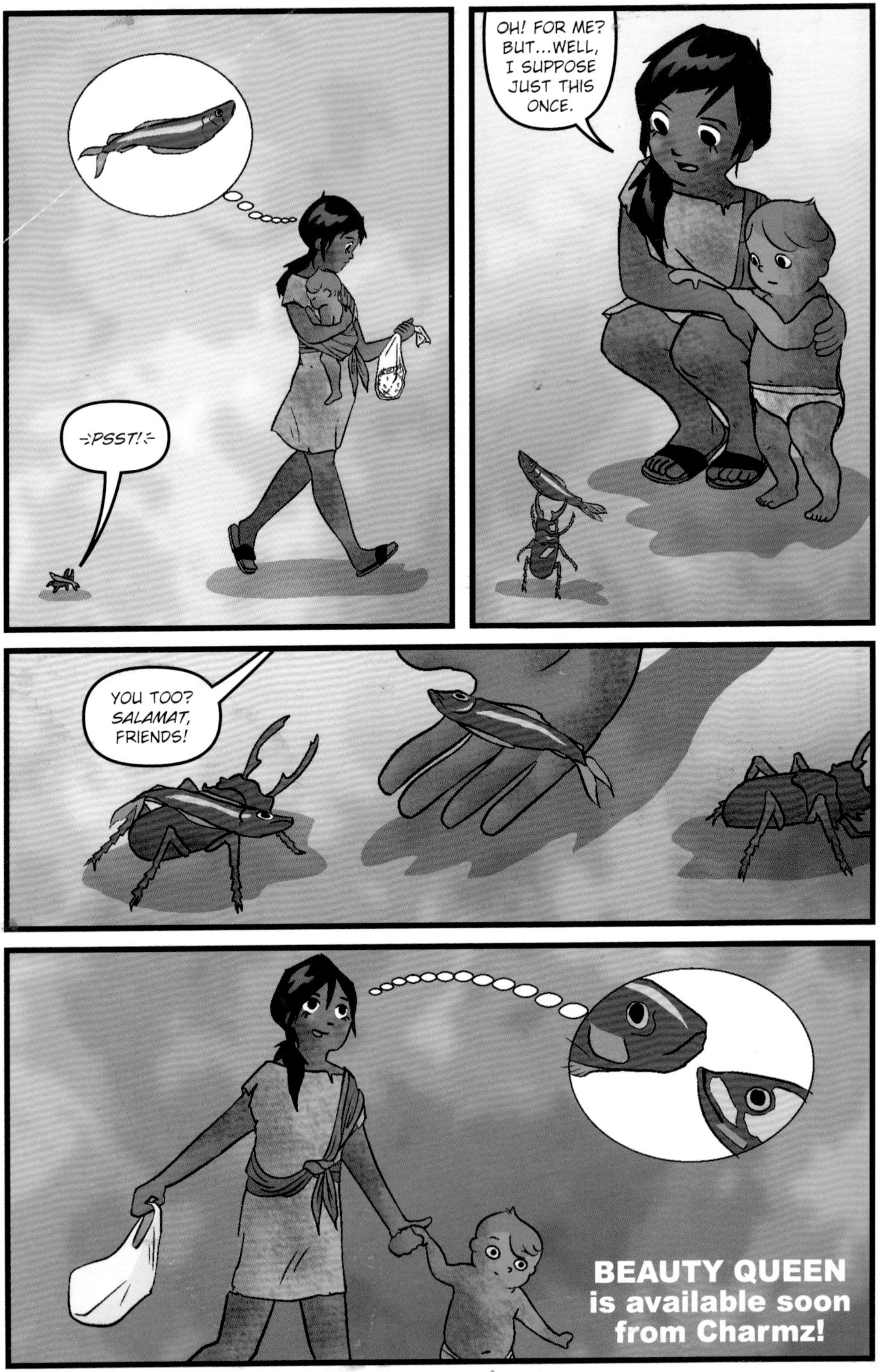
-PSST!-
OH! FOR ME? BUT...WELL, I SUPPOSE JUST THIS ONCE.
YOU TOO? SALAMAT, FRIENDS!
BEAUTY QUEEN is available soon from Charmz!